The Eleventh Commandment

෨ ෪

A
John Singer Sargent/Violet Paget
Mystery

෨ ෪

Mary F. Burns

Published by Word by Word Press
San Francisco, California

Burns, Mary F.
The Eleventh Commandment

ISBN: 9798402398092

Printed in the United States of America
Text Font: Garamond
Titles Font: Perpetua Titling

Violet Paget, c. 1880
Born October 14, 1856, Violet Paget was Welsh-English, and like the Sargent family, hers travelled throughout Europe and Great Britain, keeping company with artists, writers, intellectuals, and many socially prominent people. She was a prolific writer, using the pen name Vernon Lee, and she and John Sargent were close friends from childhood—they met when they were ten years old, in Rome. Violet died in 1935 at her villa, Il Palmerino, near Florence.

John Singer Sargent, c. 1880
Sargent was born on January 12, 1856 to American parents living in Florence, Italy. Sargent became the most sought-after portrait painter in Europe and America from the early 1880's to his death in 1925. He produced some 900 oil paintings, mostly portraits, and 2,000 watercolors, which became his preferred medium.

The Eleventh Commandment

Based on a True Story

PROLOGUE

I CAN SEE HIM AS HE DESCRIBED IT TO ME, that strange day back in '84, in March, in Paris—I told him I could picture it completely—so John kept talking, describing, getting it out of his system. He said he had been incessantly drumming his fingers on the armrest in his first-class train compartment as it sped on its way from Paris to Haarlem in the Netherlands. It was mid-February when he took that trip; at night, nothing to look at through the windows, only the reflections of the gas lamps near the door—he'd turned off the ones nearer to him, he said.

It was off-season; he was alone. He crossed his legs; uncrossed them. Stood up, undid the buttons of his coat, arranged his overcoat on the seat beside him, sat down again to the continuing, soothing rhythms of the wheels on the track.

The portrait of *Madame X* was still driving him mad—I knew this at the time, even without him telling me—and it was a mere two months before he had to submit it to the Salon. The original painting had been scraped and re-painted, touched up, layer upon layer—it was beginning to craze all over, sending out sparks as light hit the varied surfaces. He'd started a copy, hoping to re-create it all in one fell swoop, make it work.

He said he had needed to see the Franz Hals again—the master's portraits that had inspired him the previous summer with exactly what he needed to capture the insouciant, troublesome, arrogant beauty of Madame Gautreau—the insufferable minx, in my not very humble opinion.

He'd taken the night train, telling no one; he planned to come back in three days. He had smiled, thinking of Albert de Belleroche and Paul Helleu—they had gone with him in August, good and true companions. This time, he needed the time to himself. Though winter, he would find warmth and solace in the extensive exhibit of Hals's works at the Haarlem City Hall.

And of course, he'd had no idea whatsoever that he—and I—would subsequently become embroiled in an international scandal, a seething tribal and religious conflict involving ancient and modern theft, fraud, revenge—and death.

Possibly suicide, but more likely, murder.

Violet Paget
Il Palmerino
Fiesole, Italy – 1928

ONE

Paris – Tuesday, 11 March 1884

THE PACKAGE ARRIVED UNCEREMONIOUSLY ENOUGH, delivered to the door of John's charming house near Parc Monceau—plain brown wrapping, tied neatly with string, about the size of a volume of Trollope. I happened to be there, up on the studio floor with its large windows and the smell of paint and linseed oil, when Guido, John's truculent *major domo*, brought it in with other parcels and envelopes and set it on a side table near where I was sitting.

Unabashedly curious, I picked it up—there was no return address, which seemed odd.

"Look at this, Scamps," I said, calling my old friend by his childhood nickname. I chuckled. "It's addressed only to 'The famous portret painter, John Sarjeant, Paris, France'."

John put down his paintbrush and quickly cleaned his hands on a small towel hanging from the easel.

"It's a wonder it got here at all," I remarked. "Given the chaos that is the French mail." I smiled at him. "But clearly, your growing fame made it easier!"

"Let me see," he said, coming over to the table. We made a funny pair standing next to each other—John a good foot and more taller than I, brown and bearded and broad-shouldered to my scrawny, bird-like frame, wire spectacles perched on my nose and wrapped in a shapeless black dress—I was trying out the new, daringly *avant-garde* fashion of not wearing stays, which would normally serve to "perfect" my figure. I had little desire for such perfection.

I peered closely and made out the tiny letters of the city of origin in the stamped circle. "It's from Rotterdam, of all places," I said, handing him the parcel. I looked up at him. "Whom do you know in Rotterdam?"

He shook his head. "No one I can think of," he said with a shrug. He turned it over a few times, both of us examining it for marks or writing that weren't there. He set the package on the table, pried his pocket-knife open, and cut the string, then folded back the brown paper. Nestled in several layers of thick wrapping were some half-dozen or so blackened strips of something like leather or tarred parchment, about four inches high by maybe eight or ten inches long. We let them lay there, uncertain whether to touch them or not—they seemed fragile, possibly sticky with the tarry substance.

"Is there a note?" I touched the edge of one of the leathery strips to see if anything lay beneath it.

"Wait, here's something," John said. He carefully separated a couple of leaves of wrapping paper where a tiny corner of white paper peeped through. He pulled it out, a thin slip about five by seven inches or so. There was writing on it.

"It's stationery from a hotel," I said, pointing to a modest crest stamped in foil at the top.

"Hotel Willemsbrug," John said aloud, then proceeded to read the body of the note.

"*Dear Mssr Sarjeant,*" he read. "*I shall not forget your kindness to me last month, inviting me to dine with you, and lissening to my sad tales of woe. I hesitated long to burden you with these contents but am in great distress for living any longer, and I beg you to take great care of this and your own self whilst they are in your posession. I trust you will know what to do with them, with such friends as you have. Sincerely, with blessings. Moses S, known to you as Aaron S."*

"What on earth?" I exclaimed, much intrigued. I took the note from his hand. "It's dated last week, 6 March, that would be Thursday?" I re-read the note to myself, while John was carefully moving the leathery strips with a tentative finger.

"Is this truly someone you met and had dinner with—in Rotterdam?"

"Haarlem," John said. "We had dinner together in Haarlem." His gaze was unfocused, remembering. "Yes, strange man, foreign, I took him at first for a Russian Jew, but he said he was a Christian, from Jerusalem. Very engaging."

We both looked at the paper again.

Frowning, I tried to catch at something in the far reaches of my mind that seemed familiar—Jerusalem, *Moses S*, strips of leathery parchment—of course!

"Good Lord," I said, shocked and exhilarated. "Do you know what this is?" I pointed to the contents of the package. "What *these* are?"

John turned puzzled eyes to mine and shook his head.

"These are the fraudulent archaeological treasures that made such an uproar, last summer in London, surely you remember?" I peered closely at the leather strips. "See, very faintly? Hebrew letters, I'm sure of it, these are the…" I cast my mind back, and closed my eyes, to better see the headlines in the *Times* and the *Athenaeum*. "The Shapira Scrolls! That's what they called them. It was the only thing people talked about for nearly three months!"

John seemed baffled. "I don't recall anything about that, but then, I wasn't in London last summer. And that wasn't the name he gave me." He turned the paper over again. "Ah, I see, yes, he wrote *known to you as Aaron S.*, I remember now, but the last name wasn't Shapira, it was…" He thought a moment, then had it. "Sampson." He looked at me. "So the *M* stands for…?"

"Moses Shapira!" I said triumphantly. I gazed in awe at the leather strips. "But why in the name of all that's holy would he send these to you?" I looked at the note again. "He says he thinks you will know what to do, especially *with such friends as you have.*"

John had an odd look on his face as he turned to me. "You know, I remember—he was telling me about how he was an agent for the British Museum, in connection with some manuscripts he had sold to them, and I mentioned I had a friend who spent a good deal of time there when she was in London—in short, you!"

I pondered this curiosity. "And?" I prompted.

"Well, he asked your name, thinking, I suppose, that he might know you, so I told him your *nom de plume*—as you're getting so famous now, you see," John grinned down at me, and I cuffed him lightly on the arm as he continued.

" '*Vernon Lee?*' he repeated, and again *Vernon Lee?*' John said it with a slightly Russian accent. "Then he said he recalled actually meeting you and being very impressed."

I was astonished, and searched my memory for that encounter, buried as it was by intervening time. Something clicked.

"Yes," I said. "It was at the museum itself, at the exhibit they had mounted of two of these strips of leather." I pointed to the package on the table. "I remember now, there was such a crush of people—but Edward Bond was there—he's the head librarian at the British Museum—and introduced me to Mr. Shapira." I shook my head. "We couldn't have had more than a few minutes' conversation."

John laughed. "A few minutes' conversation with you, dear Vi, is more than enough to provide an indelible impression!"

I smiled wryly at him, then grew serious. Suddenly fearful that we could be overheard, I spoke in a lower voice, although that was clearly nonsensical thinking.

"He is warning you of danger—and he may be in danger himself," I said. "You must tell me everything he said to you when you dined that night in Haarlem." I looked again at the note.

"He says he is in *'great distress for living any longer',*" I read aloud, and turned to John. "That sounds rather dire. Did he give any such indication when you dined with him? And how exactly did you meet him?"

John was silent as we walked over and sat on a little sofa near the window, and briefly took in the lovely silver light glinting off the steep roofs of Paris, slick with rain from earlier in the day. John picked up a decanter of sherry—always to hand—and filled two crystal stemmed glasses, handing one to me. I sipped at it gratefully as he started his narrative.

"I met Mr. Sampson—Shapira, that is—as I was wandering through the Franz Hals rooms at the Haarlem City Hall, where they have an enormous number of their native son's paintings." He smiled, a bit ruefully. "I believe he was there mainly to get in from the cold, but he did show a certain appreciation for the portraits." He sipped his sherry.

"He was seated on one of the benches in front of the *Young Man with a Skull*," John continued, glancing at me. "I dare say you haven't seen it, but it's classic Hals, all rich, deep browns and burnt siennas and a flaming orange feather in the boy's cap." John warmed to his description and I let him go on. "I've always fancied it was Hals' version of Hamlet when he's addressing the skull of his father's jester, what was his name?—Yorick, that's it, *alas poor Yorick*. In this painting, the boy has the skull in his left hand, and his right hand is directly pointed toward the viewer—incredible sense of perspective that—but his eyes are glancing to his left—off-stage as it were—as if something has just caught his attention, and his soft red lips have this faint smile just starting..." John was silent a moment, seeing it in his mind's eye.

"Distracted from the contemplation of death," I interposed, "by someone more lively in the wings perhaps?"

"Yes, exactly so!" John put down his empty glass. "And that's what started our conversation, you see. As I drew near, Mr. Shapira, not even looking up at me, but clearly sensing that someone was also looking at the painting, spoke to that very point. *Look at that little smile,* he said." John sighed. "And it went on from there." He shifted his position, leaning back into the sofa and facing me more directly.

"He said he could tell I was an artist," he said, smiling a little. "Something about my hands, he said, and, I imagine, the way I discussed the Hals portrait with him—not so very hard to discern."

"Did he say anything about the scrolls? Then, or when you went to dinner?" I was impatient to hear about them.

John was silent a few moments, thinking. "He told me about the journeys he had taken into Palestine and Arabia—

with Bedouin guides and camels and donkeys—searching out old caves where ancient things—bowls and statues and parchments—had lain hidden under mounds of rocks for centuries." He shook his head in admiration and, I thought, a little envy. "How I would love to go on such adventures!"

"And you truly had no idea who he really was?" I took a sip from my glass.

John snorted mildly. "Why would you think I would know that? You said all the publicity about those scrolls—or whatever"—he waved his hand at the pile of papers on the table—"was last summer, in London." He shook his head. "You know I don't pay attention to the newspapers much, and besides, as I said, I wasn't in London at the time."

I put my glass on the table and leaned forward. "But surely he must have said something that would clarify the note he sent you—why would he be in fear of his life? Why would he warn you to be 'careful' while the scrolls are in your possession?" I looked at him with some intensity. "Think, John, he must have said *something*."

My old friend did indeed look as if he were thinking seriously, then a light broke on his handsome face. "Yes! There was something, now that I—at one point, we had gone off to dine by then, as it was late when we met, and I could tell he was rather hungry and down on his luck, you see—so I offered to take him to dinner, saying I was so entertained by his stories and experiences, you see—" He looked at me to see if I understood, and I couldn't help but smile at his kindness and care for the downhearted man. I nodded.

"We had at first been offered a table near the front window, but he asked me, very politely, if we might sit farther away, towards the back. Of course I agreed to it, but he apparently felt his request needed some explanation, for he said something like, *There has been someone following me, I believe*—he was very apologetic—*nothing serious, of course, just someone I wish to avoid.* I thought it odd, but had forgot about it til now." He mused a little.

"I thought that he was very sad, but trying to cover it up with all his talk; I could see, when he didn't think I was looking, that there was such a tiredness, an abject, almost desperate unhappiness in his face, especially when he talked about his family, particularly his daughter Myriam, back in Jerusalem. Clearly, he missed them very much—he told me how he had his antiquities shop in the Christian quarter of the old city, and in his very backyard was, apparently, the pool where Bathsheba bathed and King David caught sight of her and fell in love." He paused a moment. "He was a great storyteller—he made that Bible story come to life."

John shook himself. "I do hope nothing has happened to him."

TWO

Jerusalem – 1856

The Jaffa Gate was teeming with pilgrims and traders jostling each other alongside camels and donkeys as they made their way through this ancient entrance to the Old City. The Tower of David loomed ahead, and young Moses Shapira stopped in his tracks to gaze at it. The noonday sun was hot on the soft hat that covered his shaggy head, his beard itched, and his whole body seemed covered in sticky, dusty grime—it had been a long trip from Romania to Palestine—and he looked forward to bathing and sleeping indoors, as he had been promised would await him at the mission of Christ Church, the Jewish-Christian church in Jerusalem. His heart beat fast and felt as if it were growing big in his chest. He thought of his grandfather, buried in old Bucharest among strangers, and choked back his rising emotions. And where was his father? How would he find him among all these people, if indeed he were still alive? The Tower of the ancient king blurred and wavered as he blinked away the tears.

"It is a magnificent sight, is it not, young man?" A voice spoke from behind him, and he turned to see a respectably-dressed man, though dusty from the streets, with the unmistakable badge of the London Society for Promoting Christianity amongst the Jews—for short, the London Society for

Jews—sewn on the left lapel of his coat. Moses immediately whipped off his hat and bent his head in humble greeting.

"Sir," he said, his Russian accent breaking through his hard-learned English. "I am bount to Christ Church, havink bin baptised by Reverent George, hin Bukarist."

The older man clapped him enthusiastically on the shoulder. "Well done, my lucky friend!" he said. "I am Reverend Hefter of Christ Church, and you are most welcome!" He shook Moses' hand with great heartiness. "To think that I should be the first person you meet on walking through the Jaffa Gate—surely the Lord is looking after you…" He paused and looked him up and down. "And what is your name, son?"

"Moses Sha—Moses Wilhelm Shapira," Moses said, having to remind himself to use his Christian name.

"Well then, Moses Wilhelm," said the Reverend Hefter, taking him by the arm, "come right along with me and we'll get you sorted at the church."

With a final glance of gratitude at David's Tower—and a sudden feeling that the tower was somehow going to be prominent in his life in this city—Moses happily walked and talked with the good Reverend through the narrow, dirty, blessed streets of the Old City.

* * *

After a hot bath, then suitable though somewhat worn clothing, and a good meal had made him feel presentable, inside and out, Moses accompanied Reverend Hefter into the church and surrounding buildings. The soaring pillars inside the monumental Christ Church led the eye upwards into pale stone formed to a pointed center; stained glass windows with biblical figures and Hebrew lettering ringed the area over what looked, to young Moses, like the *bimah* in a synagogue. There were no crosses, no statues. It was much more Jewish than it was Christian; Moses felt some relief chip away at his apprehension.

The Reverend was justly proud of the achievement of a "Jewish Christian" church in the heart of old Jerusalem, in the Armenian Quarter near the Jaffa Gate, built less than ten years previously, built with funds from across Protestant Europe, particularly Germany and Great Britain.

Western Europe was trying to reclaim the Holy Land, one Jewish soul at a time.

* * *

Moses had been born in a village that constantly changed masters—Poland, Lithuania, Russia—but always remained the begrudged home of poor Jews. Nonetheless, it was a center of learning, as any Jew anywhere will make of his surroundings: young Moses attended *yeshiva*, studied Torah, disputed with teachers, and was praised for his keen mind and quick thinking. But then one day, his father left for Palestine, leaving his teenaged son to look after what was left of the family in the Pale of Settlement.

When he was nearing twenty, Moses and his father's father set out together, travelling from Ukraine to Bucharest, but there the old man died, leaving his grandson bereft—no family, no money, no country, no identity. Christian missionaries took him in and, grateful for their help, needing, perhaps, to just fit in *somewhere*, he converted. A Jewish Christian. He added the name "Wilhelm" to his own name when he was baptized.

He went to Jerusalem to find his father, inquiring in synagogues and churches alike. The latter had no knowledge of him, but a rabbi at one synagogue had a few nuggets of information. There was the name of one Moses David Shapira on the congregation list from about eight years previous, but no later entries. His residence was listed as the Street of the King, in the Armenian Quarter, which, the rabbi said, was where the poorest of the poor lived, in dire conditions. And the people who let out rooms to single men, when Moses went from place to place to inquire, treated him with great suspicion and hostility—as if they could somehow tell, just by looking at him, that he was a traitorous convert, an agent of Protestant evangelizing—and answered him curtly or not at all.

He searched in vain, and after a year or so, gave up the quest entirely. He was resigned to being alone.

THREE

Paris – Tuesday, 11 March 1884

WINTER WAS STILL HOLDING SWAY IN PARIS—the wan sunlight had already disappeared behind grey clouds, and John's housekeeper, madame Durnay, had come in to light the lamps. We stood at the table, once more gazing at the note and the strange objects that had come with it.

John glanced at Madame Durnay, who was dutifully checking around the room for empty glasses and lunch plates—she knew he didn't like being disturbed any more often than necessary, but she always came to collect the dirty dishes and empty bottles in late afternoon, and again first thing in the morning. The tray she had brought with her was filling up quickly.

"Madame Durnay," he said, smiling.

"*Oui, monsieur Jean?*" she responded, curtseying slightly, with a nod to me.

"We shall be dining out this evening," he said, and lifted an eyebrow in my direction.

"Shall we indeed?" I said, surprised—but pleased. I loved dining out in Paris. I nodded enthusiastically.

"*Oui, monsieur,*" said Madame Durnay. She gathered up a few more glasses, and quietly left the room.

"Shall we be off to our own dinner?" he said. "My treat." He smiled. "The commissions have been very good lately!"

"*Merci*," I said, preparing to find my coat and gloves, but stopped to look at the package and its contents on the table. "Don't you think we should put these somewhere? Or at least, out of sight? Mr. Shapira did say to keep them safe."

John thought a moment. "I know just the place," he said, gathering them up and folding the leathery pieces carefully back into the brown paper. He disappeared with them behind the large gold brocade curtain that hung on one side of the fireplace, and emerged empty-handed a few minutes later. I was on the verge of asking where he'd put them, but forebore—I really am not *quite* that nosy!

"But what shall you do with them?" I asked as we started down the stairs a few minutes later. "Clearly, Mr. Shapira trusts you to know what to do with the scrolls, as he said."

"I'm not sure," John said. He smiled, and held open the door for me. "Let's talk about it over dinner."

* * *

John treated us both to a lovely, multi-course dinner of such resplendence that I at first thought I couldn't possibly have enough appetite to taste every morsel—but there I underestimated myself. We began with a light German Riesling wine to accompany a delicious leek and cream soup with roasted mushrooms scattered over the top and a hint of gruyère and cumin. In between sips, I encouraged John to talk a little more about his meeting with Mr. Shapira.

"I'm intrigued by his saying he thought he was being followed," I said. "Can you think of anything else along that line that he might have alluded to?

John took a healthy gulp of wine, and gestured to the waiter to pour some more. He closed his eyes briefly.

"Yes," he said. "There was one thing, rather extraordinary, actually. I can't believe I'd forgotten it til now." He put down his glass and leaned across the table a little.

"I had excused myself for a few moments, nearly at the end of our meal, and was seeing to the bill, when I looked back at our table, and saw that there was a man seated in my place, leaning toward Mr. Samson—Mr. Shapira that is—and speaking to him very intently."

"Hmmm," I murmured. "And what was Mr. Shapira's reaction? How did he look? Did he speak?"

John shook his head. "Shapira's back was to me, I only saw that he was sitting very stiffly, and looking away from the man who spoke to him." He shrugged. "After a minute, the man got up, and with a sort of sneering look, left the restaurant. Curious!"

"What did he look like, this man?" I said. Very curious indeed!

With an artist's eye for detail, John described the man. "A gentleman, to be sure, by his dress and demeanour; very tall, perhaps in his mid-thirties? Full head of hair—didn't seem to have a hat with him, but was wearing gloves, nice grey kid gloves, they looked like; well-trimmed mustache and beard; and although the light was dim, he looked—tanned, as if he'd spent much time outdoors." He shrugged again, then laughed. "Right—at one point as he was talking to Shapira, he shrugged—and I remember thinking, oh, he's got to be French!"

I gave a little laugh at that, and we sat back to allow the waiter to remove our dishes and bring in the next one, a flavorful sole meunière and small yellow potatoes. Our idea of thoroughly talking over Mr. Shapira's situation, however, was interrupted just then by the arrival of a visitor to our table, just as we had started the second course.

"If I may be so forward," I heard a man's cultured voice say over my shoulder, "I can't help but say how delighted I am to see you both, after all this time."

I looked up into the handsome, debonair visage of Lord James Parke, Second Baron Wensleydale, with whom John and I had shared a quite remarkable adventure some five years before, in the far north of England.

"Your lordship!" I cried, and held out my hand, which he bent over most gracefully, and he then strode a quick few steps to John, who had risen from his chair. The two men embraced with great friendliness, and John gestured to a third chair at the table.

"But you must join us, can you?" John said, looking around for a companion or group of people Lord Parke may have come in with. "Are we taking you away from a friend?"

"Not at all, I'm embarrassed to say," Lord Parke admitted, taking the chair with alacrity, and seeming not at all embarrassed. "I've just arrived in Paris and was looking about me for a good meal, but hadn't come up against any friends as yet—until I so happily caught sight of the two of you across the room!" He flashed a smile at me, and nodded at John. We were all extremely pleased to see one another.

The attentive waiter had already brought another place setting and wine glass, and John nodded at his request to pour more wine into our glasses, and fill Lord Parke's as well.

"Well, a toast then," I said, "to adventures past!" We clinked glasses and drank.

We spent the next two courses catching up on Lord Parke's life and activities—a good deal of which were often to be found in the London papers, he being a very eligible bachelor, zealous philanthropist and indefatigable social presence in the *ton*. He told us he had recently been invited to join the Board of the British Museum, on account of his interest in the growing field of archaeology, and I was alert to this interesting coincidence immediately.

I glanced at John with an inquiring lifted brow—he nodded, knowing what I meant, of course—and I then proceeded to mention that John had received a rather peculiar package from Holland that afternoon that might be of archaeological significance. It caught Lord Parke's interest immediately.

"Holland, you say?" He drank a long draught of water. "Wouldn't by any chance have been from Rotterdam, would it?" He said it lightly, although he was not smiling.

John and I both stared at him, nearly open-mouthed. "Why, how on earth....?" I started to ask, and was stopped by his surprised look.

"Really? You *did* receive something from Rotterdam?" He looked unsettled now, almost grim.

"Yes," John joined in. "An odd little assortment of what Violet tells me are vastly important, though probably as much for scandal as for content—ancient Hebrew scrolls or some such."

"Not the Shapira Scrolls!" Lord Parke looked even more astonished.

"Why, what do you know of them?" I asked immediately.

"Well, not much more than what everyone knew last summer," he said, looking at me and perceiving that I knew what he was talking about. "But yesterday morning, I was at a meeting at the Museum, with the Department of Oriental Manuscripts—Dr. Rieu, who had been in touch with Mr. Shapira—" He hesitated a moment, and I felt a dreadful catch in my throat. He continued.

"Dr. Rieu had just had a telegram—Mr. Shapira was found dead in his hotel in Rotterdam, last Saturday, a bullet through his head."

FOUR

Jerusalem – 1857

MOSES WAS BECOMING ACCLIMATED to the strange and difficult City of Jerusalem—nominally run by Ottoman bureaucrats whose hands were always outstretched for a bribe to grease the wheels of commerce; fought over in the very streets by Muslims, Jews and Christians who were zealous in their protection of property and religious rights; those same streets filthy with decomposing carcasses and streams of human waste that never seemed to wash away; raucous with market sounds and what seemed to be a hundred tongues babbling and haranguing night and day, from desert Bedouins to evangelizing German preachers. The sonorous clang of church bells mixed with the high-pitched call to *salat*, the daily Muslim prayers, throughout the day and evening.

But Moses could see his future in this place—there was a stirring of interest, a curiosity, especially from Europeans, about this great center of worship for so many—and the Germans, in particular, seemed intent on finding "scientific" proof that the Bible was more than inspiration—it was history, and they wanted proofs to bolster their faith. A new world was about to open up, and he wanted to be part of it.

"I need work," he told the Reverend. "I want to learn a useful trade, you see." He was promptly enrolled in the church-sponsored House of Industry, and began studying carpentry. He was smart and learned quickly. He spent some spare time travelling on missionary journeys, trying (mostly in vain) to convert Jews into Christians, and was praised for having a deep and original mode of thinking.

Jerusalem – Two Years Later, 1859

Moses was now thirty-one years old, and not yet married. The last few years had seen him laid low, time after time, with sickness and the ague, but his periods of illness and recuperation eventually took a more fortunate turn, as he met his future wife, Rosette, who nursed him faithfully in the Anglican hospital. They had come to an understanding and would soon apply to the Council for its approval to marry.

In the meantime, Moses had seen his opportunity, and acted on it swiftly. He had risen in the favor and graces of the Church Council, and had been well-paid as librarian for a while now; the money he saved was thus ready to hand to buy a little shop on the Street of the Christians, in the old city, a very short distance from the Jaffa Gate and the Tower of David, from whose height one could look down at the whole quarter. Behind the row of shops was a shallow indentation filled with brackish water, called Bathsheba's Pool, believed to be the ancient site where King David first caught sight of the beautiful woman who captured his heart.

"But what will you sell in this shop, my dear?" asked Rosette. She was not averse to trade, or marrying a merchant, but she couldn't imagine what her Wilhelm (she preferred to use his Christian name) had in mind to sell.

"*Souvenirs!*" he said with smiling vigor. "As the French call them—little reminders of the place you visit—and here, in Jerusalem, this means things of religion—small bibles with hand-made covers, or verses from the Psalms, with pressed flowers, photographs of holy places, even coins—you know they lay all over the place, those old Roman coins, just under the dirt and the bricks."

Rosette, who was very conservative and plain in her thinking, had her doubts about the propriety of selling such things. But she had been with Wilhelm long enough now to be easily enthralled by his enthusiastic persuasion, his optimism and talent for painting a picture of a happy, successful future.

"Very well, my dear," she said.

He kissed her briefly on the cheek, and patted her hand.

"It will also be a bookshop," he said. "I will start to collect the old books that the Europeans are so fond of and want to pay much for. You will see," he said. "This shop will be very good for us."

* * *

Fate, or Providence, seemed to favor the industrious emigrant to Jerusalem, and the next decade saw him married to Rosette, becoming a father to two daughters, Augusta and Myriam, and the respected proprietor of a very popular tourist shop on the Street of the Christians.

But Moses yearned to do more than sell religious articles and souvenirs, and soon became an active agent and liaison with various Bedouin tribes, whose sheiks learned to trust the sociable and canny antiquities dealer with the treasures they were unearthing from the surrounding desert—manuscripts and scrolls, ancient pots and statues, hidden for centuries in caves and under the dry ridges of sand and rock. In addition, through journeys to Europe and Egypt, Moses was fortunate in his ability to find synagogue scrolls, often six or seven hundred years old, and medieval manuscripts just waiting to be discovered and turned into gold.

His fortune lay before him, and his name was becoming known.

FIVE

Paris – Tuesday, 11 March 1884

WE COULDN'T HAVE BEEN MORE ASTOUNDED at the news Lord Parke brought from London than if he'd told us the Queen was getting married again.

"Dead!" John repeated.

"A bullet!" I said at the same time. Our exclamations, I could see, were garnering attention from the tables near us, and I lowered my voice accordingly.

"Did this Dr. Rieu know what happened?" I said, nearly in a whisper. The waiter appeared with our *plats* of beef and venison, poured more wine, a dark and smooth Bordeaux, and withdrew. Lord Parke was as intensely interested as we were, and leaned forward to speak in a soft voice. He shook his head slightly.

"No," he said. "Only the barest information was in the cable." He frowned, took a taste of his wine, smiled in appreciation, and continued, hesitating at first. "I probably oughtn't to tell you this, but—" he broke off, smiling a little. "If I can't trust you two, whom can I trust?"

I felt quite a warm glow at this attestation from Lord Parke, and glancing at John, I could see he felt the same.

"Dr. Rieu had been in contact with Mr. Shapira in the months following the scandal," Lord Parke said. "And he had actually recommended the Museum purchase several manuscripts he—Mr. Shapira—had to sell." When we looked surprised, he nodded. "Yes, I know, it seems odd that they deemed him still trustworthy. I had felt the same, but Rieu explained to me, on an earlier occasion, that over the years, Shapira had brought them some three or four hundred manuscripts that were unquestionably authentic, and very valuable." He shrugged.

"So this Dr. Rieu received a telegram...," I prompted.

"Yes," Lord Parke said. "It was the very end of the meeting, when he burst in with the telegram and the shocking news." He shook his head in dismay. "I was, I have to say, not nearly as distressed as others in the room, who had known Shapira personally and worked with him for decades. Edward Bond, in particular, was quite cut up."

"Who had sent the telegram?" John asked.

Lord Parke thought a moment. "I believe Rieu said it was from the police chief in Rotterdam."

"One wonders why they contacted him, at the British Museum?" I said. "One hopes they contacted the poor man's family as well." I looked at Lord Parke.

"Then what happened at your board meeting?" I said.

"Well, no one wanted to linger on the subject, and it seemed inappropriate to continue the meeting as if nothing had happened, so we all shortly afterwards took our leave."

I mused a moment. "Do you think it likely that this will be in the newspapers soon?"

"Oh, I'm certain of it!" Lord Parke exclaimed. "If I hadn't left London soon after the meeting, I daresay I would have seen it in the evening papers."

"Yes," John said, twirling his wine glass by the stem absent-mindedly. "Much too horrific an event to escape the papers. Scandal and fraud, and now murder."

"Oh, no, good heavens," Lord Parke objected. "The telegram made it quite clear that it was suicide—and the consensus among the Board was that Mr. Shapira was so depressed by the events of last summer, and the consequent irreparable damage to his reputation, that he turned a pistol on himself."

John and I exchanged quick looks.

"What did the telegram actually say?" I asked quickly.

Lord Parke thought a moment. "I didn't see it myself, but as well as I can remember, when Rieu read it aloud, there was something about 'Shapira robbed himself of his life by gunshot,' something along those lines." He looked at me, then John.

"Why? Do you suspect it was actually murder?" He spoke with some asperity, and I saw the county magistrate in him rise to the fore. I began to answer when he interrupted me.

"And you say you have the Shapira Scrolls with you, here in Paris? That Shapira sent them to you?" He gave John a troubled look.

"Yes, that's what we believe they are," John said.

"But that's impossible!" Lord Parke exclaimed, looking from one to the other of us. We waited for him to illuminate us.

"The Shapira Scrolls are locked away in the British Museum," he said.

I almost laughed. "So what John has might be *imitations* of fraudulent documents? Curiouser and curiouser!"

* * *

We reconvened in John's studio after dinner, Lord Parke eager to join us and see the now possibly very questionable scrolls for himself. Madame Durnay, attentive as always, had heard us as John let himself in with his key, and anticipated that we might desire refreshments; within moments there was an assortment of sweet biscuits, with decanters of port wine and whisky ready to pour into crystal glasses, on the sideboard near the windows. Tall lighted tapers augmented the yellow gas lights, turned low behind etched glass globes for a warm and intimate atmosphere.

John disappeared behind the draperies and after a few moments returned with the package from Mr. Shapira. Lord Parke and I drew near as John swept papers and cloths aside on a large center table, and carefully laid out the leather strips. None of us touched them with our fingers, but Lord Parke took up a clean, slender paintbrush and carefully tipped some of the fragments to and fro, moving in closely to peer at them intently.

"Well," he said at last, straightening up, and laying aside the paintbrush. "I am assuredly not an expert in these matters, but from having seen the scrolls in London—albeit last year—these are remarkably like!" He frowned, rubbing his chin with one hand, thinking hard. "But I thought there were more of them—in fact, I'm sure there were at least fifteen of the strips. There are only seven here."

"Is it possible," I asked, looking sideways at John, "that the Museum returned some, or all, of the scrolls to Mr. Shapira, once the scandal died down? I mean, after all," I persisted, "they had determined they were fakes, did they not? Why would they want to keep them?"

"Very good question, Miss Paget," his lordship responded, nodding thoughtfully. "Perhaps I misunderstood, perhaps what the person was referring to was something else from Shapira, another manuscript?" His voice rose in a question; clearly, I thought, he was not sure what was the case.

John interposed, handing Lord Parke the note that had been enclosed with the leather strips. "Here is Shapira's letter that came with the package," he said. "You will see that he is troubled, and warns me to keep them safe."

Lord Parke quickly perused the short note, then handed it back to John, shaking his head. "I expect it would be important to indeed keep them safe."

John nodded. "Of course." He looked troubled. "I wish we could find out more about what happened to poor Mr. Shapira," he said. He glanced at me, and I gave him a nod.

"Indeed," I said. "Despite the seeming consensus that Mr. Shapira did away with himself, this package and note would seem to indicate otherwise." I frowned. "I suppose it's entirely too late to view the scene of death, or even the body—" I broke off as I saw Lord Parke's eyebrows shoot up in surprise, and smiled. "My dear Lord Parke, you cannot know, of course, that John and I have been exposed to not a few instances of murder and criminal behavior, in the years since we last saw you, up in Brampton. I assure you I am quite immured to the elements of violent crime and the viewing of dead bodies."

"I should not have been at all surprised," Lord Parke said. "But it has been too long since I was reminded of your curious, restless nature and your unorthodox approach to life and society." He smiled, to soften what might have sounded as a judgment. "I have missed this."

"But is it really too late?" John said eagerly. "Could we not take a train up to Rotterdam early tomorrow? We could be there by late afternoon and perhaps inquire at the hotel, or the police station?"

Lord Parke began to demur. "It really is not our concern..." but I interrupted, pointing to the leather strips on the table.

"Mr. Shapira has made it our concern, has he not?" I said. "He entrusted these items to John's care, and if he has met his end by foul means, it is absolutely up to us to free his reputation from the stain of self-murder, and bring the culprit to justice! We are 'the friends' you see, to whom Mr. Shapira refers, as being able to help John!"

Lord Parke looked from me to John, a slight smile on his face growing to a decided grin. "That's the spirit!" he said, and reached out a hand, palm down. "I'm for it!"

I laid my hand on his, and John put his hand on mine, and we as good as swore to find out the truth of the matter, starting out in the morning for Rotterdam on the first train.

Lord Parke insisted on making all the arrangements for us, which, I must admit, relieved my mind as to the comfort of the journey as well as the cost—my financial status was not so exalted as his lordship's, nor as prosperous as John's. We parted from John, and the cab dropped me first at my lodgings, and took Lord Parke on to the Hotel Westminster, where I'm sure he rested in the lap of luxury. We were all, indeed, in need of sleep and restoration.

But something wicked lay in wait that night, to shake our confidence and yet, strengthen our resolve.

SIX

The Country of Moab — Autumn 1871

"SELIM, MY FRIEND, THIS IS WHERE I AM MEANT TO BE."
Moses Shapira breathed in the sharp dawn air of the desert
as he prepared to mount his camel. His typical European
garb had been changed for flowing Bedouin robes—the
long, white, cotton *thawb* with wide sleeves, belted with a
hand-twisted leather strap; over it, useful for cold nights, he
had thrown a cape, the *abaye;* and what Moses wore most
proudly, his pale gold head scarf, secured with a rope of woven goat hair—the *agal*—ringed around his head. His wife,
Rosette, clucking with disapprobation, had nonetheless been
persuaded by her wheedling husband to sew into the front
of the *agal* a good luck talisman of his own making—a cen-
turies-old Star of David shekel embedded in a circle of cedarwood.

"Most respected sir," said Selim, his black eyes glinting
with the light of the rising sun. "The desert holds a place for
those who love her, and who come to know her ways." He
made an obeisance to the light, then gracefully mounted his
camel as Moses did the same. The valley of the Wadi Mujib—the Arnon River—lay before them, and the rising wall
of ancient caves lay beyond that.

The tightly grouped animals and guides began their cautious descent—with luck, they would make the oasis well

before noon, where they would camp until evening, when they would climb to explore the caves. The fiercest heat of the high season had passed, and each day and night grew cooler. Soon there would be rain in the mountains, and the wadis would fill with flash floods.

"Selim," Moses all but whispered to the guide as they rode side by side. "Tell me again what we are likely to find in the caves."

Selim shrugged, but leaned closer to whisper back. "More ancient things such as I brought to you in Jerusalem, many more," he said. "Pots, some only pieces; and figures—idols you call them, eh?" He glanced sharply at his client. "I know not why Christians have such liking for what they see as heathen stuff."

Moses laughed lightly. "It is the proof to them, you see? Proof that words of the Bible are true—stories are not made up, they are real, they are history!" He smiled broadly. "And all of them, they come to Moses Shapira, expert in ancient things, in Jerusalem."

A sudden flurry of activity at the head of their troop halted the whole line, a ripple of abrupt rearing of camels' heads and snorting of pack horses.

Selim prodded his camel to make its way to the front, calling out in a Bedouin dialect. A rapid and intense discussion ensued between him and the lead guide, ending with Selim riding back to Moses, his head shaking ominously.

"What is it?" Moses demanded. He had spent a good deal of money to finance this desert expedition, with the promise of fine and ancient Moabite artifacts—maybe even scrolls, he hoped—to bring back to the eager German and British and French scholars who haunted his shop in

Jerusalem. Ever since the Mesha Stele—the "Moabite Stone"—was discovered in 1868, there was a growing frenzy of interest in the discoveries of Bedouin tribes—men who knew every inch of the deserts east of the Dead Sea, and who could find the treasures that delighted the Europeans. Selim, his guide and colleague of sorts, had already brought him enough proofs of ancient archaeological riches that Moses could readily envision the caches of such gems that lay waiting under the desert sands.

He was, in fact, becoming famous for his Moabite collections—a renown that he felt would not only bring him wealth, but something else he craved even more—a respectable position among the scholarly brotherhood of religious savants of the Bible, both Christian and Hebrew.

He didn't want anything to interfere with this vision of the life he felt he deserved.

Selim leaned in to speak in a low voice. "There is some trouble ahead," he said. "A tribe who say the Wadi is their land." He frowned and spit into the sand as he said the name of the sheik who headed this tribe. "Thieves and liars, they are."

Apprehensive, Moses felt for the long knife hanging from his belt. His blood tingled and a fierce longing for fighting and bloodshed shot through him, as surprising as it was ferocious. Selim noticed the gesture, and put out a reassuring hand.

"I think a small trading will work, sir," he said, hiding a smile at his client's aggressive response. "Leave it to Selim."

Moses nodded, but still sat erect in the saddle, straining his eyes to see more of the desert men who were causing this delay. "Be quick about it, then, Selim," he said, glancing at the sky. "The day grows warm, and we need good light to explore caves." He gave the man an assessing look. "I trust your good sense to know what is necessary, no more."

Selim gave a quick nod and rode off again to the front of the line. In a very short time, less than an hour, as well as Moses could judge, the bickering and bartering that might well have gone on all day were concluded. He could see smiles and *salaams* on both sides as Selim handed over a small leather bag—coin, then, it seemed, was the medium of exchange today. Moses inferred from this that the tribe they were dealing with was more attached to a town than the desert, or they would have bartered for things of a more practical nature—cloth, dried fruit, spices, perhaps a desirable European cooking pot or silverware. Well, whatever made it happen, he was satisfied.

The Bedouin wheeled their horses with sharp, gleeful-sounding cries, and trotted off to the west, leaving Moses and his expedition to continue on their way. He and Selim exchanged relieved looks as the caravan started forward again.

Soon, by the light of a full moon, the caves beckoned.

* * *

A lantern held high threw light and shadows on the uneven walls and floor of the cave; the upper regions were lost in darkness. A handful of shards, edges pointed and sides curved, suggested the remains of broken pots. Further on, where Selim's agents had been at work, beyond a scrabble of rocks and dust, two smooth figurines lay revealed—a female and a male figure, looking as if they fitted perfectly together with each other in the timeless act of generation.

Moses released the breath he'd been holding, and chuckled. How funny the European Christians were about such idols, little household gods and such like things that women—time out of mind—tucked under the bed to bless a coupling with issue. They called them *obscene*, and pretended a scholarly distaste, but nonetheless, examined the little figures with a most prurient intensity.

He glanced up at Selim, hovering at his shoulder.

"Mother Sarah perhaps used such a charm of good fortune, no?" he said, smiling. "To get Father Abram in the mood?" They both chuckled at the expense of their common ancestors.

"Did I not tell you true?" Selim pressed, and waving a hand toward the back of the cave, continued. "There is so much more—you shall be most famous, sir, and most rich!"

Moses mumbled a quick blessing at this, to ward off the jealousy of the devil, and signed to Selim to say no more. The Bedouin guide veiled his eyes and his face even more than the darkness hid his thoughts, and the two men stepped further into the cave of Moabite antiquities.

SEVEN

Paris – Wednesday Very Early Morning, 12 March 1884

Here, dear Reader, is the account of John's adventure, as closely as I can recall from his description, and having reviewed contemporaneous notes of my own from the time.—V.P.

JOHN WOKE WITH A START—some small sound, the *snick* of a door latch? He had fallen asleep on the sofa in his study, having been too nervous and keyed up to retire immediately. He had once more surveyed his—what he hoped would be—his masterpiece, the portrait of Madame Gautreau— *Madame X*, he would call it, in discreet deference to the reputation of the famed beauty. *Although one need scarcely bother,* he had mused, it was all too clear who it was. But eventually he had fallen into a deep slumber, there on the sofa, until wakened by that little sound.

His eyes adjusted to the darkness, the fire having gone out, and he could see the mantelpiece clock by the light coming in the window—half-past three. He held his breath, listening intently for another sound; he tried not to move and betray his presence. After a few moments, he became aware of another person in the room, more like a shadow, moving about stealthily, close to the wall and the draperies, now past the fireplace, a figure slim and dressed all in black. A sudden gleam of light on metal caught John's eye as the wraith passed nearer the windows—a knife? The drapery to the inner room stirred with the touch of a hand.

The Shapira Scrolls were behind that drapery.

The thought electrified John's mind and his body leaped into action. He easily tackled the sylph-like figure—to his surprise he felt a woman's form beneath the tightly binding black clothing—and they landed on the floor in a sprawl.

A sudden slicing sting on his forearm caused him to yelp with pain, and he could feel warm blood flowing onto his white shirt, now ragged with the cut from the knife. The figure in black pushed him hard away, and scrambled up to run. John turned and with his unhurt arm reached out to grab an ankle, bringing her down to the floor again. But the intruder twisted out of his grasp with a muttered curse and a well-aimed kick at his wounded arm, making John curl up in pain. He looked back at the retreating figure in time to catch a glimpse of a pale, luminous face, and a few locks of bright blonde hair, escaped from the black cap pulled upon the woman's head. She was young and athletic—but that was all he could discern as the woman gained the door and raced away, almost soundlessly, down the stairs to the front entrance.

He rolled over and gasped as he put pressure on his wound to stanch the flow of blood—it was a surface cut, he could tell, but deep enough, and he gathered the sleeve of his shirt more firmly to hold it to where the blood seeped out, now more slowly. He managed to rise to his feet and after a moment's dizziness, downed the remains of a whisky he had left unfinished earlier in the evening.

A woman! Who could she be? Why had she come here, if not for the Shapira Scrolls? He was certain somehow that was the reason. Thank goodness he hadn't left them out on the table, where he and Lord Parke and Vi had been scrutinizing them; they might all now be gone with the woman, down the stairs and out the door. He realized, just then, that she had cursed in French, gutter language of the worst degree.

He heard footsteps running up the stairs, and the first moment's fear of the intruder returning was instantly replaced by relief at the sound of Madame Durnay's voice calling his name, and his *major d'omo* Guido shouting out as well—and then he could only laugh, a little hysterically, at the sight of his two stalwart servants, dressed in their nightclothes and brandishing fireplace tongs and a large iron pan, as they burst into the room.

* * *

Lord Parke's hired carriage rolled up to John's door to take us to the Gare du Nord for the train to Rotterdam, and we watched as John stepped out of the house, rather awkwardly holding a leather satchel, with Guido in tow carrying a small bag.

He entered the carriage while Guido handed up his luggage to the driver, who stowed it on top, and greeted me and Lord Parke. I noted John's pale looks immediately.

"John!" I exclaimed. "What has happened? You look awful!"

"And a very good morning to you, too, Vi," John said, easing himself onto the seat next to Lord Parke. He handed me the leather satchel with his right hand, and half-cradled his left in his lap.

"You're hurt," said Lord Parke. "What *has* happened?"

"I'll tell you the whole of it as soon as we are off," John said. Lord Parke tapped his cane on the ceiling of the carriage, and the driver urged the horses forward.

As John related the events of the night before, both I and Lord Parke uttered sounds of shock and dismay. Inconceivable! When he had finished his tale, we sat silent and thoughtful for some minutes.

"A woman!" Lord Parke marvelled at it.

"Quite a capable one at that," John added, lightly touching his arm.

"And this leather satchel," I said, "contains....?"

John nodded.

"And you are certain that this was what the thief was after?" Lord Parke asked, glancing at the satchel.

John shrugged. "Of course, I cannot be absolutely certain, but I cannot think of anything I possess that would tempt a thief." He shook his head, smiling a little. "Unless it was Madame Gautreau, having changed her mind about the portrait before it goes to the Salon next month."

"And that's not very likely," I said with half a wink. "It's the best thing you've done, and she'll be the star of the season!"

Lord Parke was looking worried. "Is there any possibility...do you think...we could be followed?"

That had not struck me before, but it did now, with a force. "We'll have to be extraordinarily vigilant," I said. "But there are three of us, to one of her."

"Unless she is but a tool in someone else's plan," Lord Parke said grimly. "There may be more than one to watch for."

The carriage jolted to a halt, and we realized that we had arrived at the Gare du Nord. Despite the bustle of luggage and directions to the right platform—all having been superbly arranged by Lord Parke's valet and the concierge at the Hotel Westminster, with porters and baggagemen at the ready—I nonetheless kept my eyes peeled for signs of anyone paying attention to us, and I saw both my companions' eyes constantly darting over the crowds moving at a brisk pace through the station. But I saw nothing to concern me, and very soon we were most comfortably settled in a private cabin in the salon car, with a continental breakfast, coffee and tea already waiting for us, piping hot and fresh. We settled in immediately, the train chugged its way out of the station, and we prepared to consider our plans during the five-hour journey to Rotterdam.

EIGHT

Jerusalem —January 1872
The Shop in the Street of the Christians

MOSES HAD WALKED TO THE FRONT OF HIS SHOP to answer a question from a customer, and having satisfied the woman as to the names of the pressed flowers in the booklet she was looking at, he glanced out the window and saw a man about his own age, early forties he guessed, gazing intently at an object on display. He appeared to be an Englishman, based on his dress, but Moses had not seen him before, in his shop or at the church. Yet something about him was familiar. He waited a few moments, watching the stranger; then, as the man continued at the window, Moses went round to the door and casually stepped outside. The man then glanced up, and Moses seized his opportunity.

"A wonderful day in the old city, is it not, sir?" he said most politely, waving a hand to the deep blue sky above them. "Haff you come here on pilgrimage?"

The stranger shook his head, smiled, and addressed Moses with equal politeness but an underlying testiness. "I am new to Jerusalem, sir, having just travelled from Jaffa—a dreadful business, to be sure, never seen the like of it, I must say, boys walking on all fours in some dratted village, gaping about, us travelling along like a circus menagerie, seemed to me."

He seemed to recollect himself then, and holding out his hand, introduced himself as Christian David Ginsburg of London. Moses shook his hand heartily.

"I knew you look familiar, dear sir!" he cried. "Why, your profile I saw in the newspapers, about your book on the Moabite Stone, is so like! And what a great and scholarly masterpiece! I haff read it through and through." Moses released the man's hand and made a short bow. "I am Moses Wilhelm Shapira, proprietor of this humble shop, and I welcome you with all my whole heart to Jerusalem."

Pleased and flattered, Ginsburg beamed at Moses, then turned back with suppressed excitement to the item in the window that had caught his attention. He pointed to a fragment of old-looking stone, inscribed with lettering, gesturing to Moses to come closer.

"That," he said, "that stone, it looks almost exactly like a piece of the Moabite Stone. I have seen the larger fragments in Paris, and you must know that there may very well be other pieces, scattered here and there."

"I know very well, indeed, my learned sir," Moses said, and with a flourish of one hand, continued. "Please to come inside, and you will see even more—I haff had a big shipment in the night, and you are to be the first to look them over with me."

Ginsburg was enthusiastic, but upon entering the store, he judged the light was so dim that it would be impossible to conduct a proper inspection of the stone fragments Moses put before him.

"Is it possible, sir, or do I ask too much," Ginsburg said, "for you to bring this collection to my hotel later this afternoon? There the light will be excellent, for I have a room on an upper floor, with many windows."

Moses bowed. "I would be so happy, sir," he said. "You are staying at the Mediterranean, just around the corner?"

"Why, how did you guess?" Ginsburg said, surprised.

Moses smiled. "It is the only hotel for important travellers such as yourself. The American writer, Mr. Mark Twain, stayed there, I believe, some years ago, and wrote well of the wonders of our city."

"Then I shall expect you at, say, three o'clock?"

Moses bowed again, and watched as Ginsburg, taking one more look at the stone in the window, wandered off down the street. What an opportunity!

* * *

The Mediterranean did indeed house its guests in superior rooms, and Ginsburg's was no exception. Moses had climbed three floors to arrive at the light-filled suite where Ginsburg was staying, and had now spread out a large collection of "Moabite" stones and fragments for the British scholar to examine.

His host had ordered a proper English tea to be served, including a decanter of fine sherry, of which he invited Moses to take a fortifying glass before they began their work.

The two men stood at the window looking out as the sun's rays, making their way west across the sky, threw the myriad of white buildings into stark relief of shadow and light. Ginsburg downed a glass of sherry quickly and poured himself another.

"This is my first time here," he confided to Moses. "I cannot believe it took me this long—as I begin the middle years of my life—to come to this Holy City." He eyed the antiquarian benignly. "I gather you have lived here for a while?"

"Yes, I haff," Moses said, sipping his sherry. "I arrived as young man of twenty-six—with no family, friends or fortune, but this city"—he waved a hand over the buildings—"she has been good to me, and my little shop overlooked by the King's Tower."

"Your accent," Ginsburg said, hesitating, "may I ask? Is it Russian?" He paused fractionally. "Are you—were you born a Jew?"

Moses looked at him, his eyes bright with equal parts suspicion and interest. He had learned many things about Ginsburg from other scholars, and this was one of them. He smiled. "Yes, like you, Herr Professor Ginsburg, I am a Jewish Christian—a convert to the Way."

Ginsburg flushed a bit at this, but recovered quickly. "We are a small but growing tribe," he said.

"We are, in much ways," Moses added after a moment's reflection, "true sons of the forefathers, both Jew and Christian; together we haff the faith, vision and promise in the—forgive me my words—wideness and the deep roots we share."

"And our destiny," Ginsburg said. The sherry was making him sentimental, Moses thought.

"We are brothers," Moses said, and held up his glass; Ginsburg touched it lightly with his own, and they drank to their shared identity. Then they put the glasses down, and Ginsburg rubbed his palms together in excitement.

"Now, let us see what you have here!"

* * *

Ginsburg had carefully examined every stone and fragment on the table, sometimes using an eye-glass, holding them carefully in his hand, feeling their weight, their contours. Moses stood by, not too near, watching every move, every nuance of the man's face and catching at the mutterings under his breath. Occasionally Ginsburg would turn aside to jot down some notes in a little leather book, even making drawings of some of the characters incised on the stones.

At last, in the waning light of the late afternoon—they had moved two lamps in the room to set them nearer the table—Ginsburg straightened up from his hunched-over position, and heaved a great sigh.

"I am convinced," he said, while Moses held his breath, "that these are not, any of them, pieces of the great Mesha Stele—the Moabite Stone—some of which I have had the honor of studying extensively." At Moses' slight sound of dismay, he held up his hand. "That is not to say that they are not authentically ancient fragments of another monument."

He picked up one of the larger pieces and traced the writing with one finger. "I am familiar with this character, for instance," he said. "But it is not one which appears on the Moabite Stone." He put it back down, dusted his hands, and turned to look at Moses straight on, his face sympathetic and kindly.

"I fear it is just possible," he said, "that the Bedouin have grasped the enormous value of 'ancient stone fragments'—ever since that dragoman Ganneau started offering exorbitant rewards for the smallest pieces—damn him! He's set off a whole cottage industry of breaking up monuments—some of them authentic!—and selling them off piece by piece."

He sighed, and put a hand on Moses' shoulder. "It would require more time than I have at present," he said, "to determine whether you have the genuine article here, my friend, or if you have been duped by clever desert rats."

Moses didn't say anything, but moved quietly to place the stone fragments back in the box he had brought them in. Still silent, he bowed to Ginsburg with great dignity, and made his way from the room, down the stairs and back out into the noise and dust of the street.

It was a blow, but not a devastating or irrevocable one. He considered himself to have nearly as good an eye and judgement of these artifacts as any scholar living—and he had faith in his destiny. He would just re-double his scrutiny of items the Bedouin brought him from now on.

* * *

In another street of the city, high above the old quarters and dark alleys, Charles Clermont-Ganneau, consul for the French government, sat at his desk and brooded over the fragments of the additional, real Moabite Stone that he had managed—by hook and by crook—to recover from the desert tribes who had scattered them across the land. He picked up a letter on his desk, from Christian David Ginsburg, received three days earlier, asking permission to visit and see for himself the Moabite Stone fragments in Ganneau's possession. Ginsburg had seen the few collected earlier, along with the paper-pressed "squeeze" of the monument's writing Ganneau had succeeded in wresting under the watchful, greedy eyes of the Bedouin—and nearly paying for it with the lives of his hired men—but Ginsburg was now asking to see more of it.

Ganneau would let him come to his office, maybe tomorrow—but he had no intention of letting this arch-rival of a scholar get a glimpse of these fragments. Ginsburg might translate the characters differently from what Ganneau was working on, and that would cast suspicion on the authenticity of the writing, perhaps of the stone itself—and de-value it in the eyes of prospective purchasers. No, these fragments were going to be for his eyes only.

NINE

Rotterdam—Wednesday, 12 March 1884

LORD PARKE WAS FROWNING AS HE LOOKED OUT the train window at rolling fields, brown and half-frozen in the lees of winter. John had closed his eyes for some much-needed sleep, and I was busy thinking—remembering every detail I could recall from the previous summer and autumn, about the scandal of the Shapira Scrolls—and trying in vain to recall the content of my brief conversation with Mr. Shapira himself.

"My lord," I said, leaning forward and speaking quietly, so as not to disturb John. He did likewise, an inquiring look on his aristocratic face. "Do you recall the translation of the Shapira Scrolls—I mean, from what appeared in the papers at the time?"

Lord Parke was thoughtful. "I believe it was Professor Ginsburg who translated them—he's still at the Museum, Ginsburg," he added. He pursed his lips and looked up at the ceiling.

I elucidated my question. "I mean, I recall that the text was purportedly the last address of Moses to the Israelites, before they entered the Land of Canaan, enumerating all sorts of strictures and laws and so forth, to wit, the Ten Commandments." I waved my hand in the air.

"Yes, that is correct," Lord Parke said, smiling slightly at my dismissive treatment, I presumed, of the Decalogue. He looked at me with good-humoured interest.

"You are not a believer, then?" he said tentatively. I instantly recalled that Lord Parke, as was the case with his illustrious cousins the Howards, in whose castle in Cumbria we had experienced a most magical and murderous adventure, was Roman Catholic.

"You will forgive me, my lord," I said, feeling mischievous at the use of the verb, "but no, I am not, as you say, a believer."

"But you are an ardent ethicist and humanist," he insisted. He smiled fully now. "In my book, that's as much and more than one could ask of an intelligent, thinking person in these modern times."

I nodded in agreement, and continued. "But wasn't there one special peculiarity about that translation, other than that it was deemed to be an early, if not an original, writing of the Book of Deuteronomy?"

"I recall," Lord Parke said, "that there was no mention of the death of Moses, which our 'traditional' versions of Deuteronomy all contain—and which, for many scholars now, seems to be proof enough that the prophet Moses actually didn't write it—for how could he write of his own death?"

I laughed softly, but shook my head. The fact I was seeking was just beyond my mind's reach, then it came to me just as Lord Parke started to speak again, and we spoke at the same moment.

"There was an extra commandment!" We had spoken louder in our excitement, and woke up John.

"What?" he said, sitting up straighter and taking a deep breath. "What's that you say?"

"I'm so sorry we awakened you," I apologized. "We were talking about the contents of the Shapira Scrolls, and we remembered that there were some differences from tradition, including an extra—well, I guess you could say, an *eleventh* Commandment."

"I know what it was," John said. "Thou shalt not awaken thy companions from a deep sleep!"

We chuckled at this, and I shook my head. "One difference I recall was something like, *Thou shalt not slay the soul of thy brother*—not the more general, traditional *Thou shalt not kill.*" I looked at Lord Parke for confirmation.

He looked at me, his head tilted slightly. "I remember that too, but there was also a slightly different translation of the eleventh commandment, I believe I saw it in a later translation of those scrolls," he said. "*Thou shalt not hate thy brother in thy heart. I am God, your God.*" He looked slightly apologetic. "That was written after every commandment."

I thought about the two translations. "It's a similar kind of sentiment, is it not, in the two statements? Where did you see this later translation?"

Lord Parke considered this. "I remember it was in an article for the Palestine Exploration Fund journal, by that French archaeologist, what's the chap's name...Ganneau, Charles Clermont-Ganneau, to be exact." He shook his head. "He was the major detractor in the whole scandal, by the way, awfully vehement about it, as I recall." He looked at me and John. "They're still talking about it, the Museum board, even now."

"I hadn't realized you had been so taken up with archaeology, my lord," I said. "Have you been on any expeditions?"

Lord Parke nodded, and spoke with enthusiasm about a recent trip to Egypt to visit the famous pyramids. At the end of an exciting story involving a cursed tomb, John took out his watch and noted the time. "We'll be in Rotterdam soon, but there's still time for more coffee, I hope?"

Lord Parke promptly took the hint and pulled the bell cord to summon a porter. We were soon settled with more excellent coffee and sandwiches. I decided we needed to sort through our plans.

"Where do we start, once we're in Rotterdam?" I queried my companions. "The hotel? The police station? Elsewhere?" I looked down at the leather satchel John had placed on the seat next to me. "And what do we do with that?" I shivered at the memory of what John had endured last night.

Lord Parke cleared his throat slightly. "I, er, took the liberty of contacting a friend in Rotterdam," he said. "Actually, a cousin of sorts, who knows people...in short, I believe we are expected at the Hotel Willemsbrug, to meet with an inspector of the police who is involved in this matter."

"Capital!" I said, approving of his foresight, and only slightly piqued that he hadn't told us this already. "That does sound like an excellent start."

* * *

Soon after, the train pulled into Rotterdam Station; we only had hand luggage, although Lord Parke secured a porter to carry our bags anyway. John kept a firm grip on the leather satchel as we followed the porter to a waiting carriage.

As I was idling for a moment on the sidewalk, looking about curiously at this city, new to me, my eye was caught by a sudden quick movement to my left—I saw a flash of blonde curls falling from a tight bonnet that had gone slightly askew, a slender form dressed in a dark blue dress, with a form-fitting, short black jacket—a woman, young by her active, graceful movements. She immediately disappeared into a private carriage that had pulled up a little distance behind our public conveyance. The coachman, a large man with a plain and ugly face, impatiently jerked at the reins to pull his horse out of the line, almost before the carriage door was shut, and moved into the busy road that led away from the railway station. I could not tell whether there was anyone already in the carriage, but something in the way the woman kept her head down as she entered it seemed to indicate there was no one else within.

It had happened so swiftly that although I enjoined both of my companions to attend to the woman, the carriage was out of sight within moments. We decided we would redouble our efforts at vigilance, and would keep an eye out for the blonde lady in the dark blue dress.

TEN

Jerusalem — Two Years On – 1874
The Shop in the Street of the Christians

"WHAT ISS THAT RACKET FROM HELL?" Moses Shapira rose impatiently from his cedar table at the back of his shop, and peered down a hallway crowded with sheepskins and braided rugs toward the front door. "Hassan, what iss going on?"

His servant and doorman, dressed in flowing Arabian garments to exoticize the shop and entice curious European customers, appeared caught between indoors and the street—he danced from foot to foot, the curled-up toes of his fanciful shoes twitching, as he watched in apparent fascination at some scene in the street, and attempted to relay his information to his master.

"A most extensive entourage, *alsyd* Shapira," he called out.

Moses made his way quickly to the front of the shop. "Europeans? Or Turkish poliss?"

Before Hassan could answer, Moses was at his side, peering from the relative darkness of the shop into the brilliant sunlight at mid-day in Jerusalem. The growing influx of tourists in the past decade, most of them Europeans, had resulted in the local government cleaning up the city to an astonishing degree, given what it had been twenty years earlier when Moses first arrived. Flinging the carcasses of animals from the slaughterhouses into the streets and alleys had been banned; water and sewage systems were being installed; garbage was hauled away on a daily basis. Anglican-run hospitals and hostels had diminished the legions of legless beggars and sick foreigners dying in the streets. It was actually becoming a city worth living in.

"Is that Ganneau? That devil, what does he think he's doing?" Moses scowled as he recognized the French official—and archaeological savant—Charles Clermont-Ganneau, astride a magnificent black horse and leading a retinue of riders both men and women, surrounded by servants dressed in the livery of the French consul in Jerusalem. The narrow street, with its canopy of translucent cotton draperies strung between the balconies of upper apartments, affording a modicum of shade from the burning sun, barely allowed them room enough to pass without knocking into the people who stood and gaped at the parade.

As Moses had intuited, with no little apprehension, the procession came to a halt in front of his shop. Ganneau, a thin man with handsome, haughty Gallic features—he was some fifteen or so years younger than Moses, who was now in his forties—stayed in the saddle a few moments, looking down at Moses. The two men eyed each other with restrained but mutual dislike. Moses maintained a stony silence until Ganneau finally dismounted, handing the reins to a servant standing by.

"Monsieur Shapira," the Frenchman said, nodding his head slightly in greeting.

"Consul Ganneau," Moses said in reply, also barely moving his head. He surveyed the other riders lined up behind Ganneau, who were in the process of dismounting.

Several ladies in riding habits were assisted by servants and gentlemen. Moses' business instincts overcame his dislike of his rival, and he managed a welcoming smile.

"I am honored that you and your friends haff come to visit my liddle shop," he said, with a half bow.

Ganneau didn't hide a smirk, but then spoke civilly. "My friends are so very eager to see the treasures of the foremost antiquarian—the famous Moses Shapira and his collection of Moabite antiquities—I could only escort them here myself to show them the wonders they seek."

Moses bowed and stepped out of the doorway to allow the visitors to enter. One young woman, particularly striking in a sky-blue riding habit and a fanciful hat decorated with peacock feathers, perched on an abundance of golden curls, seemed already in raptures as she stopped to survey the items on display.

"Oh, look, Charles!" she exclaimed, taking Ganneau by the arm. Her accent was British, her voice clear and low; she continued to speak to Ganneau, but now in fluent French, exclaiming over the items in the shop window. *Charming,* Moses thought, watching her. She turned to him. "You are Mr. Shapira?" Without waiting for him to answer, she held out a hand for him to shake. "Laura Simmons-Hartley," she said. Moses took her hand lightly and bowed over it.

"Tell me," she said, her eyes alight with excitement, "Do you have anything that dates back to the very time of Our Lord? I do so desire to hold in my hand something that He might have seen or even touched!"

Moses smiled kindly—he had seen this depth of enthusiasm time and again. "Of course, dear lady," he said, not glancing at Ganneau, whom he could sense was stiff with displeasure. "Come this way—I haff some Roman coins, with the head of Caesar on them—like the one the Lord Himself held up to show the apostles where they should be loyal."

"Oh, yes! 'Render unto Caesar the things that are Caesar's'!" The young woman exclaimed, her lovely blue eyes wide. She dropped her hand from Ganneau's arm and hurried into the shop. Moses gestured gallantly to the other ladies and gentlemen who were just as eager to enter and find their own treasures.

In an odd little moment of shared superiority, he and Ganneau exchanged a glance that as good as spoke their indulgent sufferance of these avid pilgrim-tourists—people who had no idea of the true value and deep excitement of belonging to the well-guarded brotherhood of archaeology, which these two men, however grudgingly, shared.

Once inside the shop, however, enmity returned. While Moses and his chief assistant obligingly showed and explained to the visitors the various items they were interested in, Ganneau stationed himself before the locked glass cabinet in which were displayed an impressive array of Moabite statues, little figurines of presumed gods and goddesses of the household, along with bits of pottery and shards with incised lettering on them—all purporting to be some three thousand years old or more.

The Moabite craze had begun several years earlier, and Ganneau had played a significant but ethically questionable role in the delivery of the Moabite Stone from the Bedouins to his government in France. His success had been marred by his impetuous and devious trading with different tribes, whose impatience and greed had resulted in the stone having been broken into dozens of fragments and strewn about the desert. Several years of painstaking searches in dangerous territories had ultimately yielded about two-thirds of the original stone, enough to allow scholars to interpret the writing and date it to the time of the Moabite King Mesha, whose battle with the Israelites in the ninth century B.C.E. was described in the second book of Kings.

The significance of this discovery had driven Moses Shapira, among some others, to the caves of Moab, which had yielded hundreds of ancient items, and as the wily Selim had predicted, had brought riches to Moses and a fair amount of acclaim as the best dealer in antiquities in the Middle East.

But as Ganneau stood before the case of Moabite figurines, Moses heard him scoffing and deriding the collection.

"I see nothing here that could remotely be from the ninth century before Christ," he said, pointing his index finger at a crude-looking statuette of a woman giving birth. "I think these are modern productions, buried in the sand and treated with oils and tannins to give the appearance of age."

There were murmurs and exclamations from his friends as he continued his impromptu lecture. Moses could not keep himself from intervening.

"Sir," he said, trying to sound calm, "I would haff you know that I myself journeyed so many, many times to the caves of the Wadi Mujib, and unburied these very statues with my own hands"—and he shook his hands in front of him to emphasize—"from dirts and rocks not disturbed since ancient times."

Ganneau looked amused; the young lady in blue, Miss Simmons-Hartley, looked from one man to the other, and seemed to discern the animosity between them.

"Mr. Shapira," she said in a decisive tone, "you mentioned some Roman coins to me. Would you be so good as to show them to me now?"

Moses bowed to her and led the way to a table where a vitrine of coins was on display, glancing back only once to see that the visitors had dispersed around the shop, and Ganneau had ceased to denigrate his Moabite collection.

For now.

ELEVEN

Rotterdam—Wednesday, 12 March 1884

THERE WAS ACTUALLY A TOUCH OF SPRING in the air when we drove through the cobbled streets of the old part of Rotterdam, towards the Hotel Willemsbrug. Although the sun would soon disappear behind still wintery clouds, at the moment there were some warming rays piercing thin clouds in an almost blue sky. It made the grey city a little less grey, but not much.

As the carriage pulled up before the worn building that was the respectable but aging hotel, and we began to alight, I looked intensely to my right and left, seeking the coachman with the ugly face and the graceful blonde in the blue dress and black jacket. No other coach drew near, but that didn't mean there were no watchers. I saw John and Lord Parke equally uneasy, and equally alert, and felt a little comforted with the idea that at least we wouldn't be taken completely by surprise, with all of us on our tiptoes, so to speak.

We were greeted by the hotel manager as we entered the genteelly shabby lobby. He executed a properly stiff bow to Lord Parke first, then to me and John.

"I hope you have had a pleasant trip from Paris," he said in lightly accented English. "I am Herr Innesbrucke." He was a man just past middle age, with thinning hair, but energetic and trim, impeccably dressed. He looked, to my eye, as if he should be better placed in a much more fashionable establishment than the Hotel Willemsbrug. Lord Parke murmured a polite response, and Herr Innesbrucke gestured to some waiting attendants to take our bags (to where I was not sure), and with an outstretched hand he invited us to follow him.

We were ushered into a good-sized room, set up for meetings, I presumed, with a large table and several chairs around it. There were three men seated there who all rose when we came in, and we were introduced to them: two policemen, and a minor official of the town who we were soon to learn was the coroner, or medical examiner for the police, Dr. Hans Voorhaven.

The policeman in charge, one Inspector Gerald Putman Cramer, was a middle-aged man, with sandy hair and keen eyes, and not an ounce of spare flesh, judging from the fit of his neat, pressed uniform. His younger colleague—I don't recall his name—seemed a fair copy of his superior. The Inspector looked with a discernible amount of suspicion at the three of us on the other side of the table.

"May I ask why you have an interest in this sad case?" He said it mildly, but it was clear that only the correct answer (to him) would allow the meeting to proceed. Lord Parke led the charge.

"As a member of the Board of Directors of the British Museum," he said, calmly, "I represent the interests of the Museum in the tragic demise of one of our chief correspondents for antiquities in Jerusalem." Inspector Cramer nodded slightly, as if to say *proceed*.

"The Museum's Department of Oriental Manuscripts had lately contracted to purchase several documents from

Mr. Shapira," Lord Parke went on. "It is possible that among Mr. Shapira's effects, we might find those documents, as well as other information regarding pending sales that were mooted between the Museum and Mr. Shapira." He leaned back in his chair minutely. "And of course, we are interested in the manner of his death, as well as wishing to, perhaps, contribute to what may be needed for a proper burial."

"And this lady and this gentleman?" The Inspector gave a brief look at me and John.

"I became acquainted with Mr. Shapira about six weeks or so ago," John spoke up. "We met accidentally in Haarlem, at the City Hall, where we discussed the Franz Hals exhibit."

"Ah," said the Inspector. "You are the artist—Mr. John Singer Sargent." It was a statement, not a question.

John inclined his head in agreement. I saw that he hesitated, as if about to say more, then kept silent. Before I could speak, Lord Parke spoke for me.

"This lady is the celebrated writer Vernon Lee," he said. "She is a particular friend of mine, and has connections with the Museum as well; I welcome her keen insights and analytical mind."

It was enough to make me blush.

Inspector Cramer tapped his index finger idly on a piece of paper he had laid on the table in front of him. He appeared to be making up his mind, and presently came to a conclusion.

"We were at first unaware," he said, slowly leaning forward, "of Mr. Shapira's full identity." He looked down at the paper, and then slid it across the table toward us. Lord Parke took it up and John and I leaned in to read the short paragraph that was written on it, in English. It read:

Statement of Inspector G. P. Cramer
for Daily Police Log dated 9 March 1884

After it was discovered at the office in the guest-
house of L.C. Wickers at Boompjes at the Hotel
Willemsbrug that a lodge guest did not come out of
his room the day before yesterday and the door was
still closed, Inspector police officer, Gerald Putman
Cramer went in to look. It was found that a guest
named Shapira had robbed himself of his life by gun-
shot. The corpse was looked at by a medical person
before it was brought to the storage known as
Drinkling. Nothing else was known about him other
than that he was married.

"The hotel was given some incorrect information, we
believe," Inspector Cramer continued, "as to Mr. Shapira's
occupation and city of residence. A later perusal of his personal documents, however, revealed to us who he was."

We all sat in silence for a few moments, Dr. Voorhaven,
the third official in the room, cleared his throat before speaking.

"I am the medical person who examined the body," he
said. "I saw that the man was wearing a gold wedding ring,
hence the assumption that he was married."

Inspector Cramer interjected, "When we looked over
his papers, although it was not until yesterday—the death
having been discovered late on a Saturday—we discovered
no information about his wife or family, or where they might
be found so that we could relay the sad news of his death."

He paused a moment, then continued. "But we saw his *carte d'affaires*, and saw he styled himself as a 'correspondent to the British Museum'."

"And how was it that you chose to cable Dr. Rieu in particular at the British Museum?" Lord Parke asked.

The Inspector looked a little annoyed at being thus interrogated. I could almost hear him saying *I'm the one asking questions here*. But the man was, thankfully, rational, and answered. "There was a letter from Dr. Rieu, in Mr. Shapira's wallet, and it was considered the quickest way to obtain more information."

"I was present when Dr. Rieu came into the Board room with the cable," Lord Parke said, "and read it aloud to all of us. We were, needless to say, shocked and concerned."

"*Have* his family been informed?" John asked. He looked pained, and I recalled he had said Shapira spoke about how much he was missing his family.

Dr. Voorhaven shook his head. "We have not yet received any information in response from Dr. Rieu, or anyone else at the Museum, so we will have to wait." He then looked curiously at Lord Parke. Ah, I thought, the Inspector's turn to ask questions.

"How is it, my lord," he asked, "that you are here so quickly? The cable to Dr. Rieu was only sent yesterday morning."

I noticed that the Inspector's calm grey eyes had gained a gleam of deeper interest. "And I understand," he continued, "that you have come direct from Paris? Not London?"

I leaned slightly forward to catch John's eye, and after a moment, he nodded slightly and answered the question before Lord Parke could speak.

"Lord Parke happened to run into Miss Paget—Miss Lee, that is—and me at dinner last evening, upon his arrival in Paris," John explained, "and when he told us about having heard, in London, of Mr. Shapira's death, it precipitated our visit here, to find out more."

"More?" echoed the Inspector. "Why would you need to know more?"

John took a deep breath, and glanced at Lord Parke, who shrugged infinitesimally. John proceeded to answer.

"Because I received a package yesterday morning from Mr. Shapira, along with a note asking me to keep the items in the package safe—that he felt himself to be under some kind of threat—and because"—John paused to take another breath—"because I myself was attacked in my own home in the early hours of this morning, in the course of an attempted robbery, probably of the very items Mr. Shapira sent to me."

Inspector Cramer frowned; the other two men looked more startled. Perhaps, I thought, they were not as experienced in criminal ways as the good Inspector, and therefore more inclined to be surprised.

"Pardon me if I am mistaken," said the Inspector, looking narrowly at all three of us in turn. He was a sharp thinker, I could see, and had made the necessary leap quite quickly. "I take it you are suggesting that Mr. Shapira did *not* take his own life?" He paused a moment. "That he was, in fact, murdered, perhaps in relation to these items, as you say, that he sent to you? And what are these items, and where are they now?"

"But that is impossible!" cried Dr. Voorhaven, interrupting before John could answer. "The room was locked.

There was every indication that it was self-harm—the pistol was on the floor next to the body, just where it should be as it fell from his hand after discharging it. The wound to his head, at such close range...no, no, it was suicide. I am certain of it."

I looked sharply at the Inspector, who seemed to be troubled. His younger colleague, who had been busy making notes in a small leather-covered book, leaned over and whispered something to him, something which made his face take on an even more strained and thoughtful look.

"What is it, Inspector?" I asked. "You don't necessarily agree with the good doctor." I considered the doctor's words, and had a flash of insight. "Something about the room being locked?

He hung fire for a long moment, then gave a brief, grim smile. "You are indeed perceptive, Miss Vernon Lee," he said. "My sergeant here reminds me that no room key was found in Mr. Shapira's possession."

"Leaving open the possibility," I said, "that someone took the key, locked the door and walked away."

He nodded, then frowned. "We must conduct a thorough search of the room—again; it is possible the key fell and is hidden in some obscure place." He started to rise from the table, as if to set off immediately.

"May we accompany you, Inspector?" said Lord Parke, rising also. "It would be an opportune time to examine Mr. Shapira's remaining documents."

"Oh, but that is not possible," said the Inspector. "All of Mr. Shapira's effects and belongings were removed, along with the body, and are not available at present to be reviewed. It is all at the police station."

We took a moment to absorb this information. I addressed the medical examiner. "And where is the body now?" I asked. "At the morgue?"

An awkward silence met my query.

"I'm afraid, that is, necessity required that we bury the body in a timely manner," Dr. Voorhaven said, spreading his hands in an apologetic gesture. "Given that we deemed it a suicide—" he broke off, but Lord Parke took up his meaning instantly.

"He was buried in a pauper's field, with no marker?" His voice rose, and I laid my hand on his arm to calm him. He looked at me, and I shook my head slightly. It would be of little use to pursue this issue at this time. Nonetheless, the Inspector attempted a further explanation.

"That is the meaning, in my report, of having taken the body to *Drinkling*," he said, and paused. "It is a place, here in Rotterdam, where the bodies of unknown persons, usually those who have drowned at sea or in the canals, are taken, and then buried in a far section of the city cemetery. There are, of necessity, no grave markers." He did not enlarge on the issue of why suicides were buried there also.

We were all silent for a few moments, contemplating this sad ending for Mr. Shapira.

"Nonetheless," I said, forestalling Lord Parke's evident indignation before he could speak again, "It would be very valuable for us to see his room, if at all possible, Inspector. Perhaps fresh eyes on the scene might bring forth other interpretations?" I smiled in what I hoped was a winning manner, but whatever was conveyed by it was enough.

"We will survey the room," the Inspector said.

TWELVE

Jerusalem — 1874
The Shop in the Street of the Christians

As a child of five in 1874, Moses's daughter Myriam was unusually precocious and observant, and she adored her father. He often took her riding on his big white horse, out into the desert and hills to watch the sun rise and feel the morning awakening. At home, he encouraged her to stand at his side and learn about the antiquities he found and sold, and the precious manuscripts in Hebrew, Greek and Latin that were prized by scholars from countries all over the world.

She was frequently at the shop, even after the family moved from nearby dark little rooms on the Russian Hill, to a much grander, light-filled house farther away—Villa Rachid it was called, built partly in European and partly in the "Mussulman" style. Her mother was happier there, as it was in a very respectable neighborhood, and her friends from Christ Church could be received much more comfortably for tea and dinner than at the old apartment. The "horrible Moabitish idols," so loathed by Moses's wife, had nonetheless brought great fortune to her husband and all the family.

But the shop on the Street of the Christians always held a strong fascination for Myriam, with its dark corners filled with colorful woven cloth, feathers and hides, and the drawers of flattened scrolls with their spidery brown writing— she started learning Hebrew at a very early age, and eventually became so adept she once corrected her father in a particularly complex translation. Her older sister, Augusta, and she were frequently enlisted to gather and press wild-flowers onto woven paper to make souvenirs for the tourists—Myriam rather enjoyed the task, although Augusta disdained the work, and detested the shop altogether.

So it came about that little Myriam witnessed her first glimpse of adult life—and adult sin—when she saw her father so taken with the charms of "the lady in blue," as she always thought of her from that day on, that he was led by the exuberance of his passions both physical and intellectual to be unfaithful for a short time to his long-suffering wife.

Myriam had come to the shop the morning after the rather fraught visit by her father's enemy, Clermont-Ganneau, accompanied by her nanny and companion, Ouarda, who would often sit outside in the back, overlooking Bath-sheba's Pool, while the child was inside with her father.

Laura Simmons-Hartley had arrived at the shop at an early hour. Moses was industrious and active, an early riser as well, and was there to attend to her personally as she took a greater tour of the contents of the shop.

"Are you interested in any particular antiquities, my lady?" Moses asked. When she didn't demur at the title he gave her, he knew he was correct in assuming she was the daughter of an English nobleman—he had consulted his book of the English Peerage the night before, and found her name and family connections. She was very young, barely twenty, but had been orphaned some five years earlier—a carriage accident that killed both her parents.

"Oh, Mr. Shapira," she said, smiling. "I hardly know—everything fascinates me so." She touched with a light finger a parchment that Moses had spread out on the table before her. "Tell me about this lovely thing—the lettering so fine and perfect—is it Hebrew?"

"It is Greek, my lady, from early in the second hundreds—a gospel of stories of Jesus, liddle known now but popular in that day—said to be writ by Thomas the Doubter, of his adventures and travels in India."

"Impossible!" said Lady Simmons-Hartley, her blue eyes wide and dreamy. "How can this be? An apostle went to India?"

"Old stories say, my lady, that the Lord Himself travelled there, as a youth, before He showed himself before the people," Moses said, beaming at her beauty and enthusiasm.

"Just as he was said to have visited Glastonbury, in my country," she responded, "when his uncle Joseph of Arimathea took him there as a child of twelve, to visit the tin mines of Cornwall, and trade with the miners."

"Just so, my lady," Moses said. He smiled. "We all want that the precious feet of the Savior walked in our land, yes?" He sighed. "But anything is possible!"

Just then her eye was caught by a movement behind the table, and she bent down to discover a little girl, with white-blond hair and large brown eyes, gazing up at her.

"Why, who is this little sprite?" she said, and put out her hand to help the girl come out from under the table.

"Myriam, child of mine heart," Moses said, affectionately chiding the girl. "I did not hear you and Ouarda come in—she leaves you here by your own?"

The girl shook her head, overcome with shyness, and merely pointed toward the back of the shop.

"Ah," said Moses, bending down to pick her up and hold her close. "She sits by Bathsheba's Pool, then? I think you should be joining her there for a time."

Lady Simmons-Hartley caught at this reference. "Really? Bathsheba's Pool? Is it near here?" She whirled around as if to see it before her. "I know that David's Tower is not too far from here, but I never dreamt—is it truly near? May I see it?"

Moses, delighted with her raptures, led her to the back of the shop, still carrying his daughter in his arms, and stepped outside, cautioning her to be careful of the slippery wooden steps. The late morning sun caused the usually brown water of the ancient shallow pool to gleam like gold, imbuing it with a lustre that gave some credence to its being the pool where the incomparably lovely Bathsheba once bathed naked, unknowing that the sight of her had struck King David with a kind of passionate madness.

Lady Simmons-Hartley gasped, then sighed, at the sight, clutching at Moses' arm. As he often had done, he began to tell the story of David and Bathsheba in his inimitable, captivating way, holding her spellbound until she was near tears at the end, with the blessed birth of Solomon, and the death of David's son Absalom as the price of his sin.

"Ah," she sighed, and leaned over the railing. "I would love to live here always, and gaze upon this sight." She murmured a few lines of poetry, and Moses answered her with the next few verses—they were delighted that they had the same taste in poets.

* * *

For six weeks, this English lady visited the little shop in the Street of the Christians, nearly every day, until one day, Moses invited her to come see the upstairs rooms, where he had special collections. She demurred, but invited him instead to come to her hotel for tea that afternoon.

At home, that night, Myriam listened while lying abed, to her mother's pacing footsteps up and down the hall and stairway, until very late, when she went to bed. Her father did not come home until almost dawn the next morning. And it happened again a few more times.

But nothing was ever said about it, at least, not that Myriam overheard, and a few weeks later she learned from Hassan, the doorman at the shop, that the English lady had returned to her country. For some time after, she observed that Moses was melancholy and seemed to drift aimlessly from place to place, not interested in his usual pursuits. Her mother went grimly about her household duties, her lips tight and her eyes unreadable. Myriam sighed for the romance of it, and imagined the Lady in Blue at home in England, dreaming of her own "King David" who had entranced her in the ancient city.

THIRTEEN

Rotterdam — Still Wednesday, 12 March 1884
At the Hotel Willemsbrug

As Herr Innesbrucke led our investigative party up the stairs to visit Mr. Shapira's room, a question occurred to me that I impulsively asked of him.

"What made you—or your staff—decide to see if Mr. Shapira was in his room, last Saturday?" I said.

The manager paused ever so slightly, then responded. "I believe someone noticed that he had not appeared for dinner the night before, nor for breakfast or lunch on that day," he said slowly.

"And this was unusual behavior for Mr. Shapira?" I pursued.

Herr Innesbrucke shrugged, then added, "Also, there were letters in his box that had not been collected, and he was always very prompt to ask about the post, while he was staying here."

"And how long had he been staying here?" I said, stepping up to come alongside him on the stairs. We had finished one flight and were apparently continuing to the next level.

"Thirteen nights, to be exact," said the manager.

"And you must still have those letters?" I said eagerly, glancing back at John and Lord Parke.

At this, Herr Innesbrucke came to a full stop, then looked down at me (most people must look down to see me, I'm so decidedly short), a puzzled frown on his face. "I don't recall"—he broke off, and looked at Inspector Cramer. "Inspector," he continued, "did your men take the letters that were in Mr. Shapira's box?"

Our little troupe stood as still as statuary, part way up the stairs to the second floor. The Inspector looked at his sergeant, who shook his head, then he turned back to the manager. "I shall check," he said, "but I do not recall taking or seeing any letters."

I threw an elated glance to my companions and was gratified by Lord Parke's approving smile.

"As soon as I let you into the room," Herr Innesbrucke said, "I shall inquire of the staff about the post."

We quickly made our way up to the next floor, then followed the manager to a room at the end of the hallway. It was adjacent to a door that led to a stairway, which I discovered by opening the door and looking in.

"Where does this stairway terminate?" I asked of no one in particular.

The Inspector and his sergeant looked a little blank; Herr Innesbrucke answered somewhat brusquely. "In the cellar," he said.

"And does the cellar," I continued in all mildness, "have a door that leads to the street?"

Comprehension dawned on the manager's face. "Yes," he said succinctly. I saw the sergeant make a note in his notebook.

We were let into the room, and the manager excused himself, saying he would return shortly. "Nothing in this room has been altered or removed except what the police took away," he said. "The police were the last ones in this room; I have strictly forbidden staff to enter until this situation is settled."

We faced the room where Moses Shapira breathed his last breath. I had prepared myself beforehand to see disarray and, probably, blood, but in actuality it was a little worse than I had imagined.

After four or five days now, the blood was almost completely dry, and had turned a dark brown color; it congealed in streams flowing from the center of the thin carpet that covered only a small part of the wood floor; the blood was shaped around the gruesome outline of where some part of Mr. Shapira's body had lain. The room itself was cold, no fire having been kept up in the unoccupied space, and dim, even with the drapes open to the sky and the river across the road. Despite the cold, that peculiar, iron smell of blood was still strong.

I stood in the doorway as my companions moved farther into the room, albeit along the sides, and I surveyed the room slowly: the bed was made, but roughly, as if someone had laid on it, but not under the blankets; there was an impress on the pillow where a head had rested briefly—I made a mental note to find out when a maid had last serviced the room; the wardrobe door was open and from my vantage point, it looked empty. There was no luggage or carrying case for documents or items—but the Inspector had said all Mr. Shapira's things had been taken to the police station. The washstand held a large ceramic bowl and pitcher, with a towel, seemingly unused, lying next to it. Two small glasses were also on the washstand, one upended and one facing down, as if it had not been used, both on little paper coasters to protect the marble top of the washstand.

"Inspector Cramer," I said, and he looked up at me from where he stood supervising his sergeant, who was on his knees, looking under the bed and other furniture, presumably searching for the missing key. "May I approach the washstand for a closer look?" He looked at the washstand, then back at me.

"I see no harm in it," he said. He then whipped out a clean handkerchief from his pocket, and handed it to me as I came nearer. "If you need to touch anything, Fräulein Lee, please use this."

I nodded, pleased with his apparent acceptance of my role, as it were, in the investigation. Lord Parke carefully stepped around the blood-soaked carpet to where I now stood before the washstand.

"What are you thinking, Violet?" I noted this was the first time he had addressed me so personally, which I thought was likely an effect of the close conspiracy into which he, John and I were gathered. I answered calmly, in a low voice.

"I'm merely looking for what there is to see," I said. I peered into the ceramic bowl and the pitcher—both dry. The towel was dry, but a little wrinkled, as if lightly used. I bent down to examine the two glasses. The upended one had clearly been used, as there were smudged fingerprints on the outside. The one facing down, as if unused, I carefully picked up with the Inspector's handkerchief, and examined closely.

"Ah," I said, and showed it to Lord Parke. "This glass has been used as well, but someone attempted to wipe it clean—and failed." I had caught the Inspector's attention, and as he came to join us, I pointed to a blur of dark red on the lip of the glass. "If I'm not mistaken, this is an imprint from a woman who has coloured her lips, probably with the latest invention from the Parfumier Guerlain—I believe they call it a 'lipstick'."

Inspector Cramer gazed at the glass in wonder and dismay. Lord Parke shook his head.

"There was someone in this room, then, with Mr. Shapira, before he died," he said. "Someone who didn't want anyone to know she was here."

There was a knock at the door, and Herr Innesbrucke entered immediately.

"Inspector Cramer," he said. "I regret to report that the letters that were in Mr. Shapira's room box are nowhere to be found. However," and he held up a dark brass, old-fashioned door key, and a white envelope. "We have found two very important items: the key to this room, and a misplaced letter to Mr. Shapira—they were both in the box adjacent to the one for this room."

The Inspector strode to the door and held out his hand for the items, and we all gathered around him to see. The first thing he did was to try the key in the door—conscientious man!—and indeed, it locked and unlocked it perfectly. Then he turned his attention to the letter which, I could see by straining a little, bore the seal of the British Museum on the back of it.

He seemed to become suddenly conscious that we were all near, and clearly waiting for him to open the envelope and read its contents. He made a movement as if to put it in his pocket, but at my gasp of protest, he turned to me with an inquiring look.

"My dear Inspector," I said, "you cannot possibly keep this information from us—why, are we not embarked on this investigation as a team? And as I can see that the letter is from the British Museum, perhaps its contents, if doubtful, can be explained by Lord Parke, who is knowledgeable in all the details of Mr. Shapira's interactions with the Museum."

Yes, I was stretching it a bit, as reminded by a slight nudge at my back from Lord Parke, and a small, discreet cough, which I took to be his way to keep from laughing.

Thank goodness my assessment of Inspector Cramer as a rational man was correct—even a man of reasonably good humour. I saw a twinkle in his eye as he suppressed a smile.

"Very well, Miss Vernon Lee," he said, and taking a pocket-knife out, he carefully slit the top of the envelope and extracted one sheet of paper. He perused it carefully, read it over again and, in deference to Lord Parke's association with the Museum, handed it to him to read.

It was from Christian David Ginsburg, the Museum's finest biblical scholar, and the man whose judgement had turned Moses Shapira from a renowned scholar in his own right to a despised fraud in the eyes of the whole world.

FOURTEEN

Jerusalem — 1874
The Shop in the Street of the Christians

"OH, THE SHAME OF IT! THE DISGRACE!" Rosette Shapira moaned the words, over and over, as her husband tried to calm her. "I knew those Moabitish idols would bring evil to us, I told you!" She continued her lament, her voice stifled only when she sobbed into her handkerchief.

"My dear," said Moses gently, "no one makes to place the blame to me—I am to them a dupe, a victim of desert criminals—not my own self a forger."

"As if that were any better! The foremost antiquarian in Jerusalem—duped by wicked Bedouins, those heathens and criminals!" Rosette wept even harder.

Moses despaired of trying to raise his wife's spirits; perhaps it was too soon to try, he thought. He had to admit to himself, though, that he felt much the same about the damage to his reputation. He stood up from the table where they'd been sitting, and picked up the latest issue of the *Palestinian Exploration Fund Quarterly*, in which his inveterate enemy, Charles Clermont-Ganneau, had written an extensive article condemning Shapira's entire Moabite collection as forgeries of modern production.

Rosette looked up at her husband, her grief stilled only by a wave of anger. "And you see what that monster insinuates about the good Christians who yearn for evidence of the truths in the Bible—that we are all besotted zealots, incapable of thinking rationally—the very thing a Papist like him would say!" Her anger grew, and she stood up, facing Moses.

"Our bishop shall hear of this!" she cried. "He'll put that wicked, ignorant, impudent man in his place!" She reached for the journal in her husband's hand as if to snatch it up and run to the church that instant, but Moses held it out of her reach.

"My dear, be calm in yourself," he said sternly. "This upset will make you ill. You must be strong."

Rosette glared at him; then, as if all strength had left her, sagged back down into her chair, and wept silently.

Moses looked at the article—it was as if he couldn't help himself from reading it again and again—and felt a deep-seated rage take hold of him. "*The worthy shopkeeper near Bathsheba's Pool,*" he read aloud. "*Who fondly imagined himself to be an expert on antiquarian subjects.* The pride of that man!"

The article detailed how Clermont-Ganneau had undertaken an investigation among the criminal sorts who inhabited the dark places in Jerusalem, and how he had induced several men to admit they had fabricated hundreds of pots and figurines in the Moabite "style" over the last several years, using clay from the surrounding land, then burying them in sand and dirt, with acid-like chemicals seeping around them, to produce the appearance of age.

"Is not possible!" Moses exclaimed aloud. "As if this could be done here, in Jerusalem, and no one to know, with eyes always looking?"

The story had spread across Europe and Great Britain, causing the heads of all the great museums—many of whom had purchased antiquarian items from Shapira in recent years—to become involved in the controversy. Delegates from these institutions were arriving weekly at the shop on the Street of the Christians, and Moses found himself deluged with questions and skepticism from all quarters.

"What shall you do, husband?" Rosette whispered, dry-eyed now. "There must be some way to convince people that that benighted Catholic"—she couldn't bring herself to say his name—"has slandered you most shamefully."

Moses had been thinking about this for some time. He nodded once, twice, then looked at Rosette with great confidence.

"I shall lead a journey to Moab, to show the museums the very places where my statues were found—that shall be of proof to them."

"But, my dear, if you are with them," she said, hesitating, "won't they fear they are being tricked, that you are leading them to what you have set up to be the origin of these idols?"

Moses thought again. "Then I shall pay for the journey, and ask Clermont-Ganneau to lead it, also with the Bedouin who know the way."

Rosette gasped at this audacious plan, but seeing the stubborn, defiant look on her husband's face, she merely sighed and turned away. He would do what he would, she thought, and they would all fall to ruin.

One thing, however, gave Rosette a great deal of satisfaction: her husband fired Selim from his employ. Ganneau's scurrilous article had named that man as having been the leader behind all the fake idols and pots, as far back as 1868—and Moses said he felt that he could not afford the tainted association.

What Rosette didn't know was that Selim had vowed revenge, no matter how long it took.

* * *

In the end, an expedition was arranged, with great acclaim for Shapira's honesty and integrity, and Clermont-Ganneau was of the party, along with agents of the great museums of Europe and Britain. But they had scarcely passed the ancient city of Jericho before they were attacked and robbed by marauders; the whole caravan was disrupted, some servants killed, and the remaining participants fled for their lives back to Jerusalem. Moses, in despair at this ruination of his plan, attempted to talk the museum agents into another expedition, but they were adamant against trying again. Clermont-Ganneau wrote another sneering letter that was published in all the papers, almost—but not quite—accusing Moses of arranging the attack in order to stop the expedition.

In the following months, the Ottoman Turks decided to lay claim to the land where the excavations had taken place, and proceeded to demand a heavy tax from the various rebellious tribes that lived there, resulting in further rebellion and skirmishes. Ultimately the Bedouin, convinced all this trouble had been visited upon them because of the desecration of artifacts found amongst the ruins of their lands, blew up what remained of the excavations with gunpowder, thereby destroying any possibility of discovering the truth or falseness of authenticity.

Moses, subdued and disheartened, kept to his shop, turning his attention more and more to Hebrew manuscripts of less ancient origin, and continuing, despite all the furor, to do a brisk business in religious souvenirs. He was adept— one might say purely lucky—in hunting out old synagogue scrolls buried under the remains of old temple buildings, sometimes several centuries old, and he was able to both translate the texts and sell the whole manuscript and translation to Christian churches and museums eager to read authentic Old Testament books and commentaries of their "elder brothers, the Jews," as they called them.

Life, for Moses and his family, seemed to be holding its breath, waiting for the next act to begin.

FIFTEEN

Rotterdam — Wednesday Continues, 12 March 1884
At the Hotel Willemsbrug

LORD PARKE QUICKLY READ THE LETTER THROUGH—it appeared to be rather short—and handed it to me. John and I looked at it together. It was dated the sixth of March, and posted the same day in London, attested to by the stamp on the envelope. This is what was written:

> *My dear Shapira,*
>
> *I have reviewed your latest to Rieu, and find it to be authentic—your translation is admirable. The twenty pounds promised will be sent to your bank, as you directed, with much thanks for continuing to keep us in mind.*
>
> *I was relieved and glad for our recent meeting—you were in better form than I had imagined, and our discussion about the mss. gave me great relief and satisfaction. I was glad that you didn't mind that I only sent you half of them, in January, and I hope that you are keeping them safe. I am eager to look at them all again soon, as there was no time this visit. Keep on the lookout for C-G. I believe he would have them all if he could.*
>
> *Finally, I hope the graciousness you have always showed me, in light of everything, still holds, and that I may continue to call myself*
>
> *Your friend,*
> ## C. D. Ginsburg

We were all silent a few moments, each with his own thoughts. John spoke first.

"Poor Mr. Shapira!" he said. "He never got to read that letter of friendship and encouragement."

"But it appears to settle one thing at least," Lord Parke said. "The scrolls were in Mr. Shapira's possession, since January at least."

"Then, what he sent me," John added, "*are* the real scrolls." He adjusted his grip on the leather satchel he had been holding all this time.

"Precisely," I said, glancing down at the satchel. "But apparently not all of them, as Ginsburg says he only sent *half* of them to Mr. Shapira. Curious."

"And also it seems that Ginsburg was here 'recently', he says," Lord Parke chimed in. "I wonder when that was—his letter is dated just two days before Shapira was found dead..." His voice trailed off, as we all wondered about that last meeting.

Inspector Cramer had been watching us and listening intently. He cleared his throat slightly.

"So these scrolls you claim Mr. Shapira sent you," he said. "I think I should like to see them."

I caught at his words immediately. "It is no *claim*," I said with some asperity. "They are still in the original packaging, Inspector, so you can see for yourself that they were mailed from Rotterdam."

He had the grace to look slightly abashed—but only slightly. We were all still standing in the doorway and the hall, where we had gathered when Mr. Innesbrucke had arrived. The Inspector took things in hand.

"If you are finished with your examination of the room, Miss Vernon Lee?" he said.

"Ah," I said, and turned back to the room. "Actually, there were one or two things more." Before the Inspector could object, I walked across the room to the windows. Bending down, I scrutinized the sills—there were no marks on them, as from shoes. The fastenings were extremely tight, and didn't look to have been touched in years. The view from the window clinched my theory—there was a sheer drop of some forty feet or more onto the pavement below, and as far as I could tell, there were no convenient pushed-out bricks for handholds or footholds to enable a person to climb down, or up, for that matter.

The policemen had watched, with some amusement but also intelligence. "Are you satisfied, Miss Vernon Lee?" the Inspector asked as I turned away from the windows.

"Yes, indeed, Inspector Cramer," I said, and smiled brightly.

"Shall we then regroup in the meeting room as before?" He looked pointedly at John. "We will examine that package you received from Mr. Shapira, yes?" He said it politely, but there was of course nothing to do but agree. We all left the room, and he locked the door behind us, using the manager's key.

My gazing out the window, however, had given rise to another thought—it was getting late, and there was a great deal more to be done.

Lord Parke had the same thought as I, and we spoke to each other simultaneously.

"I suppose we need to stay—" I started to say.

"We must look to some accommodations—" Lord Parke said.

We smiled at our concurrent thinking. I spoke in a lower tone, as he and I took up the rear of the little procession down the stairs.

"Do you think we might be comfortable here, at the Willemsbrug?" I dared to ask, knowing he was used to much superior lodgings. "It would only be one night, my lord," I said, feeling mischievous. "Can you make the sacrifice?"

He rolled his eyes! I truly did not think that was a gesture the nobility even knew how to make!

"I'm sure I'm up to it, Violet," he said. "I imagine there are a few things here you want to dig a little deeper into."

I nodded, serious now. "Yes, I want to talk to the staff—I have many questions," I said, then glanced at the Inspector, who was several steps below us. "If I don't run afoul of the local law, that is."

Lord Parke smiled at this, then said, "I'll speak to Herr Innesbrucke and see that rooms are made ready for us, shall I?"

"I should be most grateful, James," I said, boldly deciding to use his given name at last—though never in public, of course. I could tell by the smile in his eyes that he was pleased.

* * *

An hour later, having convinced Inspector Cramer that the package of "scrolls" had indeed been sent to John through the mail (and that he, therefore, had not stolen them from Mr. Shapira last week, after shooting the poor man, then returning to Paris), we were dismissed for the evening to make the best of the Hotel Willemsbrug and whatever it had to offer in the way of bed and board.

There had been a brief argument as to who should have possession of the scrolls, we or Inspector Cramer, but John and Lord Parke prevailed: they should remain with John, as he was the legal possessor of the items, by virtue of having received them at the express direction of Mr. Shapira. Inspector Cramer had shrugged, and let it be. We had, however, made an appointment to meet the Inspector in the morning at the police station, to view Mr. Shapira's belongings, which they had locked away in their storage room.

Herr Innesbrucke began to apologize as he led us to our rooms for the night, which happened to be on the same floor as the late Mr. Shapira's room, but at the other end, and all very near each other. Although we exchanged glances at this fact, none of us was inclined to protest—if they were the only rooms available, well, so be it. I was satisfied upon entering my room to see it pleasantly fitted out, and exceedingly clean in the way the Dutch have with everything, and with a stout lock on the door.

The lock made me feel a bit more secure—I hadn't forgotten the glimpse I'd had of the mysterious blonde woman at the train station, although she had not been actively in my thoughts during most of the day. By mutual agreement among the three of us, we had decided not to say anything to Inspector Cramer about the possibility of a "woman in blue" having followed us from Paris.

"Well," I said, turning to John and Lord Parke, as they had stopped outside my door to give their approval of my accommodations. "When shall we three meet again?" That brought a much-wanted smile to John's lips, and a chuckle from Lord Parke.

Herr Innesbrucke, standing by, *ahem'd* and spoke. "The dining room will be open in about an hour's time," he said. "I have reserved a table for you, located in an alcove so as to be most private."

"Thank you, Herr Innesbrucke," John said warmly, and held out his hand, which after a moment's hesitation, the manager took in his grip. "You have been most attentive, through all this dreadful situation."

Herr Innesbrucke nodded, struck by John's genial manner, as I have often noticed before—people just liked him on the spot. I often had rather more work to do to gain that affection, if I even came around to doing it.

I decided to take advantage of the general good feelings. "Herr Innesbrucke," I said, "may I hope for your approbation of wishing to speak with some of your staff this evening, or tomorrow morning? In light of the changing circumstances, it would be imperative to ask a few questions of them."

The manager hesitated, then nodded. "I shall make a list for you, Miss Lee," he said, "of all the staff members who were in the hotel on the days preceding the—discovery— and on that day itself."

"Thank you, that will be splendid," I said, and decided a brief curtsey would not go amiss. I saw John's jaw drop slightly in astonishment.

The manager led the two gentlemen down the hall to their respective rooms, and I stepped inside my own, sighing with relief at being alone at last.

I needed to think.

SIXTEEN

Jerusalem — July 1878
The Shop in the Street of the Christians

SHEIK MAHMOUD EREKAT, SURROUNDED BY AN entourage of Arabs from various tribes, walked silently but confidently through the Jaffa Gate, past the Tower of David, and up the time-worn stone steps that led to the Street of the Christians. He was seeking Moses Shapira, the respected antiquarian dealer of ancient artifacts. People in the street stood aside in awe and deference to the fierce-visaged men, desert-hardened and skillful with sword and dagger. As if a whisper of their coming had reached his ears, Moses lifted his head, where he sat at his desk in the back of the shop, then rose and made his way to the front door. He found Hassan bowing and signing *salaam* to the visitors, whose imposing presence in the shop seemed to make everything else shrink into insignificance.

Moses invited the Sheik, who was known to him from past excursions in the Moab, to sit in his office sanctuary, where two curved divans with deep cushions, facing each other, simulated the arrangement found in chieftains' tents in the desert; there were hangings of colorful woven cloths that separated the room from the public, and in the center was a bowl of rose water, and a *nargileh*—a water-pipe, which Moses kept always filled with fresh tobacco each morning.

The Sheik accepted his hospitality, and gestured for two of his men to sit with them, while the others were motioned to stand guard in the shop. The Sheikh had often provided safe passage for not only Moses, but other pilgrims who wished to tour biblical sites—he was intimately acquainted with the surrounding lands, and knew how to negotiate with the several tribes to allow the strangers to pass unmolested—for a small fee.

After spending the appropriate amount of time exchanging courtesies and inquiries about family, and sharing the *nargileh* and refreshing cooled wine, the Sheik spoke of his objective in coming to visit.

"Friend Shapira," said the Sheik, "I believe to have found a treasure of great interest to you—writings of great age, on strips of leather, found in the dry caves above the Wadi Mujib." He waited for Moses to respond.

"You take them for true writings, truly of great age, esteemed Sheik?" he asked, careful to keep his voice even and trusting.

The Sheik nodded. "I do."

"Then I am happy to see them when you can show them to me," Moses said, bowing his head.

"Tomorrow, then," the Sheik said, starting to rise. The meeting was over. "Come to my home in Abu Dis, and you will see what you will see."

Moses bowed to them, and escorted them to the door of the shop, watching as the dignified band of men made their silent way back to the Jaffa Gate.

* * *

Abu Dis was a calm, small village of some fifty houses, and fittingly, the largest one was the home of Sheik Mahmoud

Erekat. Unlike the stately silence in which his visitors had entered Moses's shop the previous day, the house was filled with people, laughing, talking, eating from a cornucopia of delicious fruits and breads that was spread out on a low table surrounded by cushions.

Moses had ventured to wear his own Arab clothing—despite the relatively short distance he had ridden horseback to get to Abu Dis—and especially, his head scarf of gold cloth, with the twisted goatskin rope on which hung the Star of David shekel, his talisman of good fortune. He saw some of the men nudge each other, and point to his clothes, but the Sheik welcomed him, and smiled as he lightly touched Moses's veil, nodding in approval.

When they were settled on the cushions, and the courtesies of refreshment were over, the Sheik made a slight gesture to one of his lieutenants, who rose and shepherded most of the other men out of the room. There were, of course, no women present—young boys had been busy running to and from the kitchens with the platters of food and jugs of wine, but they, too, were now banished from the men's meeting.

One of the Bedouin, at a sign from the Sheik, began to speak, falling into a sort of sing-song, story-telling voice that Moses knew well, and had come to love. The desert people lived outside of Time, and saw no need to hurry the telling of a good story—stories were Life, and Life was Eternal.

Some ten passings of winters and summers before the present day, the story began, *desert dwellers seeking relief from the Turkish devils fled to caves above the wadi, beyond the dead sea. There, uncovered to their eyes, were strips of leather—goatskin or sheepskin—folded up, not like scrolls, and wrapped in crumbling linen. The Bedouin, not*

*lettered, nonetheless recognized the black marks as writings of The
Word, but they had hoped for gold coins and idols made of silver, so
they tossed them aside as of no worth. But one man, more astute than
the others, thought they might be some kind of talisman, a good luck
charm, and he took them to his tent, where soon his flocks prospered,
his children grew strong, and he became a man of wealth and influence—even though he never looked at the leather strips or attempted to
understand the words on them, just kept them in a box on the altar in
his tent, with incense burning before it.*

Moses felt as if he had entered a dream, as the voice of
the Bedouin telling the story drifted around the room, min-
gling with the smoke from the *nargilah*. He listened intently,
and when the man finished his tale, he breathed out slowly.

"How can I see these leather strips?" he asked simply.

The Sheik lowered his eyes a moment, then looked up.
"It is a thing of great risk to obtain the talisman of good luck
from a man—he knows no price high enough to sell it, and
often, he places a curse on it that stays with the talisman,
should anyone take it from him."

Moses made a small, dismissive gesture with his left
hand. "I do not fear a curse, my God is not a God of cursing."

The Sheik looked slightly amused by this statement.
Then he said, "I know a man—one of those whose delight
it is to disrupt things and break the rules—he would sell his
mother for the right price."

Moses contemplated this with some uneasiness. He
knew better than to ask why the Sheik was interested in, es-
sentially, getting someone to steal the leather strips from the
"wealthy man" who considered them his good luck talisman—it was probably some old score that needed settling,

either for the Sheik, or someone to whom he owed a favor. Well, these tribal enmities were none of his business, he reasoned. If he didn't take this opportunity, the Sheikh would no doubt find someone else to take the leather strips off his hands.

"I will have them," he said to the Sheik, and they shared the *nargilah*, and clasped hands, for agreement.

* * *

By the end of two months, a small and nondescript-looking desert man had brought Moses sixteen leather strips; after their first meeting, at Moses's shop, the man said he could no longer come into the city—Moses suspected he was a wanted man—so they met in the Plain of the Philistines, far from the shadow of the walls, sometimes in the middle of the night. With the last delivery, the man said he had no more; Moses paid him the contracted amount, and that was the last they ever saw of him. As Moses had agreed, he sent a reward of money and goods to his friend the Sheik, for his help in arranging this sale.

Unexpectedly, Sheik Erekat died shortly after the last meeting; inquiries as to the manner of his dying went unanswered, and Moses was left to wonder, with some sorrow and some fear, at the brutal ways of the desert tribes.

* * *

Moses labored intensely to uncover the secrets of the leather strips. They weren't really scrolls; they weren't parchment either. The strips were folded at intervals, like an accordion, and on each 'panel' there was writing from top to bottom, with a thin blank strip above and below the characters.

The work was tedious and exacting; the surface of the strips was delicate and required constant testing with different chemicals and spirits to make the dull letters become visible. Where the strips were light brown, the characters were a little easier to read, but some broad swaths were almost black, as if covered in pitch. Moses found that dousing them with spirits would cause the letters to shine forth, but only for a short time—he raced to write down the characters he saw before they disappeared again.

He was bent over his table, working diligently, when his daughter Myriam, now nearly ten, burst into the room, clearly filled with some childish news of her own, but he forestalled her.

"Myriam, my own dear! You must hear of my most incredible discovery! Look at these strips of leather!" In his excitement, he ignored her attempts to interrupt him, and kept on. "I haff been cleaning them so much for weeks, and can you think—I'll bet you cannot—what I have made of these words?"

"Papa, Papa," the girl pleaded. "Please listen to me, I have met the young man I want to marry—"

But her father didn't listen, and continued speaking. "Just think, my dear, I hardly know myself, but I believe I haff found the original, the true Book of Deuteronomy! I haff never a dream to finding such a precious treasure as this!"

After several more attempts to be heard, Myriam gave up. She had just come back home after being gone a whole week on an expedition with a youth group from Christ

Church, and had met a young man, some eight years older than herself, with whom she imagined she had fallen in love. But she knew her father and his enthusiasms—he would pay her no mind while he was in this state.

"Papa, it seems like an immense discovery," she said to him, trying to sound supportive.

"Immense is hardly a word for it!" Moses exulted. "This may be the oldest of all Deuteronomy in the whole world! It will make us our fortune!" He pulled her closer to the table, and showed her the characters he had transcribed from the original document. "See there? It begins: *These are the words that Moses spoke, according to the mouth of Jehovah, to all the children of Israel in the wilderness, across the Jordan in the Aravah.*"

Myriam looked at the leather strips in awe. If her father was correct...? She impulsively kissed his cheek. "You *are* the King of the Desert, Papa," she said, remembering how he used to say that, when he would come back from his desert trips and excavations, packs filled with various treasures.

He continued to read his translation to her, and fill her with his dreams of the wealth and acclaim that would come to them when this treasure was unveiled.

SEVENTEEN

**Rotterdam — Wednesday, March 12, 1884
At the Hotel Willemsbrug**

ONE THING I BEGAN TO THINK OF IMMEDIATELY I was
alone, was the letter from Dr. Ginsburg. I have a photo-
graphic memory, and had been able to look at the letter long
enough for it to be imprinted on my mind. I closed my eyes
and saw the words that I sought to recall:

*Keep on the lookout for C-G. I believe he would have them all if
he could.*

Who was C-G? Wasn't there some name, knocking
about in my memory, that would suit? Of course! Clermont-
Ganneau, the French archaeologist. Lord Parke had mentioned him last night at dinner as being the main detractor
of the Shapira Scrolls last year. *Interesting.* The whole tenor of
the letter, and that little remark about Clermont-Ganneau,
seemed to me to suggest that these two men—Ginsburg and
Ganneau—had not actually been entirely sure—or truth-
ful?—about the authenticity of the scrolls at that time. Or
perhaps they had changed their minds? It would definitely
bear some looking into.

I took a little time to sort through the linen and clothing
I had brought with me, airing them out in the wardrobe, then
refreshed myself with water from the pitcher on the washstand. I gazed into the mirror at the untidy mess that was my

hair, and decided just to smooth it into place. A sudden yawn brought me to the realization that I was immensely fatigued, and I lay down upon the nicely-made bed, promising myself I would only close my eyes for a few moments. Then I would be able to think more clearly.

Twenty minutes later I awoke feeling refreshed and alert, and rose from the bed to shake out my dress, straighten my stockings, and prepare for battle. I noticed an envelope had been slipped under the door, and upon opening it, saw it was the staff list promised by Herr Innesbrucke.

I perused it quickly; naturally I did not recognize any names—the usual assortment of maids, bellboys, kitchen staff and waiters, the concierge and front desk staff. Fewer than a dozen people—to run this entire establishment! I thought it remarkable, and mused that perhaps its financial standing required a minimal staff.

A rumbling in my stomach reminded me how long it had been since we'd had any real food beyond tea and biscuits—well, we would see what the small kitchen staff were capable of, at dinner.

I sat down at the desk and took a sheet of paper from the small amount offered for the use of guests—the sight of the crest impressed on the paper reminded me of the note Mr. Shapira had written to John, and I felt a sudden sadness—whether by foul means or self-harm, poor Mr. Shapira had died in this very place not five days ago.

A gentle tap on the door caught my attention and, feeling a return of suspicion, I peeked through the peephole first—a young maid stood waiting in the hall.

"Yes?" I said, opening the door a few inches.

"Good day, miss," the maid said, looking nervous. "Herr Innesbrucke sent me here for you to talk to me?" Her voice rose, tremulously.

"Ah," I said, opening the door wider and inviting her in. "And what is your name, my dear?"

"Angela," she said, and dropped a brief curtsey.

We stood in the middle of the room; there was only one chair, and I didn't think it was proper for either one of us to sit on the bed.

"Well, Angela," I said, smiling in what I hoped was a kind and encouraging way, "what can you tell me about Mr. Shapira?"

The maid looked down at first, shyly or modestly perhaps, then turned large, liquid blue eyes to me. "He was a very kind gentleman," she said. "I was assigned to his room, and whenever I was there, he would ask about my health and my family, as if he were really interested." She smiled faintly. "He told me funny stories sometimes while I was tidying up and cleaning, although I couldn't understand everything, sometimes, on account of his accent."

I nodded but said nothing. After a moment, she spoke again, almost wistfully.

"He seemed really sad at times," she said, "especially when he talked about his daughter, who lived in Jerusalem so far away, and how he might not ever see her again."

I caught at this. "He actually said that? When was this that he said such things?"

Angela looked troubled. "It was more recent," she said. "He was looking sadder, and more tired and...afraid, I think."

"Afraid?" I repeated. "Why do you say that?"

The girl thought a moment. "Well, sometimes when I would knock on the door, instead of just opening it, as he did for the first week or so of his stay, he would look through the peephole, and then call out *who is it?* in a very gruff voice." She was silent a moment, then added, "And when he opened the door, he would look up and down the hall, and have me come inside, and quickly close the door and lock it."

"Did he have any visitors, Angela?" I asked.

She shook her head. "Not that I ever saw, miss," she said. "But then, I'm usually just here during the morning and early afternoon, and visitors generally do not come so early, yes?"

I nodded. Angela had lost some of her nervousness, but I could see she was eager to leave.

"Just one or two more questions, dear," I said. "When was the last time you saw Mr. Shapira, or came in to tidy up his room?"

She answered promptly. "It was last Thursday, miss, I saw him in the morning when I came to his room to clean and make up the bed."

"And how did he seem to you, that morning?"

She shrugged slightly. "He was much the same, perhaps quieter than usual," she said. "I did notice that the curtains were partly closed, and it was past ten when I came in—he usually had the curtains open, to let in the light—and he liked to stand at the window and look at the river, while I cleaned, and he would talk to me." She shook her head. "But he didn't talk much, that day, although he did keep looking out the window."

"And why did you not go to his room the next morning, or on Saturday?"

She looked a little frightened at this question. "He—Mr. Shapira—asked me not to disturb him on the Friday, miss—he said he would be very busy with some work all night, and would not want to be disturbed at all the next morning, as he would probably be sleeping."

"And on the Saturday?" I said, a little sharply.

"I have Saturdays off, miss, and our guests do not generally have their rooms tidied up on Saturdays or Sundays—we wait until Monday again."

I smiled at her then, gave her a coin I found in my pocket, and dismissed her, thanking her for her clarity and responsiveness.

"You're welcome, miss," she said, and turned to go. "Herr Innesbrucke says to let you know he will send up the desk clerk next, if that will be all right?"

I nodded, and as she left the room, I turned back to the desk and wrote a few notes.

After about ten minutes, another knock sounded on my door, and I merely called out, "Please come in."

To my surprise, John and Lord Parke entered the room.

"Oh!" I exclaimed, startled, though I should not have been, I suppose.

"Hello, Vi, we thought we'd amble down and see what you're up to," John said. "Sorry to startle you."

"Not at all," I said, setting down my pen. "I'm glad you are come, I have just been interviewing a maid who had the particular care of Mr. Shapira's room."

"Any enlightenment there?" asked Lord Parke. With the two gentlemen standing in the room, and I seated in the one chair, the little suite felt quite full. Before I could answer, a hesitant knock came at the still-open door, and we all turned to see a young man, clearly the front desk clerk by his attire, looking questioningly at us.

"Ah," I cried, and stood up. "Do please come in, Mr....?" He stepped into the room and gave a short bow.

"I am Josef," he said. "Herr Innesbrucke said you had some questions for me." He had a young face but old eyes, intelligent and shrewd.

I looked around at the already crowded room, and Josef helpfully suggested an alternative.

"Perhaps, madam, and sirs, if you please," he said, gesturing down the hall, "there is a small sitting room where our guests can make some tea or read the newspaper—I believe it is currently free of occupants. Shall we remove to that room?"

I gratefully accepted his suggestion, and the three of us followed him down the hall, passing by Mr. Shapira's room in utter silence. We entered a much more suitable room for a conversation, with two small sofas and a round table with four chairs. There were no other occupants, as Josef had indicated, but we closed the door, in an abundance of caution for being overheard, although Josef then said that there weren't any other guests on this floor at all—there were only five rooms, and our set occupied three of them, with Mr. Shapira's empty room the fourth.

"Now, Josef," I said when we were all settled. I smiled approvingly at John, who remained standing, and was looking at the tea things, intent on lighting a spirit lamp to heat some water. "Please tell anything and everything you know about Mr. Shapira, starting when he first arrived, which I believe was the first of March."

"That is correct, madam," he said. "I was at the desk when Mr. Shapira arrived." He looked uncomfortable for a moment. "I must ask, madam and sirs," he said, nodding at Lord Parke and John, "do you wish only straightforward facts, or is my opinion of things of any interest as well?"

What an intelligent question, I thought. This is one of those fellows on whom nothing is lost, as my friend Henry James would say.

"Both, please, my dear Josef, that is excellent," I said, nodding approvingly. "But I have one question, a very important one, that I must say I am eager to hear the answer to, and then we shall get on with your narrative."

He looked at me keenly, and nodded.

"Did Mr. Shapira have any visitors in the two weeks he stayed here? Anyone who, perhaps, inquired after him, whether he saw them or not?"

Josef glanced down at his hands in his lap, then looked up again. He took a deep breath.

"You understand, of course, that the police did not ask us these questions," he said, hoping perhaps to deflect some responsibility on his part for not having mentioned visitors. "We—the senior staff—have now been informed that it is possible Mr. Shapira did not take his own life, which is what we were told last Sunday."

"Yes, of course," Lord Parke said.

Josef sighed again. "Mr. Shapira had four visitors over the past two weeks—all of them just last week. The first, on the Wednesday, was a gentleman from London, whom Mr.

Shapira met downstairs in the lobby, and they went off into the town for most of the day. Mr. Shapira returned alone."

I nodded sagely. I would wager anything this was Professor Ginsburg.

"Then?" I pressed on.

"Last Thursday, in the late morning," Josef said, "two people came together, a gentleman, perhaps in his mid-thirties, and a lady, very beautiful and young-looking, but certainly past her first youth."

"A blonde woman?" John interjected sharply.

Josef turned to answer him directly. "Yes, sir, she had blonde hair."

"Did they give their names? Did they go up to Mr. Shapira's room?" I leaned forward eagerly.

Josef frowned. "They gave me their names, but somehow I didn't believe them." He looked weary. "You learn about that sort of thing in this business." He shrugged. "They said they were a Monsieur and Madame Eglantine. They spoke French the whole time—the man was a native speaker, Parisian I am sure; but the lady was British, although she spoke the language exceedingly well."

He shifted in his chair, and went on.

"The French gentleman asked me to send only his name up to Mr. Shapira's room—I saw that his key was not in his box, so I assumed he was there—we ask our lodgers to please leave their key here when they go out, it saves us having to always make new keys, you understand—but the boy came back after a little time, and beckoned to me to speak quietly. He whispered to me, and these were his exact words, *Mr. Shapira says he is not at home—and never will be, to this gentleman.*"

"And how did the gentleman, and the lady, respond to this denial?" I asked.

"The gentleman shrugged, but looked very displeased," said Josef, "and as they turned away, I heard the lady say to him that perhaps she should try to see him herself, alone, at another time."

"And did she come back?" Lord Parke asked, leaning forward as well.

Josef shook his head. "Not at any time that I was at the front desk, sir, but I cannot say it would be impossible for someone to slip by me, if they were watching carefully."

"You said there were four persons," I pursued. "Who was the fourth, and when?"

Josef again looked a bit uncomfortable. "There was a very foreign-looking man, an Arabian by his look, I would judge, although he wore European clothes—very oddly dressed, I must say. He came on the Friday, fairly early in the day, perhaps around ten o'clock. He spoke in English, heavily accented. I was not at the desk when he first came in, but the second clerk, not able to fully understand what he wanted, called me in from the office. When I asked the man what he wanted—" Josef's face took on an increase in severity—"he insisted that he be led to Mr. Shapira immediately, on a matter of great importance. I saw that Mr. Shapira's key was not in the box, so I assumed he was in his room, but this man would not give his name, and when I questioned him more, he became impatient and began shouting in his own language. I'm afraid we had to ask him to leave, and finally, threaten him with calling a policeman to eject him if he did not go quietly. He left then, with many a dire threat, as I took it, and a curse on the general population of Rotterdam."

"Did you tell Mr. Shapira that this person had called for him?" I asked.

Josef shook his head. "I was told by one of the bellboys that Mr. Shapira had told him to say he did not want to be disturbed by anyone, for any reason, that day or the next. I made a note of the incident, however, and intended to tell Mr. Shapira when next I saw him—I assumed that would be dinner that evening, or at the latest, breakfast the next morning, on Saturday."

I and my two companions exchanged serious looks.

"But of course," Josef said with a sigh, "he did not appear that evening or the next morning or evening, and it slipped my mind—and then, because we had not seen him for two days, Herr Innesbrucke decided we needed to check his room—and that's when we found his body, on the Saturday night."

The four of us fell silent at this point. I thought of the key and the letter. "Josef," I said, "how do you think Mr. Shapira's key, and the letter to him, came to be in the wrong box?"

Josef shook his head. "I do not remember, personally, putting away the letter or the key," he said slowly. "It sometimes happens, if the desk clerk is very busy—or distracted," and he grimaced apologetically—"that things sometimes get put in the wrong place. And as Mr. Shapira never came down to the desk again..." He left his thought unfinished.

I let my gaze wander, and noticed that John had succeeded in making some tea and was just finishing up pouring it out into cups. But something was missing.

"John," I said quietly. He turned to look at me. "Where is your leather satchel?"

He frowned slightly. "I left it in my room," he said. "But I locked the door," he continued. He frowned more deeply. "You don't think it's safe?"

I rose from my chair and made for the door.

I had a bad feeling about this.

EIGHTEEN

Jerusalem — 1878-1883
The Shop in the Street of the Christians

September 1878

MOSES WAS KEEN TO HAVE HIS DISCOVERY VERIFIED, but wary of its reception in scholarly circles. The Moabitica scandal was only two years over, and even though he had not been accused of forgery himself, his reputation had suffered. He would have to proceed cautiously.

His staunchest supporter during the furor over the Moabite idols was Professor Konstantin Schlottmann in Germany, so he wrote a long, carefully worded letter explaining about the leather strips, and included a copy of his own translation of the characters.

The response he received, a month later, was stunning. Schlottmann had shown the letter and translation to a colleague, a Professor Delitzsch, and the two men were in agreement. They wrote to Moses:

How dare you call this forgery the Old Testament? Can you suppose for one minute that it is older than our unquestionable genuine ten commandments? It contradicts the Bible...it is a hideous fraud, a sophisticated, but at the same time, crude, forgery.

Moses was crushed at first, then he rallied. The chief complaint of the two professors was that his translations were clearly deviations from the "traditional" text of Deuteronomy. But that was the point, wasn't it? That it was different—it was *original*. But he couldn't contend against the respected scholars, and although he believed his scrolls were authentic, he decided he couldn't risk pursuing the matter at that time.

Soon after receiving the letters from the scholars, Moses packed up the leather strips and took them to the Bergheim and Company Bank on David Street, and had them placed safely in the vault. He could not afford risking any more damage to his reputation, and tried to turn his attention to acquiring valuable manuscripts, for which wealthy collectors always seemed to be willing to pay enormous amounts of money. *There* his reputation was safe.

Three Years Later – August 1881

"LISTEN TO THIS, MY DEAR ONES!" Moses Shapira strode into the sitting room at their comfortable house in the better part of Jerusalem, where his wife and daughters were busy at various tasks. They looked up expectantly. Myriam recognized the journal in his hands as the latest issue of the *Palestine Exploration Fund Quarterly*—she remembered bringing it to her father a few days ago when it arrived with the rest of the post.

Her father was beaming, although his hands trembled as he started to read aloud—perhaps a good sign, Myriam thought, hoping that it wasn't another such article as their hated enemy, Clermont-Ganneau, had written a few years ago.

"This is a writing by my good friend, Claude Conder, my dears, you know him, he was here last Spring? and he writes about the Siloam Inscription, you know, that was found in Hezekiah's Tunnel, the one built by King Hezekiah to bring water into the city? Claude, and Hermann Guthe too, we had many discussions about it in this very room," he said by way of introduction. Rosette, Myriam and Augusta put down their various tasks of knitting, embroidery or writing, and gave him their full attention.

He began to read:

> *Mr. Shapira gives a different interpretation to the text, explaining it as referring to the cutting of the tunnel from two opposite ends. This we know was really how the excavation was effected, and Mr. Shapira's intimate acquaintance with the Hebrew idiom (as a Talmudist of 20 years' education) seems to render his opinion worthy of consideration.*

"There! You see, he as good as says my interpretation was correct. *A Talmudist of 20 years' education*, yes, very nicely put." Moses scanned the article, reading a few more mentions of his name here and there; a broad smile of almost ecstatic satisfaction gave his face a cheerful look that had been lacking for a very long time, and was not lost on his wife and daughters.

"Oh, Papa, that is wonderful!" Myriam said, and ran to hug him and look at the article for herself. "Your reputation will be so enhanced by Mr. Conder's praise."

Even Rosette looked pleased, and she and Augusta exchanged meaningful looks. Every step in the direction of restoring and publicizing Moses's good reputation would be of great benefit for the scheme the two of them had been working on. Moses had, in the last two years, sold a large number of important and very old Hebrew manuscripts to the British Museum, and had published articles detailing his many adventures in *Arabia Felix*, which is what the British called Yemen. He was trusted again—and the family was on solid financial grounds.

Taking a deep breath, Rosette decided this would be an opportune moment to introduce the subject.

"Wilhelm," she said, "I am very glad that you have made such progress in recouping your reputation, and being seen as the true scholar that you are." She plunged ahead. "As a scholar, you of course must see the benefit of a good education for your daughters, and Augusta, you know, is at the age when intensive study and the introduction to other girls from good families are most important."

Moses looked up from his journal, one eyebrow raised. He looked from his wife to his eldest daughter, a slight smile playing about his lips. "And what haff you two been cooking up?" he asked, but not at all sternly.

"Oh, Papa!" cried Augusta, holding her head high. "There is a boarding school in Berlin, Mama knows all about it, the best families place their daughters there, and I could learn to speak German properly, and dancing and painting, and all sorts of..."

Her mother interrupted quickly to add, "And studies of greater importance, too, theology and literature, even science."

The room held the silence for a full minute. Myriam, still with her arms around her father's waist, looked at her mother and sister—this was the first time she'd heard of this plan. Augusta and Mama were always closeted together or sitting in corners, talking intensely, she had noticed that of course, but she assumed—well, she hadn't quite known what to assume they were discussing, just things that older girls needed to know? At any rate, she was surprised, and wondered if a boarding school was also in store for her, some day.

When her father finally spoke, it was in a cheerful, kindly voice.

"Well, well, we shall have to discuss this, my wife," he said, and looked appraisingly at his elder daughter. "You have been growing up without my noticing it, dear child—I see it is indeed time to give some thought to your future." He disengaged himself from Myriam's embrace, and walked over to where Augusta sat at the table. Bending down to kiss her cheek, he nodded once or twice, then left the room, still clutching the journal in his hand.

Rosette looked triumphant, and smiled at Augusta. Myriam felt a little wary, even a little frightened, wondering if this was the beginning of many changes to come.

July 1882

"Papa, here is a heavy package for you today," said Myriam, entering the room upstairs where her father spent his most productive hours, poring over and translating ancient manuscripts. The one he was working on at the moment was a commentary by Rambam—the famous Rabbi Moses Mai-monides (may his name be for a blessing)—on the text of Genesis.

"Thank you, my dear," Moses said, a little absent-mind-edly. He pointed to a side table. "Place it there, please, I will look at it later."

Myriam, always intrigued by packages, read the return address aloud. "Christian David Ginsburg, British Mu-seum," she read. "Papa, it's from London!"

That caught Moses' attention, and he carefully put down his delicate implements, then eased himself off the high stool with a sigh and a hand at his back—he was getting older, fifty-two this year, and the many long trips on camel-back, horseback and just hard walking through deserts and mountains had taken their toll. But the months he had spent in Yemen, far from his family for nearly a year, had proved fruitful beyond his imagining. The scattered colonies of poor Yemenite Jews in Southern Arabia—where few Europeans visited even now, to say nothing of four years ago—held priceless riches of sacred manuscripts that Moses managed, in his inimitable way, to carry off with him back to Jerusa-lem. People, he had learned, would break the rules if the temptation was great enough. He had described those ad-venturous journeys in several journal articles over the years, but had not revealed how he had actually obtained the man-uscripts—that, he felt, would have to remain between him and his God.

He slipped the edge of his pocket-knife under the string that bound the package, and unfolded the wrapping. A letter addressed to him lay on top of a beautifully bound book, whose gilt lettering informed him he was looking at a copy, in German, of Friedrich Bleek's *Einleitung in das Alte Testament*. He picked up the envelope while Myriam traced the gold writing with a tentative finger.

"*Introduction to the Old Testament*," she translated, and looked up at her father, who nodded and patted her head with his free hand. He read the letter with increasing interest.

My dear Shapira,

I am delighted to inform you of the Museum's decision to purchase your collection of one-hundred-forty-five manuscripts of the Karaites community, on the basis of having examined the three manuscripts you sent to me a few months ago. Your recent article in the Athenaeum about that community, describing their strict adherence to the Jewish law only as presented in the biblical texts (without reference to any rabbinic commentary) made an enormous and positive impression upon the Board members, and Dr. Rieu of the Department of Oriental Manuscripts, in particular.

Moses pressed the letter to his chest and smiled in relief and gratitude. Glancing at it again, he read quickly through the banking arrangements that Ginsburg suggested, and then came to the final paragraph.

The book I have sent you with this letter is a very special one, published in 1869, as it started a revolution in biblical criticism and analytical thinking. Several scholars, DeWette and Wellhausen among them, have since amplified Bleek's theories and added greatly to the scholarship about who exactly wrote the Bible, and when—the answer is becoming clear in one regard: it was most certainly not written by Moses, and also not in his lifetime! I think you will enjoy reading it, my friend.

Sincerely,
C. D. Ginsburg

Moses put down the letter, picked up the book, and began reading. Slowly he made his way to a big chair near the window, reading as he walked to it. He was soon lost to everything around him, including Myriam, who stood to one side, watching him in silence and love. After about twenty minutes, he looked up and saw his daughter standing there. He motioned for her to come stand beside him.

"Myriam, my dear," he said, drawing her to him and kissing her cheek. "This book changes everything, everything!"

But Myriam, despite her father's elation, felt a tremor in her heart, a foreboding of what the future actually had in store for her father, and all her family.

NINETEEN

IN MY SUDDEN CONSTERNATION about the leather case with its precious contents, I nearly dashed my tea cup and saucer to the floor as I stood up quickly and headed for the door. Just as I opened it, a noisy commotion—shouting and scuffling—broke upon my ears, and as I opened the door wide, with John and Lord Parke and Josef all joining me, we saw two footmen running toward a strangely dressed, foreign-looking man who was bent on one knee in front of Mr. Shapira's room, as if he had been peering through the key-hole!

"Hie there!" cried Josef, and he burst from behind us to join his fellows in securing the man. John raced past me and Lord Parke, and headed straight for his own room at the other end of the hall. Lord Parke—rather over-protective, in my view—held on to my arm, as if to keep me from joining the fray, but it was all quieted down in a few moments. Josef and the two footmen held the man firmly in their grip as they pulled him to his feet. I noticed something metallic and shiny in his hand, and called out, fearing it was a knife.

"Be careful! He has something in his hand!"

Josef grabbed the man by the wrist and, twisting it deftly, caused him to yelp in pain and drop the item.

Stepping a little nearer, I saw that it was some sort of thin metal shaft, not a knife, thank goodness. Josef kicked it in my direction, to keep it out of the man's hands, and I drew out my handkerchief and picked it up to examine it more closely.

"Perhaps some kind of lock picking implement?" I murmured to Lord Parke.

The captured man began to wail an Oriental-sounding lament in a high, quavering voice.

"Quiet, you!" Josef said, giving him a shake. He peered closely at the miscreant. "I recognize you!" He looked at me and Lord Parke, grimly. "This scoundrel was the one who attempted to see Mr. Shapira last week, the one we threw out the door to get rid of."

"Shapira, yes!" The man caught at the name, nodding vigorously, speaking a few words of broken English. "Must see, talk Shapira!"

"What do you want with Mr. Shapira?" I asked, boldly stepping forward. The man, who was standing quietly now, though still firmly held by the hotel staff, looked sideways at me, his eyes mostly cast down, and shook his head. He pointed at Lord Parke.

"Him. Not female." His accent was extraordinarily thick, but I believe those were the words he spoke. Then he repeated himself, this time in heavily accented French. Josef responded immediately in the same language, and after some back and forth between them, too low for me to catch much of it, Josef looked up at us, satisfied.

"He says he came to find Mr. Shapira, yes, last week, and tries again this week. He says he has good news for him, but he must see him for himself."

I spoke in a low voice to Lord Parke. "Then it would appear he doesn't know of Mr. Shapira's fate."

Lord Parke nodded, and whispered back. "We might learn more from him before we tell him that, do you think?"

I nodded in agreement, and motioned to Josef that I needed to speak with him. He made sure that the man was securely held, then stepped over to me. I whispered that he should not tell the man that Shapira was dead, and then asked if we could bring him into the sitting room to question him further.

Josef gestured to the footmen to bring the man forward, and we all returned to the sitting room. I looked down the hall to see John coming out of his door, the leather satchel tight under his arm. Thank goodness! I waited for him to arrive at the door.

"Everything good?" I whispered, and he nodded.

"We're going to question this man," I said, and lowering my voice more. "He doesn't know about Shapira. But he won't talk to a woman, so you'll have to ask the questions—in French, all right?" John looked slightly bemused, then nodded again, and we walked back into the room.

This was not a comfortable situation, and we did not sit down. I could see that Josef was nervous—he probably wanted to call the police—but I didn't think this would take long, and after we were through, he could do as he saw fit with this intruder in the hotel.

So as to not further test the man's cultural disinclination to converse with a female, I stood off to the side. John took the lead, and spoke slowly and distinctly in French.

"What is your name, sir?" he said. Oh, that John, always so polite!

The answer came back clearly enough for me to understand. "Selim."

"Ah, Mr. Selim, then," John said. "Why do you want to see Mr. Shapira?"

No response. The man's face was like a dark brown stone, impassive and etched with fine lines from, I imagined, years exposed to desert sun and sands. His clothing was simple but, to my eyes, exotic—a white robe, belted in leather, and a dark cloak over his shoulders. He wore a headdress, like a woman's flowing veil, with a twisted rope ringed around his head and across his forehead, made of something that looked like animal hair. His eyes were black and inscrutable—I could discern no emotion in them, not fear nor surprise nor even cunning.

"Pourquoi devrais-je vous dire?" Selim spoke coolly, as if he had decided, after all, that we were harmless and he had the upper hand. *"C'est mon affaire."* I discerned that his French was far better than his English, and when he spoke calmly, I could understand him quite well.

"You must speak to us because you were caught trying to break in Mr. Shapira's room," Josef said sternly. "That is *my* business."

Selim lifted an eyebrow slightly. "You would not let me in last week when I asked politely, and Necessity drove me to try other means."

I had a sudden idea, and spoke before I thought too much about it. My feminine tones sounded high and thin in this room full of men.

"Do you think Mr. Shapira has something that you want? Something you think belongs to you?"

Selim lowered his eyes. *"Je ne parle pas aux femmes."*

"Then you will tell *me* the answer to her questions," John said.

Selim looked at him appraisingly, then shook his head. "I will only talk to Mr. Shapira," he said.

I puffed out a sigh of frustration. John looked at me questioningly, and I nodded.

"Ce n'est pas possible," he said. He crossed his arms and leaned back a little. "You see, Mr. Shapira is dead. He died five days ago."

The shock on Selim's face was real, I could swear it. His mouth dropped open, and after a moment, he shut it firmly again. His eyes narrowed.

"Do you speak the truth?" he demanded.

"Why should we lie to you?" Josef spoke up. "I was the one who found him, dead in his room, last Saturday night."

Selim frowned, and a fierce light came into his black eyes. "He has cheated me of my revenge!" He shouted the words, and suddenly pushing hard against the two footmen who held him, he made a dash for the open door.

He didn't get far. Josef and Lord Parke both took after him instantly, and gained on him before he was halfway down the hall.

"There's for you, you blackguard!" Josef cried, giving Selim a swift kick behind his knees, bringing him down with a thud. He shouted back to his staff. "Send for Inspector Cramer, now, Johann!" and the younger of the two footmen sped off to fetch the policeman. Josef and the other footman secured Selim once again, removing their belts to bind his feet and hands. While they were thus engaged, I saw—once again—a shining piece of metal emerge from a pouch in the man's voluminous cloak, and as they dragged him to a standing pose, it fell out.

A wickedly curved knife in a silver, hand-tooled sheath lay on the floor. Lord Parke bent to pick it up, and looked at it in wonder. Then he handed it to Josef.

"I imagine Inspector Cramer will be interested in this," he said. He turned then to come back to stand by me and John, straightening his mussed clothes.

I look at both of them approvingly. "You've both been magnificent!" I said. "What an amazing turn of events!"

"What do you think he meant by 'revenge'?" John asked.

I shook my head. "I expect that will be for Inspector Cramer to figure out. And he may very well have been after the leather strips. But one thing seems clear," I continued, "Selim did not know that Mr. Shapira was dead, so he didn't have anything to do with his death—he happened along too late to enact his revenge, we can assume. If he had killed him, he would be long gone, back to Arabia, by now."

We stood a moment in grim silence, watching as the men took Selim away, now completely subdued and docile, to await his fate at the hands of the Rotterdam police.

"I'm starving," I said, taking a deep breath. "Shall we go down to dinner? I rather imagine the good Inspector will want to talk to us, and I'd just as soon have some nourishment before the interrogation begins."

TWENTY

Jerusalem — May 1883

MOSES HAD BARELY LEFT HIS UPPER ROOM at the Villa Rachid for the last three months, turning the day to day management of the shop over to Hassan and the clerks. After reading through Bleek's massive work on the Old Testament, he obtained copies of articles by Julius Wellhausen that theorized the Torah had been composed by four different authors—which he termed the Jehovist, the Elohist, the Priestly writer, and the Deuteronomist. These scribes, whoever they were, were definitely not Moses—and they were said to have edited, added to, and changed the scripts they worked on, numerous times over the years.

Those scholars who had so hastily and arrogantly dismissed Moses's leather scrolls—on the very basis that they conflicted with what the Prophet Moses wrote—they were wrong! The leather manuscripts might very well be an authentic, early version of Deuteronomy. Moses was elated.

Late in March, just before Easter, he had hastened to the bank vault where he had placed the leather strips nearly five years before, and carried them home to his upper room, where he proceeded to once more examine them minutely, bringing the latent characters to life, sharpening and improving his previous translations, until he felt he had something solid to show other scholars.

By great good chance, there was an eminent German scholar visiting Jerusalem in his role as consul in Beirut, just as Moses was coming to these more favorable conclusions about the scrolls: Professor Paul Schroeder. He sent a note to inquire if he might meet with the consul.

"Herr Professor," Moses said, bowing his head slightly as he addressed the consul in his hotel room one afternoon early in May. "It is very gracious of you to see me without introduction."

"Moses Shapira of Jerusalem needs no such introduction, I assure you," said Schroeder, giving a short bow in return and then offering his hand to shake. "Please, have a seat, I am looking forward to having a good discussion with you about many things." He gestured to a comfortable set of chairs near the large window overlooking the City. "I have arranged for some refreshment to be brought here soon, I hope you will share the repast with me?"

"You are most kind, sir," said Moses, and took a seat. He had brought with him four of the most legible leather strips, and they were safely wrapped in linen, inside a box of cedarwood that he had designed and made himself, especially to hold the strips.

The two men spoke about biblical scholarship, with Moses mentioning his excitement and encouragement upon reading Bleek's book, as to some translations he had done on some ancient scrolls in his possession.

"I haff what I believe to be a very early, if not most earliest, version of the Book of Deuteronomy, on these scrolls," Moses said.

Schroeder raised a brow. "Indeed? And did you find Bleek's theories of use to you in determining this?"

"Very much so," said Moses. He drew out some papers from a leather satchel, and placed them before the professor.

They were his hand-written translation, in modern Hebrew, of the words on the leather scrolls. Schroeder picked them up and started reading, falling silent as he continued, with only a nod of his head or a muttered exclamation as he quickly perused the pages. When he finished, he set them down in his lap and looked at Moses in amazement.

"There is no mention here of the law against worshipping in any place other than the Holy Temple, here in Jerusalem," he said, looking intently at Moses.

"Exact!" Moses said, certain triumph in his voice. "Bleek, and others, say that law was much later added to the text—impossible for the Prophet to haff written, as the Temple did not exist for him!"

Schroeder scanned the text again eagerly, finding other instances of differences between the traditional text of Deuteronomy, and Moses' translation.

"And these scrolls that you have extracted this translation from, where are they? May I see them?"

Moses smiled, and placed the cedar box on a small table between them. With some little show of ceremony, he unclasped the box, opened the lid, and carefully drew out the four linen-wrapped items. He glanced at Schroeder. "Perhaps there is better light for you to see?"

Schroeder nodded and stood up, leading the way to a table close to the window, looking north, with a diffused but bright reflected light into the room. Moses spread the four pieces of leather scroll upon the table, and stepped back so Schroeder could approach. The professor had snatched up a magnifying glass and proceeded to scrutinize the strips very closely, humming slightly under his breath—Moses thought it was something of Bach's—but otherwise silent for many minutes. Finally, he straightened up, laid down the magnifying glass, and turned to Moses.

"Congratulations, my dear Shapira," he said, and took him by the hand to shake heartily. "These are unquestionably the real article! I would stake my reputation on their authenticity! What a prize you have discovered for our entire community!"

* * *

From that day forward, Moses was a changed man. Professor Schroeder's approval and support gave him courage and confidence to take his fabulous discovery to the wider world. Rosette would barely listen to him after a while, as he talked of nothing else; she was taken up at that time with outfitting their daughter Augusta, who had been sent to an expensive boarding school in Berlin, and who wrote almost daily of her need for dresses, hats, and shoes—and all required to be of the latest fashion. Professor Schroeder's family were very kind to Augusta, and she wrote with great enthusiasm about the dinners and parties at their mansion in Berlin, to which she had been invited often.

So Myriam was the one to whom Moses confided his hopes and dreams; she sat with him in his upper room as he continued to refine his translation, and helped him write letters to scholars in Berlin, Halle and Leipzig, to introduce his great find. The first letter—fully ten pages of extensive explanation—was to Professor Hermann Strack at the University of Berlin, at the department of Old Testament Exegesis and Semitic Languages, one of the foremost scholars of the time.

"Myriam, my child," he said to her one day early in May, after dispatching this letter, "No more need for us to spend long days in the stuffy shop, scratching texts on olive-wood covers for tourists' prayer-books! And for you—" He caught her up in his arms and they danced around the room. "We will travel all the wide world, you will see the wealth and beauty and glory of other great cities! Will you like that?"

"Oh, yes, Papa," she answered, happy to support him and see him, after so many troubles and setbacks, hopeful for the future. "People will see that you are a serious scholar, too, as you deserve so well."

"Yes," he said, becoming solemn at the thought. "I know it will bring to me a position in some fine university, how not? And then, at last," he said, his face turning dark with anger, "that insolent dragoman Ganneau will see all his tricks against me are so much nothing."

The shadow of the family's great enemy, Charles Clermont-Ganneau, always lurked at the edges of their life—they viewed him as the most evil of men, treacherous and spiteful. Myriam had once asked her mother what a '*dragoman*' was— to her it seemed it meant he was part dragon, part man! But Rosette, knowing to whom she referred, would not tell her, and forbade her daughter to speak of him.

When Myriam asked Ouarda, her nanny, what the word meant, she said, with a sniff, that it was some kind of arrogant European government official, a go-between for negotiations, someone who knew many languages and 'how to get things done.' This was all very mysterious to the girl, but it didn't make her hate their enemy. She had been very impressed by him on his black horse that day he came to the shop with all his friends—how adventurous and romantic he looked, especially when he stood next to the lovely Lady in Blue! She wondered what had become of the Lady? But when she thought of how cruelly he had treated her father, she was persuaded that he was indeed a ferocious enemy.

Despite his eagerness to show the leather strips to other scholars, Moses soon disappeared once again for nearly a month into the deserts of Egypt, in search of manuscripts his Bedouin contacts had told him of. The morning he left for that expedition, a bright and sunny June day in 1883, Myriam was there to watch him mount his great white horse in the stableyard. He wore his Bedouin clothes, which made him look handsome and dashing, and gave him a youthful vigor as almost nothing else could. She asked him if his old collaborator Selim was still helping him. He scowled and addressed her sternly.

"Do not mention his name to me again, child! It was Selim who schemed with our great enemy to say the Moabite idols were fakes—it was Selim who builded the very ovens and figures that he showed to Ganneau, as if they had been what made my collection! No, I hope never to see the faces of those evil ones again."

And with that, he urged his horse forward, followed by the long line of guides and hired servants tending the pack horses and camels. Myriam stood watching them until they disappeared at the bottom of the hill and out of sight, and she returned to the house, sighing for the chance to have adventures of her own. She had just passed her fourteenth birthday.

Neither of them could know that this would be his last journey into the desert world that he so loved.

TWENTY-ONE

**Rotterdam — Wednesday Evening, March 12, 1884
Dinner at the Hotel Willemsbrug**

WE THREE WERE A RATHER SILENT GROUP as we sat in the private alcove that Herr Innesbrucke had so thoughtfully reserved for us. I was surprised, as I looked around, that the dining room was nearly filled with people—surely all of them could not be staying at the hotel? When I saw more diners arriving at the door, and the host taking their evening wraps from them, I could only conclude that this restaurant was somewhat of a destination for, perhaps, people who lived in the surrounding area, and didn't want to venture far on a blustery Spring night. The menu was more simple than extensive, but so far everything was quite delicious and well-prepared. John and Lord Parke were making fast work of the first bottle of red wine—of which I'd only taken a small glass, though not watered-down—and looked to be moving on to a second bottle in very short order.

A respectable-looking older woman was the hostess for the restaurant, greeting the arrivals and beckoning a smartly-dressed waiter to show them to their tables. She gave a discreet glance our way every once in a while, whether checking if we needed anything or just keeping an eye on us, I wasn't sure. I couldn't imagine that our collective interference in the Shapira Affair, as I'd begun to refer to it in my own mind, was in any way welcome to the establishment, or the police, for that matter.

"Well," I said aloud, "think of the devil and he appears." My companions looked at me as if I'd suddenly started sprouted horns, so I smiled and nodded toward the door. They turned in time to see Inspector Cramer divesting himself of his overcoat to the smiling hostess. We all watched with interest as the policeman strode over to our table.

"Good evening, *mademoiselle, messieurs*," the Inspector said, a short half-bow accompanying his greeting.

"Inspector," I said, inclining my head graciously. "Won't you please join us?" There was a fourth chair at the table, and he accepted with alacrity.

"We have nearly finished our *plats*," John said, "but would you care to order something for yourself?" He motioned to the hovering waiter to take away the empty wine bottle and open the other one.

"Or perhaps you would like to start on dessert?" I said, thinking to myself that I could imagine no person less inclined to eat sweets than the lean and serious Inspector. But he overturned my expectations.

"Thank you, you are most kind," said Inspector Cramer, smiling the least little bit. "I have had my dinner, but would be delighted to join you for dessert and coffee."

When we were settled with coffee, digestifs and ample servings of a delicious pound cake with fruit sauce and whipped cream, I decided it was time to ask the Inspector a few questions.

"I hope you have joined us this evening, Inspector," I began, "with the intention of providing us with information you may have gleaned from that scoundrel Selim, since he was hauled off into the custody of the police earlier today?" I smiled at him and took a sip of coffee. "As delightful as your company in and of itself may be."

He smiled at my archness, which was as I had intended. "Miss Vernon Lee," he said, "you have a most interesting way of speaking—perhaps it is the way of all eminent literary persons?"

Lord Parke laughed. "I assure you, Inspector, Miss Vernon Lee's 'way' is entirely her own—entirely original!" He tipped his wine glass in my direction as a salute, to which I nodded graciously.

Then we grew serious. The Inspector leaned forward a little and spoke in a low voice.

"We are lucky to have access to a university professor who is fluent in Arabic, and although Selim spoke a more obscure dialect, they were able to understand one another, and the questioning went well."

Dessert was forgotten (or very nearly) as we all leaned in to hear.

"It appears that this Selim has a long history with Mr. Shapira, dating back some decades, when he would accompany him—or rather, lead him—on expeditions into the various desert and mountain lands of Palestine, Egypt and Arabia, in search of precious antiquities. He grew a little boastful, I must say, especially after we allowed him some food and drink—our interpreter told us what his dietary restrictions were, religious sort of thing, you see," the Inspector said, and we all nodded. "He claimed to have found any number of ancient manuscripts, pottery, statues of gods, *et cetera,* and said he'd been the cause of many a European's success in archaeology."

"Did he mention anyone other than Mr. Shapira?" I asked eagerly. The Inspector gave me a curious look.

"Yes, Miss Vernon Lee, as a matter of fact, he did." He took a small notebook from his vest pocket and consulted it. "Let's see, some Germans—Peterman, Klein—and a Frenchman, Clermont-Ganneau." He put the notebook down. "He was especially vituperative about Clermont-Ganneau, on account of some skull-duggery or other he claimed the Frenchman had perpetrated against him." He shrugged, and took a sip of his coffee. "Said the same of Mr. Shapira—that he'd cheated him of his good name, fired him from his employ, in fact."

"Do you think he had anything to do with Shapira's death?" Lord Parke asked. He held up the bottle of wine with a questioning look—John nodded, and he re-filled his glass. The Inspector and I both declined, and Lord Parke filled his own glass.

"I own that I think it very unlikely," said the Inspector, frowning. "It seemed clear that he sneaked in to the hotel with the intention of speaking to Mr. Shapira—perhaps even of exacting revenge on him with that dreadful knife—and that he had no idea that he was already deceased."

I frowned as well. "How did he come to know which room was Mr. Shapira's?" I asked.

"Ah, yes, we thought of that, too," the Inspector said, without a hint of condescension, for which I admired him—he was treating me as an equal. "He said that the previous week, before he tried to see Shapira, he had waited outside many hours, and twice saw the man looking out of his window, gazing at the river. So he was able to work out which room it was."

We fell silent for a few moments, thinking about this turn of events, and what danger Mr. Shapira might have been in, had Selim succeeded in gaining access to him the previous week. Not that it mattered now. I roused myself and drank some more coffee.

"Have you charged him with anything?" I asked. "Is he still at the police station?"

The Inspector nodded briefly. "We are merely holding him overnight, to make sure of some details of his story." He shrugged. "The hotel has declined to press any charges, and indeed, there is little to charge him with, as he hadn't actually broken into the room—he was just found in the hall." He picked up his wine glass absently and put it down again. "We will let him go in the morning, and he will be warned to leave the country immediately, which our interpreter said is Selim's intention anyway—he has nothing to stay for here, he says."

John spoke up for the first time. "Did he make any mention of the leather strips? Does he, by any chance, know they are in my possession?" he said, glancing down toward the leather satchel at his feet—he was determined not to let it out of his sight.

The Inspector shook his head decisively. "I don't think he knows anything of the sort," he said. "I asked him straight out if there was any particular thing he was looking for in Shapira's room, anything he thought might be there that he wanted to have in his own possession—but he seemed puzzled by the question. He shrugged, told the interpreter that there was nothing Shapira had anymore that was of interest to him, especially after the disgrace in London—yes, he did mention that, and laughed, actually laughed, at the poor man's misfortune in that regard." The Inspector looked as if he did not approve such lack of sympathy.

I shook my head. I remembered quite clearly the devastating letters and articles in the papers following the rejection of the Shapira Scrolls by the British Museum—they were brutal. The poor man was driven out of town, scorned and abused as a fraud and an arrogant, over-reaching trickster. There was more than a hint of virulent anti-Semitism, of which I entirely disapproved.

The restaurant was beginning to empty out, and I felt overwhelmed with fatigue—it had been a long day. John and Lord Parke, and indeed, the Inspector as well, looked as tired as I felt. But I had (at least) one more question.

"Inspector, you have been very forthcoming, and I thank you with all my heart for allowing us to follow this investigation with you," I said, pulling up some energy to make this last exertion. "We look forward to viewing Mr. Shapira's effects at your office tomorrow, of course, but I have one more question before we all leave for a good night's rest. Did Selim make any mention of the lady and gentlemen who inquired of Josef at the front desk about Mr. Shapira late last week, the tall Frenchman and the apparently British woman who spoke excellent French? If he was on the lookout for Mr. Shapira, he might have seen them approach the hotel, for they came just the day before Selim tried to talk to Mr. Shapira."

The Inspector consulted his notebook again, as if to make sure. "We asked him that question, too," he said. "But the man looked very cagey, and wouldn't say much. Nothing about any lady at all, and then he muttered the strange word *'dragoman'*, that *'devil dragoman,'* he said. But he refused to say anymore." He looked at the three of us. "Does that term mean anything to any of you?"

We shook our heads—it was indeed a puzzle.

With a cordial good-night to the Inspector, John and Lord Parke and I made our weary way back to our rooms, too tired to speak more than wishes for a good night's sleep. But I turned back from my door to call softly to John.

"Put a chair under the doorknob, my dear friend, won't you? In addition to locking the door?"

He smiled and nodded. Lord Parke, hearing my admonition, added another thought.

"And be sure to check the wardrobe right away, to make sure no one is hiding in it," he said, half laughing.

He shouldn't have laughed.

TWENTY-TWO

Germany —June - July 1883

MOSES HAD RECEIVED A REPLY TO HIS LONG LETTER to Professor Strack at the end of May, which he read upon returning from the desert in early June.

"*It is not worth your while*," he read aloud to his family from Strack's letter, "*to bring such an evident forgery to Europe.*" His face was dark with frustration.

"But he has not even seen the scrolls," Myriam protested, knowing how stung her father must be at this arrogant rejection.

"He will change his mind, once he sees them," Moses said after a moment's thought. His wife shook her head ominously, and muttered under her breath something about *coming to no good*, but only Myriam heard her. Moses was already striding about the room, making plans aloud about whom he would see, along with Strack.

"I shall go first to Berlin, to see Herr Professor Strack, and make him see reason," Moses said.

"I hope, Wilhelm," Rosette interrupted, her voice calm but with an edge to it, "that you will find a moment to give to your eldest daughter there?"

Moses stopped for a moment and gazed at his wife. "I haff hope I will be able to do so," he said, not very convincingly.

"There is a special reason for you to spend a little time with her—and perhaps the Schroeders, too," Rosette persisted. She pulled a letter out of her apron pocket and tossed it on the table. "It seems that she and young Paul Schroeder may be coming to an understanding, very soon, and it is only right that you should discuss this with Herr Professor while you are there—we cannot let such a thing go on in the hands of the youngsters alone."

Moses looked at her, amazed, then smiling, and said, "Nothing better to me than for Augusta becoming part of that good family." He walked over and kissed his wife on her cheek—something he hadn't done in a very long while. "It is up to you, I think, that this happiness comes to us?"

Rosette coloured prettily—she was still a handsome woman—and *tut-tutted* her husband away. "Thank the Lord that we are able to provide her with a significant dowry," she said, and turned back to her sewing.

Myriam looked on in wonder—such momentous news! She turned to her father.

"Oh, Papa, do visit them, I'm sure Augusta will be very happy that you are there to rejoice in her good fortune!"

"Very good," said Moses, "Herr Strack first, then the marriage talking afterwards."

Rosette had to be content with that order of things, but she at least felt confident that Moses would keep his word.

25 June 1883 – Berlin

"For the third time, I have no need to look at these forgeries!" Strack thundered as his fist met the table between him and Moses in the professor's study at his home. For a young man of only thirty-five, Moses thought, Strack had quite the physical and mental presence, and would have been intimidating if not for Moses's having twenty years and more on him, and decades of experience facing down dangerous Bedouin chiefs and scurrilous bandits.

The man continued his rant. "Your interminable letter explained more than enough about the questionable venue of these items, and I do not care to be made to play the fool, like Schlottmann, with those Moabite atrocities you convinced him were authentic!"

"But Herr Professor Schroeder was very clear in his judging," Moses started to say, but Strack waved a hand at him in dismissal.

"Schroeder is a *linguist*," he said, as if that were a bad word. "A *poseur* who thinks he knows antiquities just because he can read Phoenician."

The two men glared at each other for a few moments, then Moses, with great dignity, picked up the leather fragments he had taken out of his carpet bag, bowed politely, and left the room.

Later that evening, dining at the Schroeders, he did not repeat the insults, completely unfounded, that Strack had thrown out against his friend—and now, Augusta's future father-in-law. The two men had spent considerable time in Schroeder's library before dinner, discussing and dismissing Strack's intransigency, with Schroeder urging Moses to continue on to Leipzig to meet with a group of young scholars and antiquarians of his acquaintance there, at the best universities. Moses did not need much urging, and after a further day or two visiting with the newly engaged couple and drinking toasts to their future, he packed once more to continue on to Leipzig.

29 June 1883 – Leipzig, Hotel Hauffe

Moses's recent good fortune allowed him to take a room at the recently built, magnificent Hotel Hauffe in Leipzig—set in the midst of an enormous park, the five-story building could accommodate hundreds of guests, and boasted several restaurants and two ballrooms. Visiting diplomats and well-known international scholars frequently stayed at the Hauffe, and Moses was not surprised to recognize more than one representative of a European museum with whom he'd had cordial dealings, as he strolled through the gorgeous lobby.

He wasted no time—the very next day he brought several of the leather strips to a good friend of his, Hermann Guthe, who was soon to become a full professor of Old Testament Exegesis at Leipzig University, though he was only thirty-four years old. Guthe was delighted to see him.

"My dear Shapira," he said, kissing him on both cheeks in an unusually effusive greeting. "You are most welcome! What brings you to Leipzig, my friend?"

"I seek your help," Moses said, "and your expertness for some items I haff found that I believe are worthy of a scholar's attention."

Guthe's eyes lighted with interest. "Excellent! You always have something to liven up the day, Wilhelm."

Moses smiled and shook his head. "I want first to tell that I took them to Herr Strack, in Berlin, a few days ago."

Guthe looked wary. "And—"

"He would not even look at my manuscripts," Moses said. "He was strong in his mind right from the start that they were not real, and not worth his time."

"Ridiculous!" Guthe said firmly. "What kind of scholar dismisses such a thing out of hand, without even the courtesy of looking—and from someone like you!" He patted Moses on the shoulder. "Come, let us see what you have—I'm certainly willing to see what it is."

Moses opened his handbag and took out three leather strips, laying them carefully on a table near the windows, where there was a strong light from the summer sun. Then he stepped back, and waited while Guthe peered closely at the manuscripts.

"So, Landberg was right, these are amazing," Guthe said. He straightened up from the table.

"Landberg? Herr Doctor Carlo Landberg?" Moses inquired, startled. Guthe looked a little embarrassed.

"Yes, I should have said—Landberg wrote to me a few weeks ago, he'd heard from Schroeder about these leather strips of yours—they're causing a great deal of excitement in our little circle you see, despite the great Strack's contemptible behavior." Guthe turned back to the strips.

"There are more? May I see them all?" Guthe spoke rapidly in his enthusiasm. "And may we get Eduard Meyer to come as well? He's out of town today, I happen to know, but will be back late tonight—we can all meet tomorrow and discuss this."

Moses smiled faintly. "So you think there is some possibility they are the real thing?"

Guthe shrugged, but smiled broadly. "That remains to be seen—we must have a very careful and exact examination, with a number of respected scholars—but yes, I think it's more likely than not that they are what you say they are—manuscripts from at least the sixth century B.C., maybe the ninth—the oldest known to date."

They arranged to meet at the Hauffe the next day.

* * *

That evening, sitting at a small desk in his comfortable hotel room, Moses wrote in a little book of blank paper in which he had begun to keep track of the process unfolding around his leather strips. He knew his writing ability was limited, especially spelling, especially when he wrote in English, as he tried to do most often, and other times in German; but he wanted to preserve the events he felt were historic in their nature, and in which he played so key a part. Tonight he wrote:

H. Guthe gives me hope that the authentiknes of the lether manuscrips will be showed by the best scholars in Leipzig; they will publish the result, and my originel Deuteronomy will get the aclaim that is its due. Thanks be to God.

2-3 July 1883 – Hotel Hauffe

Over the next few days, Guthe and his colleague Meyer scrutinized the leather strips, which had been laid out on a large table in a meeting room at the Hauffe—most of the strips, when unfolded, were between one and three feet long, though only four or five inches high. There were different degrees of decay and crumbling, especially at the extreme edges; some of the "pages" were connected at a fold, while others had become separated. While they worked, Moses relayed to them what he had already determined—that the strips were actually two complete copies of the same writing—and this resulted in Guthe taking the first half (seven of the strips) and Meyer the second half, to make a better comparison of the two sets of writing.

"This is impossible!" Meyer exclaimed at one point, frustrated by the impenetrability of the black, tarry layer that covered what they presumed was lettering underneath—on Guthe's half, this same section was clearer, against a light brown background.

"I haff used spirits of alcohol, when I looked at them," Moses said, but the two younger men shook their heads.

"We need to call in Franz Hofmann," Guthe said, and explained to Moses, "He's an expert in chemistry, with a degree in medicine—his advice will be sound."

Hofmann came the next day, and after conducting several experiments with oil, ether and alcohol, he decided that applying a small amount of alcohol with a delicate paintbrush would be best. When asked eagerly by all three men what was his opinion of the leather manuscripts themselves, he replied only, "I find nothing suspicious."

Which was good enough for them to continue.

At the end of the day, another noted Orientalist, Adolf Erman, arrived at the hotel, having been urged by telegram to come and view the manuscripts for himself. Although his initial response to the invitation was skeptical, upon his arrival he was impressed and astounded.

"If these are not the genuine article," he declared after examining them, and hearing what the others had to say, "I will eat every one of them myself!"

Moses's entry in his little book that night reflected the enthusiasm his colleagues had engendered in him:

I coud not ask for better men than these who are making me full of confidanz for the truth of the manuscrips. What a trezure I have found, and what riches will come to my famly.

He could not foresee how the next two weeks would turn the wheel of his fortune yet again.

TWENTY-THREE

Rotterdam — Wednesday Night, 12 March 1884

I HAD NO SOONER TURNED INTO MY OWN ROOM at the Willemsbrug when I heard a shout from down the hall. Both Lord Parke and I ran out of our rooms in time to see a slight figure, dressed in black—clutching John's leather satchel tightly—scramble through the doorway of John's room and race for the stairway that led to the cellar.

Stunned, we failed to move for a few precious moments, allowing the thief to gain the door to the stairs and escape from our sight. My first thought was for John, and I ran quickly to his open door. By the dim gaslight in his room, I could see him struggling a little to rise from the floor.

"John, good God! James!" I cried, turning back to Lord Parke, who had been about to run down the stairs himself. "James! Come here, John needs help!"

He turned back and we both entered the room. In the event, we could see that John was not injured, but had only had the breath knocked out of him. We helped him to rise, and as he fought to regain his breathing, we exclaimed over the inconceivability of this second attack—and theft!

"The thief took the scrolls," I said, dismayed. "Perhaps I should not have stopped you, James, from following him."

John spoke up, wheezing a little. "*Her*," he said. "It was the woman—again—I think—the same one."

"Well, it's fortunate we made the switch when we did," Lord Parke said. I gazed at him intently. He didn't look very disturbed about the theft.

"She didn't actually take the scrolls, then," I said, making an intelligent guess.

Lord Parke nodded in agreement. "They are safe in my room, locked in a case and hidden away." He smiled at John, who was recovering apace.

"It was his idea, though," Lord Parke said. "He thought if he carried the satchel around with him, then the thief—if she were going to try again—would have to wait until he returned to his room—and then we might be able to catch her. Drat the woman, though, for being so clever! I thought she'd wait til the middle of the night!"

John nodded. "She caught me completely by surprise, and hit me with the door when I was entering the room." He shook his head—almost in admiration, I thought. "She has some remarkable abilities, I'd say."

Lord Parke frowned. "I should have gone into the room with you," he said.

I looked from the one to the other. "Well," I said at last, "but you are both to be congratulated for thinking so smartly ahead of time—you saved the scrolls." I looked anxiously at John. "Are you all right then?"

"Yes, yes, I'm just fine. I don't think she'll be back tonight, right?" He seemed to muse a moment. "One wonders how she got into the room."

We examined the door lock and I saw faint scratchings on the brass around the keyhole. "She seems to be an expert picklock, along with everything else."

Lord Park laughed. "You ought to know, Violet." I smiled at his reference to my own burglaring abilities, with which he'd had some acquaintance five years ago, on our first adventure.

Assuming that by now the woman had gotten thoroughly away, we decided that the best thing to do was to retire for the night, and prepare for our visit in the morning to the police station before catching the train back to Paris.

Thursday, 13 March 1884 – Rotterdam Police Station

Inspector Cramer was chagrined to learn of the thief's thwarted attempt to steal the manuscripts, although much relieved at the gentlemen's quick thinking and planning ahead of time.

"But how did she slip by my men?" He frowned, and his ever-faithful sergeant scribbled for a bit in his notebook. "I had them stationed at the front and back doors." He glanced sharply at me. "And even at the cellar door, *Fräulein* Lee," acknowledging my discovery the day before. He said something, in Dutch I thought, to his sergeant in a lowered voice; I assumed some underlings would be in for some serious questions later.

I was amused by the ease with which the Inspector switched languages—French, Dutch, German, English—and wondered if utility and practicality were the primary drivers of which language he employed, or did his emotions sometimes impel him, for instance, when he addressed me variously as *Miss*, or *Fräulein*, or *mademoiselle*? It would make an interesting study.

But there were more important things to focus upon at this moment. The sergeant had left the room temporarily and now came back with a paperboard box containing Mr. Shapira's effects, along with a small, battered leather suitcase. A black overcoat hung over one arm, and he placed it on a table along with the box and the suitcase. Then he said something only the Inspector could hear, after which the Inspector addressed us all.

"There is a matter to which I must attend immediately; I hope it will not take much time," he said, bowing his head apologetically. "But you must feel free to look through these belongings of Mr. Shapira—we have an inventory of them."

I smiled inwardly to think that he was warning us that he would notice if we happened to take anything—as if we would think of doing such a thing!

We waited until the Inspector left the room, then turned to the box on the table.

"What do you hope to find here?" Lord Parke asked me. I shook my head.

"I have no idea of anything," I said. "Let's just see what he left behind."

I motioned to John to look through the suitcase. "A gentleman should look through his clothing, it seems to me," I said. "You would know what should and shouldn't be there."

I took the lid off the box, and Lord Parke and I peered inside. There wasn't much there. "Lord Parke," I said, "if you would be so kind, perhaps you can make a list of these things as I take them out, one by one?"

He readily agreed, and looking around, seized a pen and some paper from a nearby desk, then sat down, pen poised, to take down my words.

"A hairbrush and comb...tooth powder and brush." I set them on the table.

"A copy of the Old Testament," I said, rifling the pages quickly. "In Hebrew...and a copy of the New Testament, in Greek and English." The box was nearly empty.

"Some postcards, blank, of famous sights of Berlin, Amsterdam, London." I put them on the table and frowned. "Wouldn't you think there would be letters, say, from his family? Or correspondence with his business colleagues or the museums?"

Lord Parke looked up at me, nodding. "Yes, one would think so—I know he's been in contact with Ginsburg and Rieu in London."

"John, what have you got?" I said.

He shook his head. "Just what you would expect. Some underclothes, two pairs of stockings, two shirts—clean and ironed, just back from the laundry I'd guess—a pair of trousers, two collars, both quite worn. One set of cufflinks, gold by the look of them, but simple."

"Look for false pockets or something," I directed. John felt carefully along the bottom inside edges of the suitcase—nothing.

"What about his overcoat?" I said. "Anything in the pockets?"

Lord Parke leaped up from his chair to rifle through the coat. "Empty," he said.

I picked up the final item in the box, which was a plasticine bag with a label on it: *Items in pockets and on his person.*

It gave me a moment's pause, realizing that these were things found on Mr. Shapira's person as he lay dead on the floor of his room.

"What's wrong, Vi?" John asked, seeing me standing quite still, the plasticine bag in my hand. I shook myself free of morbid thoughts. "Nothing really," I said, with a wan smile. "Just feeling a trifle ghoulish."

I tipped the contents of the bag out onto the table, and named them aloud as Lord Parke wrote them down.

"A watch, engraved *To W.M.Shapira, with esteem, Rev. Hefter*...a handkerchief, no monogram...one gold wedding ring, with a date, presumably his wedding date...some currency of various countries, doesn't add up to much...and this envelope." I held the last item very gingerly, as it appeared to have splashes of blood on it.

John and Lord Parke came nearer to look at the envelope, which was addressed to Dr. C. David Ginsburg, British Museum. It was empty inside.

"There's a postage stamp on the envelope," I said.

"He must have intended to send a letter to Ginsburg," John said.

"So where's the letter then?" Lord Parke said.

We were mystified at this odd occurrence. I looked more closely at the back flap of the envelope.

"I don't think this was ever sealed," I said. My two companions each took a look themselves, and nodded their agreement.

"So someone—maybe even Mr. Shapira—took the letter out of this envelope...but when, and why?" Lord Parke said.

"Maybe he hadn't written the letter yet?" I suggested. "Maybe he prepared the envelope first, then didn't actually write the letter?"

"Or maybe he *had* written the letter, but hadn't yet put it in the envelope," John said. "Perhaps it was just sitting out, on the desk, and someone took it, not realizing there was an envelope?"

We three stood there, contemplating all the options. "We need to ask Inspector Cramer exactly where this envelope was found," I said at last. "It is a bit crumpled, and as you see, there is blood on it, so my guess is that it was found under the body—perhaps it fell on the floor when—someone—snatched it up from the desk? Or wrested it away from Mr. Shapira?"

"One thing seems certain," Lord Parke said grimly. "Whoever took that letter, and has it now, was likely the last person to see Mr. Shapira alive—and could quite possibly be his murderer."

We looked from one to another with heavy hearts, and then I said what we were all, no doubt, thinking.

"Where are all Mr. Shapira's documents? Letters from his wife? Ancient manuscripts he had promised to sell to the museum? His diary—surely a businessman such as he would have a diary, for appointments and notes?"

John and Lorde Parke looked as puzzled as I felt.

"Someone has made off with a lot more than just that one letter," I said.

TWENTY-FOUR

Berlin, Germany — 4-14 July 1883

KARL RICHARD LEPSIUS, HEAD OF THE ROYAL LIBRARY at Berlin, glared at the young man standing before him. Lepsius was seventy-three, and feeling every minute of those years on the morning that Adolf Erman came to see him about some bothersome old fragments he was over-excited about. These youngsters and their fantasies!

He sighed, and bid Erman to be seated. As the daylight streamed into the high-ceilinged room that was his office, lined with books and manuscripts, and Erman began to describe in detail the manuscript he had seen, he couldn't help himself from catching some of the younger man's enthusiasm for this discovery.

"Eighth or ninth century B.C., you say?" he queried.

"Yes, I saw them myself, the characters are in every respect like the Mesha Stele—proto-Hebraic," Erman said, trying to keep his voice even—he knew the old man didn't like an emotional fuss.

"We must speak to the minister before we commit to anything," Lepsius said.

Erman took this to be a very positive sign.

But the old man turned his still-keen eye on him. "Who else knows of this? Dillmann? Sachau? Who?"

Erman tried not to stammer as he sought for the best answer. "No, no, they have no idea, just Guthe and Meyer, they're with Shapira in Leipzig, they're doing the work."

Lepsius grunted. "Shapira, is it?"

Erman held his breath—was this going to be bad?

The old librarian smiled faintly. "Despite some mis-steps, Shapira is a good man." He leaned back in his chair, more relaxed now. "I'll inquire—you get me more information—find out what Guthe and—Meyer you say?—find out what they think they have there."

"Absolutely, sir, I am in close communication with Guthe, you'll get a full report."

Erman rose from his chair, clicked his heels and bowed a half-bow to the eminent man, and took his leave before anything could reverse Lepsius's current good feelings.

He immediately sent a letter to Guthe in Leipzig.

Wednesday, 4 July 1883

My dear Guthe,

I have spoken with L. who is interested, but he urgently wishes that others don't get involved, especially not Althoff. He wants to try with the minister directly. So, please write to everyone you have written so far that they must feign ignorance of the matter—with old L., a lot depends on it. Shapira must turn to him, he has good prejudice for him.

P.S. I pretended not to know whether Dillmann, Sachau, Nöldeke, etc., had been written to.

More soon, Adolf

By Saturday, Erman had written several more letters to his friends in Leipzig, each one more alarmed than the previous one. Sachau had been to see Lepsius, so the old man knew that he, Erman, had prevaricated. Then other scholars showed up, talking about the Shapira manuscripts, in varying degrees of indignant scoffing or amused derision. Lepsius was vacillating. *He is afraid and can easily be frightened,* Erman wrote.

More scholars entered the fray—one in particular, Georg Ebers, a noted Egyptologist nearing fifty, was excited but cautioned his younger colleagues to be careful: *Where Shapira appears, it smells a bit sticky...be doubly cautious...doubly suspicious. I'm so happy for you, but I'm a little afraid,* he wrote to Eduard Meyer on 10 July.

The older scholars were all too cognizant of the evil that had befallen their former colleague, Schlottmann, whose over-enthusiastic endorsement of Shapira's Moabite statues had ruined his reputation and brought embarrassment to the country, which had paid out some thousands of marks for the collection ten years previously.

Moses sat by in the room where Guthe and Meyers were testing and examining his Deuteronomy, and he heard all this back-and-forth with as much equanimity as he could muster. Finally, he could brook it no longer.

"I shall go myself to Herr Lepsius," he said. "He knows me. All will be well."

Tuesday 10 July 1883

Moses stood at the gate to Herr Lepsius' home in a garden-like neighborhood of Berlin, his carpet bag—a capacious satchel made of brocaded carpet figured with leaves and pomegranates in brilliant reds, yellows, greens and blues, with wooden handles fitted with an iron catch—with its precious contents secure in his grip. He felt as if his Fate were awaiting him inside the ornate mansion, but he did not fear it. He had faced down many a foe in his lifetime, and he was ready for one more. He did feel that he was on the cusp of an earthshaking change in his life—he was confident that this would be the crowning achievement of all his efforts.

He opened the gate and walked up to the front door, where he was admitted by a solemn butler who took his hat and coat, and led him to a well-furnished sitting room. In a few moments, his host appeared at the door.

"My dear Shapira," Lepsius said, and taking his hand, shook it heartily.

"Most respected sir," Moses said, deeply gratified at the respectful welcome.

"I invite you to make yourself comfortable here, in this room, Schramm will get you anything you desire, while I and others will be examining the, ah, the manuscripts, in my study, will that be all right?" Lepsius spoke quickly, as if to forestall any objection on Moses's part. But Moses saw the value of the scholars being by themselves. His friend Adolf Erman was to be part of the group, and he knew he had a champion there. Lepsius himself seemed cordially inclined, which also seemed a good sign in his favor.

"Yes, yes of course, it will be fine," Moses said.

"Good, good," Lepsius said. He looked at the large, colorful bag, still in Moses's hand. "And the, uh, the items are in there, are they?"

"Oh, of course," Moses said. He handed over the bag, but not without a moment's chagrin at letting them out of his sight. He told himself he was being foolish.

Lepsius took possession of the manuscripts, shook Moses's hand once more, and made to leave the room.

"We are all assembled," he said. "Hopefully, we shall have some conclusions to share with you—I'm sure it won't be long—we have Meyers' and Guthe's reports to work with—we just need to see a little for ourselves."

Moses nodded agreeably, but felt the anxiety returning. As the door closed behind the great Egyptologist, the man who had coined the term *The Book of the Dead*, Moses prayed, something he found himself doing more often these days. *For your Glory, O Lord...let this come to pass.*

* * *

Adolf Erman became aware rather quickly that he was the only one of the four other eminent scholars in the room who was convinced of the authenticity of Shapira's manuscripts. Lepsius was mostly silent as the others—August Dillman, Eduard Sachau and Moritz Steinschneider—hemmed and hawed, peered and poked at the strips, then snorted and derided the items they were scrutinizing.

In the end, even Erman found himself wondering if his own enthusiasm was misplaced, and conceded that the group could not, in good conscience, support a recommendation to the government to purchase the manuscripts. There were too many questions, too many flaws—and perhaps, although this was hinted rather than said outright, too much history telling against Shapira. They had taken a mere hour and a half to come to this conclusion.

Lepsius took the young scholar aside as the other men left the room, and said, "It is up to you, my young friend, to tell Shapira our answer."

Erman could see it was useless to protest. Lepsius walked him to the door of the room where Shapira waited, and wished him good luck. With a deep breath and a sigh, Erman knocked lightly on the door and went in.

* * *

Moses shut himself up in solitude for a few days, fuming over the treatment he and his manuscripts had received, then roused himself to his more usual optimism. He spent some time with his daughter and the Schroeders—to whom he gave little hint of what Erman had told him, merely that the scholars would be publishing their findings in due course. Professor Schroeder, perhaps guessing somewhat of the truth, urged him to take the manuscripts to his friends at the British Museum, where Moses was sure to receive a respectful welcome. So, on Saturday, the 14th of July, with his suitcase and his carpet bag of precious manuscripts, Moses Shapira embarked from Berlin across Europe, heading for London once again.

TWENTY-FIVE

Rotterdam — Thursday, 13 March 1884

INSPECTOR CRAMER WAS BACK IN THE ROOM where we had surveyed Mr. Shapira's belongings, and he was frowning.

"I do not recall any such things being found in his room," he said, when we asked about documents and letters. He looked at his sergeant, who shook his head.

"Don't you think that's odd?" I asked. "A man such as this, gone many months from his family, surely there would be letters, at the very least?"

He nodded, frowning some more.

Poor man, I thought, here he was all set with a mere suicide and now he's got us foreigners barging in and upsetting everything. But justice must be served.

"And then there's this," I said, holding out the plasticine packet with the blood-stained envelope in it. He took it from my hand warily. "Can you tell us where *exactly* this was found, when you entered Mr. Shapira's room last Saturday?"

The Inspector and his sergeant conferred in whispers, then he answered, "It was found under the body."

I nodded, satisfied.

"And why, may I ask, Miss Vernon Lee, is that of interest?" Inspector Cramer looked weary, but I could detect no sarcasm in his tone.

"There is no letter in the envelope," I said. I looked to my companions, who nodded encouragingly. Lord Parke spoke up.

"We are led to surmise, Inspector," he said, "that someone was with Mr. Shapira in his room, and took the letter from him, either before or after he died, and that this person either came after Mr. Shapira shot himself, or..." he left the thought hanging in the air.

"Or else was there when it happened..." the Inspector said, adding to the options.

"Or else murdered Mr. Shapira, took the letter, and perhaps other documents as well, and left," John said.

We all were standing in the evidence room, gazing at each other and the envelope in Inspector Cramer's hands.

"But," he said, with a deep sigh, "there is no way of knowing which of these scenarios is true." He looked up at us, his gaze firm. "The hotel staff saw no one suspicious, the door was locked, we simply do not have enough solid evidence to think this is anything but a sad and tragic suicide."

He placed the envelope back in the box, and motioned to his sergeant to do the same with the other items.

"Miss Vernon Lee, gentlemen," he said, with a short bow to all of us, "the Rotterdam police thank you for your interest and your insights, but I believe this matter is officially closed." He shook our hands, bowed again, and he and the sergeant left the room, taking the evidence with them.

We three looked at each other in near astonishment. Then Lord Parke shrugged. "Word from on high, one assumes," he said. "The Inspector has been shown the lay of the land, in no uncertain terms."

* * *

The sun was breaking through the grey clouds of late morning, and a soft wind was rising, bringing the scents of Spring with it into the town. We returned to the Willemsbrug Hotel to pack our things and prepare for the journey back to Paris. Each of us, I believe, had a heavy heart and a frustrated mind over the many puzzles and unanswered questions that still plagued us about this affair.

We alighted from our carriage and walked to the front door of the hotel. Lord Parke consulted his watch as we entered the lobby. "We have a little more than an hour before we need to be at the train station," he said. "Shall we meet down here in about forty minutes?"

"I'm going to speak to that maid, Angela, again," I said abruptly. "She would certainly have been aware of any bag or case of documents that Mr. Shapira would have had in his room."

Lord Parke looked at me ruefully. "I'm afraid it won't do much good to know one way or the other," he said. "If there were such a bag, it's long gone by now."

"I understand," I said. "But I have to make certain, don't I?"

John put a comforting hand on my arm, and nodded.

I watched them mount the stairs yet again to the rooms above, and turned to the front desk to ask after the maid. Luckily she was there, and a clerk sent someone to find her and bring her to me. I chose a small sofa in a far corner of the lobby, which was deserted anyway at this hour, and waited for her.

Angela came swiftly, and curtsied as she stood before me. I invited her to be seated, and although she demurred for a moment, I insisted.

"I just have one or two questions, my dear," I said, and she nodded expectantly.

"Can you describe to me the kind of luggage, or bags, that Mr. Shapira had in his room, and perhaps the kinds of things that may have been spread out on his desk, when you would go in to clean and tidy up the room?"

Angela was quiet for a few moments, then spoke. "He had a smallish leather suitcase, for his clothes; after he had hung the clothes in the wardrobe, or put them in the drawers, he kept the suitcase on the floor next to the wardrobe. Then there was a medium-sized carpet bag, very beautiful I thought it was," she said, smiling a little, "with figured patterns of leaves and pomegranates, brilliantly colored red and green and other colors, and lovely carved wooden handles."

I knew it! I tried to keep my voice even, despite my growing excitement. "Did you ever see what was in that carpet bag?" I asked.

She nodded. "Several times, when I would come in and Mr. Shapira was in the room, which was fairly often as he didn't go out much, he would have that bag on the floor next to him as he sat at his desk, and I would see him take out or put back various kinds of documents—some of which looked very old, like parchment with writing on it—and he would be looking at them at the desk, using a magnifying glass."

"Thank you, Angela, that is very, very helpful," I said. "Just one more question," I said. "Do you recall Mr. Shapira receiving anything like personal letters, while he was here?"

She nodded eagerly. "Yes, miss, there were several times when Josef, at the front desk, would ask me to take up the post to Mr. Shapira in the mornings, as I was going to his room anyway, and I noticed many times there were letters from far away places," she said, coloring a little. "It was because of the stamps, miss," she was apologetic, "the ones from Jerusalem in particular, were so beautiful and different, I couldn't help looking at them."

I nodded and smiled, as if I shared her interest in stamps. "Excellent, again, very helpful, my dear," I said, and rose from the sofa. "Thank you for taking time from your duties to answer my questions."

She curtsied and went back to work, while I slowly walked to one of the windows and looked out at the city streets—people were walking by, some idly, some with seemingly great purpose. The clouds had cleared off altogether and the sun, though cheerful, was throwing light on dingy brick walls and some street trees that had as yet to show any signs of new leaves. I thought of Paris, and how the parks there had already shown signs of greening.

It seemed as if weeks had passed since John received that package at his studio, and yet it was but three days! Thinking of the time made me realize that I had planned to end my sojourn in Paris tomorrow, when I had a ticket on the ferry from Calais to Dover, and then on to London, to stay with my dear, dear friend Mary Robinson, at her parents' home in Kensington. Heavens! All my regular endeavours and interests of writing and publishing rushed back into my brain. I was on the brink of publishing my first novel, *Miss Brown*—and had final decisions to discuss with my publisher in town. This business of murder and ancient scrolls had completely obliterated thoughts of my own life and activities.

I turned from the window and quickly made my way up the stairs and to my room; packing would be only a few moments' work, but I felt eager, nay anxious even, to be moving and getting on with my life. What was it, after all, that we could do for poor Mr. Shapira? I knew the three of us would talk it over further on the train back to Paris, but at the moment, I did not feel sanguine that any action we could take would make any difference now.

Even as I looked forward to getting back to my real life, however, I felt a pang of sorrow and then a *frisson* of anger. Whoever had done this to that poor man—and I was convinced that someone had indeed killed him—should be brought to justice somehow. I took comfort in thinking that John and Lord Parke would probably feel the same, and that we might yet find some way to solve this perplexing mystery.

TWENTY-SIX

London, England — Tuesday, 17 July 1883

AS HIS TRAIN NEARED THE CANNON STREET STATION in London, Moses reflected yet again on the conversation he had with Adolf Erman in the renowned librarian Lepsius's study the day before. Erman had been visibly disconcerted, but tried to reassure him.

..... *"Lepsius—I told you, he is easily frightened off, he's very conservative in his thinking—afraid of new things, you see," Erman had said. "The others, well..." he hesitated. He looked down, embarrassed.*

"My old reputation is a ghost behind me, even for the next generation?" Moses said, trying to sound a lighter note.

Erman nodded. "Lepsius did make a reference to the, uh, the Moabite statues, I'm afraid," he acknowledged. "But he defended your role in it, that is to say, your own ignorance of the fraud that was practised on you at the time."

Moses took a deep, steadying breath. "And you, Herr Erman, what do you think? And what do Guthe and Meyer say to you on this matter?"

"Oh, well," Erman said, trying to sound heartier than he felt. "I still think there's plenty of time and work left to do to determine authenticity." He skirted his own opinion. "Guthe wrote me just yesterday that he has started on his paper, and is quite enthusiastic in your favor."

Moses nodded; that made him feel marginally better. "But the answer here," he said, with a finger pointing to the heavily carpeted

floor, "*is that there will be no asking for funds to purchase my scrolls,*
here in Germany?"

Erman nodded sadly. "*I'm afraid that is the case, sir.*"*....*

Moses came back to the sense of the present, the train
rocking slowly as it began to slow down for the station. Erman had suggested that he take the scrolls to London, where
among other numerous friends at the Palestine Exploration
Fund and other such organizations, the British Museum itself was open to Moses Shapira as an important and valuable
partner and agent in its quest for antiquities. In the past six
years alone, the Museum had purchased some three hundred
manuscripts from Moses. He thought of this with increased
confidence and satisfaction.

But he wanted to see one person in particular before he
approached the British Museum directly—where he knew
his old friend, Christian David Ginsburg, would very likely
end up being the final arbiter of the authenticity of his
scrolls—and he wanted to do some advance reconnaissance
and gather as much support as he could before approaching
that lion's den.

Suitcase in one hand and his carpet bag of priceless
manuscripts in the other, Moses confidently checked into
the recently built Cannon Street Hotel, across from the station. It was a stately, five-story edifice modeled on the ornate
Renaissance style of the sixteenth century—and so strong
was his belief that his fortunes were on the rise again that he
asked for a large room on an upper floor, where he was soon
settled in comfort and style.

My deer Rosette, and deerest little Myriam—he wrote immediately to his family—*soon our lives will have fame and a fortune of*

*a millyon pounds from the British Museum directors. Maybe I will sell
off the whole shop, as unwirthy of my attenshun any more—or perhaps
I shall make it a free gift to Hassan, what do you think?"*

At home in Jerusalem, Rosette rejoiced over this news,
and started making serious plans for her daughter Augusta's
trousseau and wedding to the son of Professor Schroeder,
to take place in Berlin in January of the coming year. She
began ordering renovations to their own house, and new furniture to replace things that, in her estimation, were looking
rather shabby. She and Myriam looked forward to Moses's
happy and encouraging letters, few and far between though
they had been.

Friday, 20 July 1883

"Mr. Besant will see you now."

Moses turned from the window of the handsome offices at 1 Adam Street, which were the headquarters of the
Palestinian Exploration Fund. The young clerk at the front
desk, his fair hair brushed to a sheen and his cravat impeccably tied, gestured for Moses to follow him through a doorway that led to a long hall, at the end of which was Walter
Besant's inner sanctum. On the walls were hung framed
photographs of various PEF members on location of famous archaeological sites throughout Egypt, Palestine, and
Arabia. Moses recognized all of the sites—indeed, he was in
two of the photographs—and, with a secret smile of confidence of having been long "in the know" as people said, he
approached Besant with a gratifying sense of his own experience and importance.

He was not going to repeat his more humble approach to the Germans—here, he felt he was securely among his equals. He believed in his Deuteronomy scrolls, and he would make others believe in them as well.

The young man tapped lightly on the open door to Besant's domain, and said, "Here is Mr. Shapira, Mr. Besant." With a quick bow, he went back down the hall.

Besant rose from behind his desk and came around to greet Moses with a smile and an outstretched hand.

"What a surprise, Mr. Shapira," he said, motioning to him to be seated. "I had no notion of your being in London at this time."

Moses sat, placing his carpet bag on the floor next to his chair. "I haff just come from Berlin," he said.

Besant nodded expectantly. "Yes?"

Moses took his time, glancing around the well-appointed office with its high, narrow windows letting in a mere sliver of summer light on the deep carpets, polished mahogany shelving and oak furniture. The bookshelves held more ancient pots and statues than books, and Moses thought he recognized one of his own Moabite figures.

"I haff brought with me," he said, forming his fingers into a steeple before him, "a document that will make students of the Bible and Hebrew scholars reconsider their ways." He let the statement stand.

Besant narrowed his eyes slightly. He was well acquainted with Shapira, his shop, his expeditions—and his mistakes and missteps in regard to fraudulent items. But the man was, all in all, trustworthy—Ginsburg at the British Museum spoke well of him. "Yes?" he prompted.

"What I haff here in this bag," Moses continued, "will throw a flood of light upon the Pentateuch."

With a stifled sigh, Besant smiled. "May I see this document?"

Moses hesitated, keeping up the suspense. His hands parted and he waved one hand toward the carpet bag on the floor. "It is sheepskin, and the writing on it is close to the Moabite Stone, which, as you know, I am most familiar with," he said. He held up a finger to mark the next point. "But—there is importance in translation, some things new, some things different, next to the traditional text of our Deuteronomy."

Besant couldn't help himself—this was too damned interesting! "Mr. Shapira—my dear Moses—please let me see this document." He leaned forward in his chair.

Hiding a smile, Moses bent down and extracted one leather strip from his bag, careful to choose one that had a lighter background, upon which the black letters would show most clearly. He laid it carefully on Besant's desk, then leaned back in his chair.

Besant turned up the gas lamp on his desk to throw a greater light, and picking up a magnifying glass, let it hover above the leather strip. After a few moments, he looked up at Moses, his face alight with wonder. "The characters are Phoenician, no doubt of it!" he said softly. He carefully touched the edge of the strip. "This could be three thousand years old!" he said, and sat back in amazement. "If this is true, we must tell the world!"

Moses allowed himself to smile fully at this statement. It was exactly what he wanted to hear.

Tuesday, 24 July 1883

There was a second, small meeting at the PEF—Moses had insisted that Captain Claude Reignier Conder, a military man, friend and artist who had sketched many of Moses's sites and treasures in the past, be invited before any others to view the scrolls in the presence of Besant. Moses promised to write out a full account of how they had come into his possession, which he brought along with him the next day, to meet the two men at the PEF office again.

Upon seeing the leather strips, Conder was beyond enthusiastic—he was ecstatic. "What an inestimable treasure!" he exclaimed, and the three spent some time discussing the possible interpretations of the text, with Moses supplying many of his own translations.

They were all agreed on two things: one, Shapira's dramatic and intriguing account of the origin of the documents should be offered to the *Times* for publication; and two, Dr. Christian David Ginsburg must be shown the documents, and he would be the final arbiter of its importance.

A meeting with Ginsburg, and other scholars, was set for Thursday, 26 July. That evening, after Moses returned to his room, replete with a sumptuous dinner and gratified by his colleagues' approbation and plans, he wrote once more to Rosette and Myriam.

My deerest ones, the Lord favors those who beleeve in His way and who perseveer in the paths of knowlege and right. There is a meeting set now with my dear frend and colleege Dr. Ginsburg, who I have no dout will prove the erth-shaking importance of my Deuteronomy scrolls. My dears, we are going to be welthy beyond our dreems.

TWENTY-SEVEN

Back to Paris — Thursday, 13 March 1884

WE WERE A GRIM AND SILENT TRIO on the journey to Paris, each with his own thoughts, although with the same comfortable accommodations that we had enjoyed on the way up to Rotterdam.

I amused myself for a moment trying to imagine what my two companions were thinking. John, probably, was looking ahead to the bustle of sending two portraits in the next few days to the Salon this year—it was getting close to Varnishing Day, usually around the 1st of April—and I knew he had still been feeling unsatisfied about that portrait of Madame Gautreau. He had won the status of *hors de concours* a few years ago, and therefore his entries were not subject to initial judication—they would accept anything he chose to offer—but there was still judgement waiting.

Lord Parke's thoughts were a little harder for me to discern, not knowing him nearly as well as I knew John. Likewise his Lordship's present pursuits, beyond this misery of Mr. Shapira, were unknown to me. I wondered if perhaps he was in a way to getting married soon—he had been an eligible bachelor for some years now, and a young lord of independent means must be in want of a wife, as our dear Miss Austen so wryly said. I found that I had been gazing upon his handsome face, albeit absent-mindedly, as he sat across from me, and he must have felt the focus of my eyes on him, for he looked up suddenly and smiled.

"You have a speculative gleam in your eyes, Miss Paget," he said, reverting to form in a more or less public place. "I would be delighted to know of what you are thinking."

Caught for a moment off guard, I nonetheless answered with spirit, not being one to shy away from admitting an honest interest in one's friends.

"Oh, my lord," I said carelessly, "it occurs to me that, not having heard anything to the contrary—and you know, John's sister Emily is quite the scholar of such things—I'm wondering if you have any thoughts of marriage at present?"

The effect of my question was more than I had hoped—Lord Parke positively sputtered and turn quite red. John turned to look at me with a muttered remonstrance. "Vi, really?" Then he turned to regard Lord Parke with a somewhat troubled countenance.

"I swear you are the devil himself when it comes to knowing things, Violet," Lord Parke said, although not at all angrily. In fact, he started to laugh. "You'll be pleased to know, then, that there is something like that in the offing—although with all deference to Miss Emily Sargent—I don't expect that any news of such a connection will have filtered out into the town as yet." He glanced at John, and his smile dimmed somewhat. "There are certain kinds of expectations of such a one as I," he said, then shook off the thin shade of melancholy. "She is a most estimable young lady."

"Do not be alarmed," I said. "I will not importune you for any details—that would be too rude, indeed." I glanced at John, and caught a glimpse of a fleeting emotion across his face, so quick I couldn't tell if it were sadness or hilarity.

"But I will offer my congratulations in advance of the event, and wish you all possible happiness, though in a state of which I have no desire to partake."

John echoed my good wishes, and we all sat smiling at each other for a few moments. Then John frowned, and spoke aloud.

"Not to throw a damper, you see, but," he said, "do you know if anyone has made arrangements to inform Mrs. Shapira of her husband's death?"

Lord Parke sobered instantly, and nodded in the affirmative. "I sent a telegram last night to Ginsburg at the British Museum, and his reply indicated they would enlist some PEF representatives, along with the British consul, already there in Jerusalem, to call upon her and break the sad news."

I leaned forward; it was time to deal with this situation. "Did you ask him whether the Shapira Scrolls are still at the museum?"

Lord Parke nodded. "Half of them are, he told me," he said.

I nodded. "That comports with what he said in the letter we saw, does it not? So, what shall we do with the ones we have here?" I looked from one friend to the other.

Lord Parke touched the leather briefcase that sat next to him on the seat; he still had possession of the Shapira Scrolls that had been sent to John. The two gentlemen exchanged glances, and Lord Parke spoke first.

"John and I have discussed this, and what with all this mystery, and death, and thievery, we have decided the best thing to do is to bring the documents back to the British Museum, to Dr. Ginsburg." He looked at me just a trifle fearfully, as if anticipating an objection on my part. When I said nothing, Lord Parke spoke again.

"I can easily put off the slight business I had in Paris, and so I plan to return to London tomorrow," he said. "I'll personally deliver them myself within a few days."

I smiled at him, and then patted John's hand. "I think that is an excellent plan," I said. "They'll know what to do with these things." I glanced at the briefcase, and made up my mind.

"I shall accompany you, Lord Parke," I said, "if that is agreeable to you. I am expected in London tomorrow evening, in Kensington, and can be sure of the leisure needed to attend at the delivery of the documents to a safe place."

"I would be honored for you to accompany me," Lord Parke said, and I think he mostly meant it.

John squeezed my hand and nodded. "I think that's a wonderful idea, Vi."

I felt satisfied at this plan—although I did not tell either gentlemen the reach of that plan. "I am very much looking forward to meeting this Dr. Ginsburg," I said. "Very much indeed."

* * *

Lord Parke's man was waiting for us at the Gare du Nord, so of course everything was swiftly and properly taken care of—we were whisked away in a carriage sent from the Hotel Westminster, dropping John off first at his home and studio, with promises from him to come to London in the next few days if he could; then I was taken to my *pensione* in the sixth. All arrangements for the next day fell into place.

"I shall call for you at ten sharp then," Lord Parke said as I alighted from the carriage, his man having leaped down to open the door for me. I thanked him, then turned back to thank Lord Parke.

"My dear Lord Parke," I said. "Words cannot express how grateful I am for all the trouble you have gone to, getting involved in this escapade with us, and scrambling from house to hillock in pursuit of what I am not sure." I held out my hand and he held it in his own.

"Miss Paget," he said earnestly, "Violet, life would be so much duller without my acquaintance—may I say friendship?—with you and John. The gratitude is all on my side."

I nodded graciously. "At ten!" I said, and stepped away from the carriage, watching it as it rolled off, the horses stepping smartly along the cobblestone street. With a sigh, I turned to the door of the *pensione*, where I saw that my arrival in such a handsome equipage had drawn the notice of not only my landlady, but two or three other guests of the establishment, all peeping out of the first floor drawing room windows (or what passes for a drawing room in a Paris *pensione*).

Not being inclined to suffer through their hints and attempts to question me, I hurried up the stairs to my room on the third floor, where I quickly surveyed what would needed doing in order to arrange and clean my clothes, and get everything packed up in order to leave in the morning.

As I worked, I thought about the events of the last few days, going over and over in my mind the various bits of information—both present and missing—that formed the structure of this remarkable situation. It struck me that none of the three of us had mentioned "the woman"—the Lady in Blue, as I thought of her. Had she left the field, defeated at last? Or was she even now here in Paris, planning another attack? However she had known to search for the documents at John's studio in the first place—and then again in his hotel room in Rotterdam—surely she would be flummoxed now as to who exactly had the documents in their keeping? The lack of documents in John's room at the Willemsbrug might lead her to suspect he had passed them to another. It seemed unlikely she could get at Lord Parke in the Hotel Westminster hotel, and I assumed he would have his valet in the suite as extra insurance against such an attempt.

Was I in danger of a midnight intruder? The thought gave me pause as I folded my dresses and wrapped the few pieces of jewelry I had in their velvet cloths. I looked around the room—it was small, mostly taken up with the bed and a wardrobe, but with a little sitting area next to a bay window that overlooked the street. The bathroom facilities were down the hall, so there was nowhere anyone could hide in this room unseen.

I went to look out the window and noticed for the first time how close it was to a large, strong branch of a tree just outside. I made sure of the latch on the window, and drew the curtains against the remaining brightness of the day. No sense in giving myself away if anyone happened to looking up to see at what window I might be standing.

I checked the lock on the door, it was a sturdy bolt and there was a chain and slot as well—I would make sure it was thoroughly fastened before I went to bed tonight.

Feeling well fortified, I returned to my packing and told myself that I would have my landlady accompany me to my room after dinner tonight, just to be sure. I didn't say to myself that *nothing would happen*, as that generally leads to something very definitely happening. So I merely thought, *it's not very likely that anything untoward will occur*—and had to be satisfied that therewith I had defended myself from the mischievous tricks of the minor gods.

TWENTY-EIGHT

London — Thursday, 26 July 1883
At the British Museum

WALTER BESANT HAD INFORMED Dr. Ginsburg that they would meet at the PEF; Shapira would bring the scrolls and his copy of their history and provenance, and Captain Conder and Besant would, of course, be there as well. Ginsburg would be invited to peruse the leather strips at his leisure.

It was to be a small meeting of the keenest minds on the subject. In the event, as Besant said later to his wife over dinner, "the whole of the British Museum, so to speak, with all the Hebrew scholars in London, turned up."

Moses was not intimidated, nor was he displeased. His old friend Ginsburg greeted him with affection and respect, and the other men who gathered in a large meeting room at the museum were known to him either personally or by reputation. Ernest Budge was the keeper of Egyptian and Assyrian antiquities at the museum; Professor William Wright had edited three volumes of the Catalogue of the Syriac Manuscripts; Thomas Lewis was not only a chairman of the PEF, but a professor at the University College of London; and finally, the famous Scottish artist William Simpson was there, known for his decades of service during various wars, expeditions of the PEF, and as a correspondent for the *Illustrated London News*. Moses thought briefly, and with great satisfaction, that there would come from this meeting a fair amount of publicity—he knew the general reading public of London would be agog at the news of his discovery. He noticed Simpson sketching throughout the meeting, and secretly hoped there might be one of himself.

"Gentlemen, esteemed professors," Moses said, standing mid-way down the long end of a large oak table; no one had taken a seat, but had pushed the chairs to the sides of the room. He placed his colorful carpet bag in the center of the table, and an expectant hush fell upon the assembled scholars.

"What I am about to show to you was discovered in ancient caves of Moab, and the content of its writing will forever change the way we understand the Hebrew Bible." Moses couldn't help himself—the natural performer in him blossomed under these dramatic circumstances, and he relished being the center of attention—and deservedly so, as he thought. He made a concerted effort to use his very best English, and minimize his still existent Russian accent.

He brought his fingertips to his lips, as if thinking something over, then he said, "I offer this exceptional discovery to the British Museum for the price of one million pounds."

No one even blinked.

Moses opened his carpet bag, reached in and lifted out a handful of the leather strips, then in an almost reckless and jaunty way, lightly tossed them onto the table. As the scholars leaned in to look at them more closely, Moses narrated the story of their discovery, much as he had rehearsed it to Besant and Captain Conder two days earlier.

"And here, on this strip, you see this character?" Moses pointed to a very clear set of characters on a light-colored piece of the leather strips. "At first I thought it was to signify the Phoenician meaning of *idol*, but later knew it better, after much research, and found that it meaned something else."

Questions flew thick and fast, and Moses did his best to respond. At one point, in an excess of showmanship, he pinched off a tiny bit of leather from the very edge of one strip, and passed it around for the others to examine more closely.

William Simpson, with a touch of sarcasm, noted to another man, "That tiny bit must be worth five hundred pounds if the whole is a million!"

As the scholars reviewed the leather strips, the excitement grew—Moses could see they were impressed, awed even, and seemed positively influenced by the tenor of his presentation and the support of Besant and Captain Conder.

But Moses had something more in store for them. When one of the men picked up a dark and blackened strip, protesting that this was entirely unreadable, Moses pulled out a bottle of home-made spirits from his carpet bag, and proceeded to demonstrate how, with a light brush over the scroll, characters began to appear where there had been nothing visible. The amazement and exclamations of the assembled audience were very gratifying.

Having done his best, Moses stepped away from the table now, leaving the discussion in the hands of the gathered savants.

"This is a remarkable illustration of the arts as known and practiced in the time of Moses," Thomas Lewis said. Most nodded in agreement.

Professor Wright proclaimed, in the end, what it appeared that everyone was thinking: "This is one of the few things which could not be a forgery and a fraud!"

After some three hours of looking and discussing, the group were unanimous in naming Dr. Ginsburg as the one to be in charge of a thorough examination.

"For as long as it takes," Moses said, agreeing with them completely. With a little pang, however, he placed the leather strips—his companions for these long, long weeks of tension and work—into a strongbox that Ginsburg had brought in, and handed them over to his old friend. They would remain in his keeping, under guard in the British Museum, until his stamp of approval would settle the matter once and for all. The carpet bag seemed forlorn now, empty of its precious contents, when Moses picked it up to leave the room.

But it wouldn't be long, he thought, then all would be proved, and the thought cheered him. Moses almost grinned as he thought of the German scholars, and what they would think, when the announcement was made.

Friday, 3 August 1883

Less than a week later, the newspapers had gotten wind of a biblical discovery of historic importance—the *Times* of London ran a lengthy article that began, *"The surprises of archaeology are magnificent and apparently inexhaustible. It is continually bringing forth things new and old, and often it happens that the newest are the oldest of all."*

Moses read the article several times—he was not altogether pleased by what it said—far too much discussion of the "Moabite forgeries" and his having been the dupe of desert criminals in the past, and a good deal of ambivalence as to the authenticity of his scrolls.

He was sitting in his suite at the Cannon Street Hotel, it being just after noon on a hot and sultry day in London—the air outside was an insult to one's lungs to attempt to walk and breathe in it, and although his rooms were also warm, at least they smelled better than the city streets. But he was getting increasingly restless, and feeling too alone in the great city, awaiting his Fate.

A discreet knock on his door roused him from his reading yet again the *Times* article, and when he proclaimed "Enter", a bellhop in a fanciful uniform with gold trimming and a jaunty cap brought him a card sent up from the front desk. It read:

Lady Laura Simmons-Hartley

There was a family crest above her name. He turned the card over to see a short written note under the printed announcement of the lady's at-home hours.

Fridays -- Three to Six pm

Please come today! At 2:30

Moses felt his heart beat just a little faster, and he looked up at the boy waiting in front of him. "The lady is not downstairs, is she?" Even as he said it, he knew that would be absurd. The boy shook his head. "No, sir, it was delivered by a footman."

"Of course, of course," Moses said and, digging in his pocket, he produced a small coin and flipped it to the lad who caught it in mid-air, grinned and departed.

It was nearly one o'clock. Moses calculated he had time for a bath to freshen up, trim his beard and dress, then go to Lady Laura's residence in Mayfair.

He had been there on two previous occasions, when he had visited London—once, soon after Lady Laura's visit to Jerusalem nine years ago, and again, just two years ago, on an extended business trip to discuss terms with the British Museum's Department of Oriental Manuscripts. He had fond memories of those visits.

He looked at himself in the mirror for a moment and judged that, despite all his desert trips and strenuous life, he was holding up very well, at fifty-three—his black hair only showed a few streaks of grey, and his figure was trim and upright, though he was a large man.

He began to look forward to seeing her Ladyship again.

* * *

As he left his room about an hour later, he had no sooner gained the lobby from the main staircase when the front desk manager, catching sight of him, hurried to his side and motioned for him to step behind a large potted palm near the staircase.

"Mr. Shapira," he said in a low voice, "the papers are full of your story! Everyone is so excited," he continued. "However, it is clear that the reporters have discovered you are staying here, and several of them have showed up this morning looking for you."

Moses was amused, gratified and only slightly alarmed. He peered cautiously through the palm fronds into the lobby. "Are any of them here now?"

The manager looked severe. "We insisted they leave the hotel, of course, but they are waiting in the street, I believe."

"Very good, very good," Moses said. "I thank you for your kind concern. I will see if I can leave without being seen."

The manager bowed and returned to the front desk. Moses squared his shoulders, adjusted his hat, and walked out to meet the press.

TWENTY-NINE

Paris to London — Friday, 14 March 1884

DESPITE WAKING ON THE DAY BEFORE the historically ominous *Ides of March*, I felt no presentiment of any evil to befall me other than a possibly rough crossing on the ferry from Calais to Dover, which, in the event, was relatively calm and smooth.

Lord Parke's carriage was prompt; his valet was, as usual, organized and efficient, and the train delivered us to the Port of Calais with time to spare before boarding the ferry to England. It was a luxury I could really get used to enjoying, having all my luggage seen to, without a moment's care on my part. I travelled, of course, without a lady's maid, not having the wherewithal to do so, but also having nurtured that independence of mind and body that "modern women" have begun to introduce to the sisterhood of unattached ladies who must make their own way in the world. I said as much to Lord Parke after we had been settled in the better dining area of the ferry, and were at last underway. We were served a remarkably edible luncheon of poached fish and roasted potatoes, with asparagus and lemon; a refreshing white wine accompanied it well.

"I find it remarkable," said he, after listening to my disquisition on Life as a Woman in These Times. "No young woman of my acquaintance would even dare to imagine she could travel alone on trains and ferries, stay at *pensiones* in big cities, unescorted—and yet, here you are, unscathed, unmolested, unconcerned about doing all that—and having a grand old time of it!"

I admit I had my reservations about his glowing account of the single woman's life in society, but I didn't want to disabuse him entirely.

"Oh, my lord," I said. "I expect that many a young woman *of your acquaintance*, as you say, has actually had the daring to imagine such a life for herself—surely they are not *all* so enthusiastic about marriage and children as the only course of action they are allowed to follow?" I took a last sip of my wine, and glanced out the window at the passing sea.

He was silent a moment at this, and seemed suddenly downcast. I perceived in an instant what must be on his mind.

"And gentlemen, too," I said quietly, "of your acquaintance—their lives, though able to be lived in a much broader sphere than ladies, are also circumscribed, plotted out to the last year, with expectations of behavior defined and codified?"

Lord Parke looked at me directly and nodded. "I'm grateful that someone understands," he said. "That *you* understand is not a surprise, of course, but I welcome the comfort that comes with knowing a friend can discern one's difficulties in life, without making a fuss." He straightened his shoulders, as if shaking himself back into harness. He motioned to the hovering waiter to pour more wine.

"I believe John mentioned that you are on the brink of publishing your first novel?" he said, turning the subject firmly. "I shall subscribe to it the instant it is out—will it be in chapters over time, or will it make a grand entrance on the literary scene all at once?"

"Oh, the latter certainly," I said. "I have made it clear to my publisher that I have no patience with teasing the reading public with serials that go on from month to month—how is one's attention to be gained and kept? No, my novel, though I believe it will be made available in three volumes, due to its length, will be published and available all at once."

"Three volumes? Goodness," exclaimed Lord Parke, "do you intend to challenge the volubility of Dickens? I see I shall have to set aside a good week or more to enjoy the work with the strictest attention and enjoyment!"

We discussed the literary scene in London for a while, and I told him about my dear friend Mary Robinson, a poet of no little renown, and he said he had read her first book of poems with appreciation, and expressed a desire to meet her, which gratified me greatly. We left the dining room soon after to find seats near a window, and for a while we were both silent, watching the water rushing by as the ferry plowed its way through the Channel. Lord Parke held fast to his briefcase with the leather strips in it, and as my eyes fell upon it, I wondered again about Mr. Shapira and his tragic end.

"I have been trying," I said abruptly, but in a low voice, turning to Lord Parke, "to recall the very short conversation I had with Mr. Shapira, last August, when I visited the Museum to get a glimpse of the leather strips they had put on display. Mary Robinson was with me, too."

Lord Parke turned his eyes from the grey water back to me. "And?"

I grimaced in frustration. "I was introduced to him by the head librarian there, Edward Bond, whom I know fairly well, and we were in the midst of a crowd and couldn't hear very well," I said. "I have the impression of a very tall man—of course, nearly everyone is tall to me!—with a black beard and heavy brows, but with lighter hair and blue eyes. He seemed very self-possessed, I recall thinking at the time."

"What gave you that impression?" Lord Parke asked, curious.

"Oh, just that with all the people swarming around, even some photographers constantly begging him to stand in front of the display, or turn this way or that way, so they could take a photograph—he was very calm, even gracious, and allowed any number of gushing young women to exclaim to him about this or that verse of the Bible—and write his name in the front—extraordinary, that, I thought."

Lord Parke laughed lightly. "It is amazing to me, I admit, how zealous and enthusiastic a certain kind of religious believer can be, about a text or a phrase in the Bible, and what it means, or whether what is printed in the King James bible is to be believed as the actual Word of God."

"I agree with you there," I said. "Does it not occur to people that, first, they are reading the Bible in a language different from the one it was written in originally, that is, English not Hebrew, or Greek in the case of the New Testament, and therefore is liable to contain any number of errors and mistranslations? And second, the German scholars have long provided us with evidence that not only was the Bible *not* written by *one* person, say Moses (leaving the Deity out of it altogether), but by several people over centuries of time, and edited and changed and added to and re-worded to fit better with the times?" I paused to take a breath, and continued. "They are *stories*, not facts—although there *may* be some historical veracity to *some* of the events or persons mentioned in the stories, I admit."

"And you are most gracious to admit that," Lord Parke said, a twinkle in his eye.

"But such a fuss was made over Mr. Shapira's scrolls, which were to have changed all one's notions of what was said in Deuteronomy, and the Ten Commandments, as we recall, and it was all for nothing, alas, poor man," I said.

I looked at Lord Parke speculatively. "Do *you* think he was a fraud?" I asked. "Do you think he deliberately and knowingly somehow manufactured those scrolls and tried to foist them on the scholarly community? How could he think he could get away with it? And most importantly, if they are inauthentic, why is someone going to the lengths we have witnessed to obtain them now?"

Lord Parke shook his head. "I am not able to judge in the matter of authenticity," he said. "All I know is that the best minds in that area of study determined they were not authentic." He was silent a moment. "But it does seem to me that if he attempted a fraud, it was brilliantly done."

We heard the blast of the ship's horn, signalling it was nearing the coast of England, and looked out the window for a glimpse of Dover's majestic white cliffs.

"At any rate," Lord Parke said, "I would welcome the opportunity for you to ask that question of Dr. Ginsburg, when we meet with him next week, as soon as I can get an appointment."

THIRTY

Jerusalem — Late August 1883

"ONE MILLION POUNDS!" Rosette said those three words aloud, over and over, until her voice seemed to catch in her throat, and she closed her eyes and prayed.

Myriam, watching her, knew she was praying to be forgiven for thinking too much about money—or perhaps for being too proud and gratified by her husband's descriptions of the success he was enjoying in London.

The girl felt no such scruples. She was just fourteen, and filled with romantic dreams about what the family would do with such incredible wealth. Her father had enclosed one brief newspaper article that he had cut out from the *Times* of London early in August. There in old Jerusalem, her family were always far behind in the news of the greater world, especially Europe and Great Britain, as the ships bringing the post and the newspapers often lagged by a month or more, but especially as her mother did not subscribe to any newspaper, but relied upon seeing copies in the church library or discarded ones from the hotels.

His letter told them he had made an initial presentation to the directors of the British Museum, and that there was no doubt in his mind that they would purchase his manuscripts for the price he asked.

"Now we can truly plan for Augusta's trousseau," said Rosette, a happy gleam in her eye.

As inklings of this great good fortune coming to the Shapira family began to spread throughout Jerusalem, Rosette and her daughter began to notice a marked difference in how people treated them. They were of course respected and even liked before this, but people had paid them no special attention, and Myriam could remember, with great pain, hearing an occasional slight directed at her father—"only a convert" one person said, and "still a Jew on the inside"— which hurt terribly. She could never bring herself to repeat those words to her father, whom she adored without question, and only muttered half-formed curses about those people who said such things, as her nanny Ouarda would do.

When they went to church now of a Sunday, every one would bow to them, as if they were royalty, and during the week Villa Rachid would receive more visitors than ever it had seen, to sit at tea, admire the artifacts and furniture, and offer their seemingly sweet but slightly acidic congratulations on Moses's brilliant success, *at last*. Myriam may have been young, but she was well able to discern the envy and spite behind all these ladies' compliments and good wishes.

For her, the promise of wealth beyond her dreams brought with it a blossoming of philanthropy—for other visitors to Villa Rachid soon came to plant themselves at the gates, beggars and cripples seeking assistance, as well as representatives of various charities, asking for funds. Their obliging German bankers, aware of Moses's mission to London, happily granted Rosette's requests for loans and advance monies at reasonable rates.

Myriam was extravagant and almost reckless, in love with being "Lady Bountiful" and doing good. She would walk around the poor quarters of the city, followed by a groom carrying bundles of clothes and baskets of food, and leave them at the door of poor folks who were too proud to ask for public relief. Once, her mother tried to restrain her good works, but she only laughed at her and said, "Oh, mamma, it's so lovely to do good! And besides why shouldn't we, when we are going to be so rich that we shan't know what to do with our money?"

Rosette shook her head, but with a small smile that she tried to hide from her daughter. She and Augusta wrote to each other steadily, nearly every day, and Augusta's letters were full of the balls and dinners she was being invited to, and the dresses and hats she needed to buy. Rosette gave instructions to the German bankers to keep up the account in the Berlin bank so that Augusta could have the money she needed.

Occasionally there was a letter from Frau Schroeder, Augusta's mother-in-law to be, praising her goodness, her vivacity, her dancing, her conversation, and stating how pleased they were that Augusta was going to be a member of their family, and also how wonderfully Moses's success in London would add to the prestige of both families. She clearly depended on the proceeds of the sale of the scrolls to help enable her son's acceptance of an honorary appointment at the University—and Augusta would be the wife of a prominent professor!

Rosette was mostly content, and mostly happy, but every once in a while Myriam would catch her at her prayers, and hear her asking for blessings to keep misfortune away.

The girl would then approach her gently, and put her arms around her neck, murmuring that all would be well, but her mother only gave a heavy sigh.

"Oh, my Myriam, all this seems too good to last; it makes me afraid, terribly afraid."

Even Ouarda looked with an evil eye on her master's good fortune. When Myriam tried to show her a sketch of Moses that had been published in one of the newspapers, she wouldn't look at it. "Dear one," she said, "you know quite well that whoever allows his portrait to be taken is caught in one of the devil's traps and throws down a challenge to fate."

But Myriam refused to let her superstition and prejudice cloud her blue skies, and continued with her good works, and kept on thinking of her father in London, meeting with important people—maybe he would meet the Queen!—and also, she wondered if he and the Lady in Blue ever met, there in that strange and distant city, the center of a great empire. Was he sitting next to her, even now, in some English drawing room, telling her again the story of King David and Bathsheba? Or perhaps, she was married now, and had children, and they would only meet as friends, if at all. She sighed for the romance of it; she was still very young.

Most of all, she dreamed of the travels she and her father would take, once he was home again.

It never occurred to her that she had already seen her father for the last time.

THIRTY-ONE

Paris — Friday, 14 March 1884

Having departed Paris, dear Reader, I cannot have witnessed my friend John's activities whilst he remained there, but I think, from what he told me, that this is a fair account of what occurred. —V.P.

HENRY JAMES RANG THE DOORBELL to John's studio promptly at a quarter to eight o'clock that evening. It was a meeting that had been planned the previous week, when the two met at a *soirée* at a mutual friend's. Mr. James had been greatly taken by the young artist, and practically invited himself to John's studio, after which they were to go out to dine. John, cognizant of the older man's influence in London society—as well as Paris, Florence and Rome—was delighted to have him.

Luckily, John had been reminded by his housekeeper, upon his return to Paris, that Mr. James was to call the next day—he having sent a brief note on Thursday afternoon, just before John arrived home. The note read:

Might I have a glimpse of the famous—or to-be-famous—portrait of Madame Gautreau? Everyone is already talking about it. Yrs. H. James

John clambered down the stairs to open the door himself—better he than Guido, who was possibly a little drunk. "Good evening, my dear Mr. James!" he cried, and held out his hand, American-style, then he recalled at the last instant something Mr. James had said about the "crushing hand-shakes of our fellow Americans," so he lightened his grip considerably.

Mr. James, though not yet forty, moved like a more elderly man, and John accompanied him up the stairs to the studio with much pausing for breath at the landings. At length they reached his studio.

"What a lovely space you have here, Mr. Sargent," Mr. James said, gazing around keenly. "How happy you must be in your creations, here, above the fray and bustle of the streets below."

"I daresay you, too, must have such a retreat," John replied. "A writer's study, all brown and dim and crammed with books, yes?"

Mr. James inclined his head and smiled. "Do you see that in your painter's eye?"

John looked at him, critically, as if sizing him up as a subject. "Someday, I shall paint you, shall I, Mr. James?"

Mr. James demurred. "Our Puritan forebears would no doubt consider it frivolous idolatry," he said, and smiled just a little.

They had some sherry, and a little sit-down so Mr. James could rest, but soon he was up and about, looking at all the paintings ranged around the room. He had not yet approached the portrait of Madame Gautreau, propped against a far wall.

"I saw, last year in London," he said, his voice echoing slightly in the high-ceilinged room, "your splendid *Doctor Pozzi at Home*, at the Academy. Did you know that he had been placed in the same room as the two Cardinals? So many red garments, the effect was rather sanguineous."

John nodded, but stayed silent, encouraging him to go on—he knew Mr. James was a frequent contributor to cultural journals of essays on art and literature, and he wanted to hear what he had to say.

"The Cardinals have had poor luck this past year," Mr. James continued. "Cardinal Manning having been sacrificed simultaneously to Mr. Watts, whose effort is less violent than that of Mr. Millais, but not more successful." He paused a moment, peering more closely at a portrait of Albert de Belleroche, a particular friend of John's and a fellow artist. "The best that can be said of Mr. Watt's portrait of Cardinal Manning is that it is not so bad as his portrait, at the Grosvenor, of the Prince of Wales, of which I shall say no more, as I fear it would expose the artist to the penalties attached to that misdemeanour known to English law as 'threatening the Royal Family.' "

John laughed aloud at this pointed sally, poured himself another sherry and brought another to Mr. James.

"But your flamboyant physician," the writer said, taking the glass and lifting it in salute, "out-Richelieus the English Cardinals, and is simply magnificent."

"Did you see my Venetian studies, at the Grosvenor?" John asked him.

"Yes, most wonderful," Mr. James said. "I thought the figures of the women, sitting in gossip over some humble, domestic task in the big, dim hall of a shabby old palazzo, were extraordinarily natural and vividly portrayed." He gazed at his sherry, then looked up at John. "You have seen and captured that part of Venice which the tourist does not know, and which only such as you and I, wandering the narrow walks in the shadows, have the heart and the sensibility to observe, and to love, observing."

John, often at a loss for words, touched his glass to that of Mr. James in acknowledgement of their fellow feeling. They walked over in the direction of the portrait John most wanted him to see. He held his breath as Mr. James looked at Madame Gautreau, with her slightly lavender-grey skin, her clinging dress and tight bodice, her right arm twisted almost unnaturally as her hand bent to rest on the little table—and the diamond-crusted strap of her dress fallen part way down her arm.

"I see a shadow of Franz Hals in this portrait," Mr. James said at last, and John started, amazed. "The brown tones, the little table, the vagueness of place and the faint shadow behind the figure."

"That is absolutely correct, sir," he said. Excitement fed a rare volubility, and he spoke with passion. "I had despaired of finding the right background, through dozens of interminable sittings, until I went on a sort of pilgrimage, up to Haarlem, and was happily inspired by the master."

"It is a fitting tribute," the writer said, but he said no more about the portrait.

Later, over dinner, the conversation turned to what was most on John's mind at the moment, the remembrance of viewing the Hals paintings in Haarlem having made him think anew of Mr. Shapira. He knew Mr. James lived in London, and decided to ask him if he had been aware of the scandal the previous summer. The writer answered promptly.

"Indeed, how could one not be aware of the Shapira Scrolls last summer and fall? The papers were full of the story for months." He lifted his glass of wine to admire the gleaming ruby color, and took a careful sip.

"Did you go see them, at the British Museum?" John asked eagerly. "I was not in London during that time, so was completely ignorant of the whole affair then."

Mr. James looked at him curiously, his mild grey eyes calm and friendly—it was that look that always, he knew, prompted confidences and secrets from people who sat and talked with him—a tremendously fruitful source for his novelist's brain to tap for characters, motives, descriptions, and stories.

"Alas, I did not," he said quietly. "And now? Is it of some special interest to you now?" He leaned back a little in his chair; the restaurant at which they were dining was quiet; they were coming to the end of their meal, and ordered two glasses of brandy.

John proceeded to pour out the whole story of the Shapira Scrolls—everything that had occurred since the beginning of the week, and Mr. James listened most attentively.

"I am acquainted with Lord Parke, a fine gentleman," he said, when John had finished the story, with another round of brandy ordered in the meantime. "And of course, Miss Vernon Lee, your friend and mine, a most prodigious and formidable mind!" He smiled. "It is quite extraordinary to consider her, and you as well, in the role of amateur investigators in this matter." Then he grew serious. "But what do the two of them imagine can be done in London, other than to place the scrolls in the keeping of the British Museum? It appears, from what you have told me, that the police in Rotterdam consider the matter a suicide, and thus no longer to be investigated."

John shook his head. "I'm not at all sure, but I must say, I wish I were there with them to see this through." He smiled ruefully. "As soon as I can deliver *Madame Gautreau* to the Salon tomorrow, I have half a mind to go to London myself and find out what's going on. It's a wretched business," he added, drinking down the last of his brandy. "I have taken a little studio there, you know, in Chelsea, with a friend, Edwin Austin Abbey, perhaps you know him?"

Mr. James signalled for the waiter. *"L'addition, s'il vous plaît,"* he murmured as the man bent to attend to him.

"I do know him," James affirmed, turning back to John. "Excellent fellow! You should definitely come to London," he said with decision. "Your talent is much needed there, and I would be more than happy to introduce you to dozens of people who would be delighted to have you paint them."

John thanked him profusely but started to demur.

"Nonsense," said Mr. James. "I shall set up some dinners where you may be introduced—you are already much talked of, you know," he continued. "The ladies, in particular, are wild to have you 'do' them in oils." He laid a hand on John's arm. "Do say you will come? I will be returning to London in two days' time, and all will be arranged."

John smiled and surrendered. "As you wish, Mr. James," he said. "I shall be forever in your debt."

Henry James smiled, and paid the bill.

THIRTY-TWO

London — Friday, 3 August 1883

LADY LAURA SIMMONS-HARTLEY STILL LOOKED, to Moses's eyes, scarcely older than when he had first seen her in Jerusalem, nine years before, as a young girl of nineteen. Her eyes lighted up invitingly when he walked into her drawing room; having come at the stated time, he found himself alone with her.

"My dear Shapira," she said, staying seated but holding out her hand, which he came forward to take and bow over.

"My dear Simmons-Hartley," he said with a smile—it was a little joke they had, calling each other by their surnames, as if they were professional colleagues. Somehow it seemed even more intimate that way.

She gestured for him to be seated in a chair adjacent to the little sofa on which she sat, and they spent a few moments simply looking at each other.

"You haff not added a day to your blooming looks," Moses said softly.

Lady Laura smiled, then shook her head. Her golden blond hair was loosely captured in a French twist that accentuated her elegant neck. "Flatterer," she said, then tilted her head slightly. "The years and your travels have etched their story in your face, my friend," she said, "but it only serves to make you look wise and experienced and manly." Tiny wrinkles appeared at the corners of her vivid blue eyes when she smiled, but were quickly gone.

"What is all this I read about you, now, in the papers? You are the man of the hour, despite the nasty suspicions of the *Times!*" She snatched up the paper from beside her on the sofa, and read a paragraph aloud:

"If, moreover, the supposed fabricator is also himself the scribe, it is evident that he is not only a very ingenious artist, but also a very accomplished scholar, and one can only regret that he has engaged in an industry which has placed him at the mercy of an Arab who would steal his mother-in-law for a few piastres, and is likely, therefore, to enrich no one but Mr. Shapira."

"How can you bear it!" she exclaimed. "Such a left-handed compliment, as the saying goes, deeming you both ingenious and accomplished, yet insinuating you must be a fraud nonetheless!" She threw the paper down in disgust.

Moses was touched by her indignation, and gave her a grateful look.

"With such supporting from you, I cannot pay mind what the brigand press have to say," he said, and half-sighed. "All depends on Ginsburg."

She looked at him shrewdly. "It's in his hands then, to determine authenticity?" She leaned forward, intensely interested. "Tell me all that has happened, do please, Shapira. I long to know all the details."

He looked pleased, but doubtful. "It is a long story," he said, glancing at the clock on the mantel. "Are there to be other visitors?"

She waved a hand in dismissal. "I have given instructions that I am to be denied this afternoon, so we have hours ahead of us to talk." She rose from the sofa and pulled a cord next to the fireplace. "We shall have some tea, shall we, and perhaps something stronger? You see, I have ever so many questions," she said, smiling so earnestly and charmingly that Moses once more lost his heart to her. He sighed inwardly at the thought that perhaps this was to be an affair of the mind only, this time around, but schooled himself to be satisfied that here, at least, was one woman whose mind and soul were at one with his, when it came to the ever-restless search for the knowledge of antiquity.

Their refreshments were served, and they spent the next three hours in intense discussion. When he at last rose to leave, he was rewarded with an embrace and a warm kiss full on his mouth, a remembrance of past kisses that seemed to hold the promise of more.

* * *

But Moses Shapira was not the only visitor to Lady Laura's drawing room that day, for not half an hour after he had taken his leave, a hired carriage drew up before her Mayfair mansion, and a tall, lean and well-dressed gentleman in his late thirties alighted.

Something about the way he stood and looked around him, the cut of his clothes, the tilt of his hat, his lip slightly curled as he drew on his gloves, revealed he was a Frenchman. The carriage continued on its way, and the gentleman walked to the front door and pulled the bell. He was welcomed inside, and soon was announced to Lady Laura by her butler.

"Mr. Charles Clermont-Ganneau, my lady," the servant said, and withdrew.

"Charles," she said, turning from the window where she had been gazing out at the garden. He approached her slowly, his eyes fastening upon hers as he came near. He touched her cheek lightly with one hand, and she lifted her face willingly to his fierce embrace. But they parted moments later, and she smiled knowingly. She spoke in French.

"We have much to discuss, *mon amour*," she said. "He has told me everything."

* * *

That night, when Lady Laura was alone in her bed, she was visited with some pangs of conscience. She truly did like Moses Shapira, but she was, she knew in the darkest part of her, in thrall to Clermont-Ganneau. Both men were brilliant scholars, as well as adventurers and risk-takers—a thrilling combination, for her, of physical prowess and intellectual acumen. She sighed as she tossed and turned in her comfortable bed, but it was a sigh equally mixed with delight as with chagrin—she wanted them both, she wanted it all—she dreamed of adventures and expeditions, of danger and romance—but she was tired of simply dreaming—she wanted something to happen.

She and Clermont-Ganneau had discussed at length about how he would approach the men at the British Museum—he knew them all well—and have the opportunity to see these so-called ancient scrolls for himself. He had assured her he was already convinced they were trash—fraudulent tripe served up by that upstart Jew who always seemed to be getting in his way with his claims and his seeming piety.

Lady Laura shook her head, remembering how heated her French lover had become, growing red with anger as he inveighed against his rival—not that he would even dignify Shapira with the title of rival! But Lady Laura thought he went too far, and that his prejudices clouded his otherwise rational thinking. She reserved her own opinion to herself, however, and let him rant. She was sure he had no idea, of course, that she had anything more than a casual but professional acquaintance with Shapira. It had been Clermont-Ganneau's idea for her to invite him to visit that day, to which she had pretended to be disinclined, but gave in after he had made promises of a certain delightful nature.

It was decided he would visit Ginsburg early in the next week, announcing himself as on a mission from the French government to investigate the Shapira Scrolls—surely they would allow him, a respected scholar and archaeologist, to see them without demur.

However, Lady Laura thought, something about the way Shapira, whom she knew fairly well, had talked about the scrolls earlier that day, suggested to her that if *he* had anything to say about it, Clermont-Ganneau wouldn't get within six feet of them.

She almost smiled to think of it.

THIRTY-THREE

London — Saturday, 15 March 1884

I WOKE ABRUPTLY TO THE WARBLING SOUND of birds in the back garden, mixed with subdued street noises of carriages passing and the general rumble of the town. *Oh yes,* I thought, I'm at Mary's house now, in Kensington, my brain struggling to free itself from the snares of a long-awaited sleep. Lord Parke had kindly left me at Mary's doorstep, although he declined to go in, pleading the late hour and his being unknown to the family, but he promised to call in a day or two.

Mary and her sister Mabel were at the door to greet me as they sent the footmen out to gather up my luggage, and I was met with such kindness and affection from both of them that my heart swelled with friendship and gratitude to be among such good people. I longed to get Mary to myself and tell her all that had occurred during the last week—I had had no time for writing, and she was wild to know what had kept me from my usual, almost daily, correspondence with her. There had been no time or opportunity to discuss anything after I arrived so late.

Well, she'll hear it all after breakfast, I thought as I threw back the covers, luxuriating in a fire already set up and warming the room—I hadn't even heard the maid creep in—and began to dress.

There had been considerable unpleasantness, about a year previous, primarily between me and Frances, Mary's mother, but her father George as well. Suffice it to say—as they have both long since apologized most sincerely—that all has been forgiven if not completely forgotten, and I have tried very hard to erase from my mind their unfounded and insulting suspicions about my "unsuitability" as a friend to their daughter. This very invitation to stay at their house while I was in London was proof enough of their contrition, so I felt I could descend to the comfortable breakfast room that morning without any unsettling feelings or untoward tensions.

Mary was always an early riser and had begun her second round of tea by the time I made my appearance at the breakfast table. She jumped up and greeted me with a most affectionate embrace, and bade me sit down while she made up a plate of food for me from the side table.

"You see you have me all to yourself, dear," she said as she assembled scrambled eggs, fresh toast, rashers of bacon and sliced fruit on a large plate. "My mother and father were called away two days ago to my mother's sister, in Oxford, who is feeling poorly and wanting company," she continued, placing the very abundant breakfast before me—more than I usually ate, I am sure, but as I suddenly felt famished, I was happy to begin devouring.

It is just possible that my increase in appetite and good spirits resulted from the news of the Robinsons' absence.

"And where is our dear Mabel?" I said between mouthfuls of egg and bacon. There is nothing like a substantial upper-middle-class, conventional household for providing one with equally substantial comestibles, I always say.

"My sister is out and about early this morning, and begs your forgiveness, today is her day for volunteering at the women's shelter, where she teaches a class in sewing."

"Very commendable," I said, knowing that both Mabel and Mary were inveterate volunteers for good causes throughout the capital, and especially in helping to provide services for poor women.

"And how is *Miss Brown* coming along?" Mary asked, as always showing her keen interest in my writing.

"Exasperating as usual," I said, and shook my head. "I have a meeting this afternoon with my publisher—I'm sure we'll be arguing again about this, that and the other thing." I swallowed some cocoa meditatively. "I do wonder at times if I should allow anyone to read it before it's published." I looked at her hopefully. "You, for instance?"

Mary smiled and shook her head. "After my own horrible experience with novel-writing last year, I cannot in the least put myself forward as any kind of critic of the genre— I must content myself to be a reader only, of finished works." She looked at me fondly. "And, my dear, you know you probably wouldn't like what I would have to say."

I opened my mouth to dispute the charge, then closed it. Last June, when the two of us had decamped from Kensington at the height of her parents' unhappiness with me, we spent nearly three weeks at a darling little cottage in Kent. There I had read some portions of my nascent work to her aloud, and she was exceedingly discouraging. She warned me that my depiction of characters in the "aesthetic" way of life was too transparent, and my friends would be insulted and offended. I laughed at her then, and I still held to my sense that no such thing would happen. It would not do to discuss it at this late date—the book would be finished soon.

She allowed me to eat some minutes in silence, while she sipped her tea, then she burst through all restraint.

"All right then, dearest, you must tell me—what *has* been going on that you couldn't write to me? Except for one cryptic post card from Rotterdam! And mentioning Lord James Parke as a travelling companion! What on earth have you been up to?" She leaned forward across the table with sparkling, inquisitive eyes, her porcelain skin flushed a lovely pink, her light brown curls falling across her brow—leaving me almost breathless at her still quite youthful beauty. We share a birth year just months apart, and so will both be twenty-eight this year—but she looked nearer twenty, as compared to brown little me looking well past thirty, I vow.

"Well," I began, drinking the rest of my chocolate and taking my time, just because I could. "Do you recall last August, what the newspapers were all full of at the time?"

She looked nonplussed. "Newspapers? Last August?" She frowned. "Do give me a better hint, Vi, I beg you."

"Well, not that it's your favorite subject," I said—knowing full well that she was as agnostic as I when it came to religion and a Deity—"but you may recall a tremendous to-do about some ancient biblical scrolls found in a desert cave by a man from Jerusalem?" I stopped there and waited for her mind to find the reference, which she did very quickly.

"Oh, yes!" she cried. "The Shapira Scrolls! I remember that very well—you and I went to see them at the British Museum, did we not? And that poor man, Shapira, I remember the letter he published in the *Times*, upbraiding the man at the British for having ruined him, nay, betrayed him, I believe it said." She shook her head, then looked at me. "So how are you connected with that curious and awful scandal from last year?"

I proceeded to tell her the story from the moment of the mysterious package arriving at John's studio to my arrival last night on her door step. I barely noticed that the servants kept coming in, replacing tea and coffee, whisking away the food and empty plates, until finally, about an hour or so later, the two of us were left to ourselves in the brightening day to wonder and exclaim over the whole strange proceeding.

"And what is it that you have in mind to do now, Violet?" she asked, looking at me most penetratingly. "I know you, and you can't possibly be considering this matter as finished, can you?"

I smiled at her fondly. "Of course not!" I said. "Lord Parke is going to arrange an appointment for us next week with Dr. Ginsburg at the British Museum—to bring him the leather strips, and to ask him quite a few questions, you can be sure."

Mary looked thoughtful for a bit, then spoke.

"And you say that neither you, nor John, have any idea who the 'Lady in Blue' could be—as you so whimsically call her?"

I shook my head. "We only know she is likely British, but speaks excellent French, is young and lithe and quite apparently, reckless and even dangerous—to undertake such tasks and perform so devilishly well at them."

"And this woman would understandably be connected," Mary pursued, "in some way with the study of archaeology, or of ancient biblical texts and artifacts?"

"Yes, I would imagine so," I said. I looked at her intently. "Mary, what are you thinking?"

She looked at me with a faint smile. "Only that I know a young woman, blond, lithe, and frankly, rather reckless, who is also very interested in and collects ancient biblical artifacts—and who speaks exquisite French! We attended the same lyceum for a time, in Switzerland."

"And this lady's name?" I said, practically quivering with excitement.

"Lady Laura Simmons-Hartley," Mary said. "And she lives in Mayfair."

THIRTY-FOUR

London — 10-13 August 1883

THE NEWSPAPERS HAPPILY FED THE CONTROVERSY over *The Shapira Scrolls*, as they unanimously titled the leather strips. Dr. Ginsburg had released an initial translation of part of the text, the first of three to come, which was printed in its entirety in nearly every paper and journal. Moses read them all, every morning and evening, with resulting mixed feelings of confidence and anxiety. He had no one to talk to, and he was too nervous to write to his family. Finally, he was driven to pay a visit to Lady Laura again, after first sending a note to her residence, requesting permission—he felt too diffident of his reception to appear unexpectedly.

He received a reply with the return of the hotel's messenger:

My dear Shapira, you are always welcome. Come anytime.

Yrs. S-H

Inspired to greater confidence by this show of friendliness, Moses hastened to Mayfair, dressed well and fashionably (the best clothiers being more than eager to dress him on credit, given his expectations). He attempted to avoid the dirt and squalor of the streets, intensified by the summer's heat, by taking a hansom cab from the hotel. That was only partially successful, as the city's traffic inhibited any chance of a quick journey from one street to another, and Moses at last arrived with a fine sheen of perspiration dampening his face and neck. Stepping into the cool marble hall of Lady Laura's mansion afforded an immediate relief, however, and he had regained his sense of well-being by the time he was ushered into her drawing-room.

This time, they were not alone.

"Ah, Mr. Shapira, do sit down and refresh yourself," said Lady Laura as she extended her hand in greeting. He bowed low, taking her hand briefly, and took a seat near the window, open from floor to ceiling upon a cool, green view of a well-manicured garden, shaded by stately, spreading trees.

"Allow me to introduce you to my particular friend, Lady Emily Allerton, and my cousin, the Honorable James Simpson." The two persons thus introduced smiled and murmured at Moses, who nodded his head in greeting. "They are exceptionally delighted that you are come to visit," Lady Laura continued, "as they both have a keen interest in biblical era archaeology and manuscripts."

The gentleman seemed very young, even younger than the two ladies, and was perched on the edge of his chair in a rather anxious way, his high collar and cutaway coat, although the height of fashion, contriving to make him more of a mannequin than Moses imagined the poor young man perceived.

"I am indeed gratified that you are visiting today," Lady Allerton said, leaning slightly forward in her chair. She was young and attractive, but also had the light of a strong intelligence in her face. "I was so intrigued by Dr. Ginsburg's translation of the text, particularly in regard to the geography of the Israelites' journey as described in Deuteronomy—

your marvelous version seems to make so much more sense!"

Moses smiled—this was a primary aspect of the ancient text that was much talked about in the more serious papers and journals.

"You are correct, my lady," he said, taking a sip from the glass of cold lemonade that a maid had held out for him. "How it came to be so jumble about in the later text is perhaps the real mystery."

They all laughed at this small witticism, and Moses went on to explain more about this issue, with both Lady Allerton and Lady Laura interrupting with questions as well as speculations. The young Honorable was apparently more comfortable staying quiet; Moses could see that all his attention was for Lady Laura, with whom he seemed to be besotted.

After an hour's discussion of the scrolls, both the gentleman and Lady Allerton rose to take leave, but a glance from Lady Laura told Moses she wished him to stay. When they had the drawing room to themselves, she turned to him with a smile.

"So, my dear Shapira," she said. "How is the famous Dr. Ginsburg coming along? He seems to be tantalizingly slow, does he not? Are you at his side continually, looking over his work?" She looked up as a servant entered the room but before he could speak, she said, "I am not at home, Burton," and the butler bowed and left. She turned again to Moses with an inquiring look.

"You have so much true sight, my dear Simmons-Hartley," he responded. "I agree that the process is slow like agony, but alas! I am not allowed to be companion to Ginsburg as he studies my manuscripts." Moses sighed, then shrugged.

"I understand a scholar needs to concentrate, and that often is best done all alone," he said, finally relaxing into the comfortable chair by the window. "But how I wish I could be there, next to him, to hear his commenting—even if only to himself!—and see what he makes of the strips."

Lady Laura looked sympathetic. "It is as if your children were being raised by someone else, and you are not allowed to talk to them or be with your offspring."

"How well you put it," Moses said, looking at her in admiration. "Yes. I feel...alone."

They were silent a few moments, then Lady Laura spoke. "But surely, the great Ginsburg does not deny you access to his chambers altogether?" She busied herself with some pamphlets that were strewn on the low table in front of her while she spoke. "Surely, he must be telling you something about what he thinks?"

Moses shook his head. "He keeps me in the darkness as much as the great public—you haff seen the papers," he said. "All jumping this way and that way—much *ifs* and *perhaps* and *might be's* in his writing." He leaned forward, a troubled look on his face.

"But one thing there is of trouble to me—so many papers haff some little details about how Ginsburg is doing his examination—where are they coming from? Who is saying this detail to the papers, if not Ginsburg himself? And why would he do that?"

Lady Laura looked at him keenly. "Why should it not be Ginsburg himself?" she said. "Do you not think that he is an ambitious man? And eager to put himself forward as the great expert who will have the final word in this matter?" She made an unladylike sound of contempt. "There should be other scholars involved, it seems to me—this should not rest on the word of one man alone."

"Other scholars?" Moses repeated, his brow knitted. "I am, I hope, as good a scholar as many who haff seen these strips for themselves, and I hope my word would stand for something."

"To be sure," Lady Laura said promptly, in a soothing tone. "But you have *interest*, people will say, and therefore it must be up to others to determine authenticity." She waved a hand. "I say nothing about the *translation* of the text, that may be as it may be, interesting as it is. I mean only the establishment of the *date* of the documents."

"Perhaps you are right," Moses said, after thinking it over. "Perhaps I ought to say to Ginsburg to haff another such scholar as he to give the second opinion—just to be sure."

Lady Laura watched him thoughtfully. "Do you think it's more likely than not that Ginsburg will declare them authentic? Or is it possible that he may think the greater glory—for him—lies in his uncovering a clever fraud?" She held her breath, hoping she had not gone too far.

Moses shook his head, and tried to laugh. "In my deepest heart of hearts," he said, "I myself am sure they are the real thing. But I cannot say for another man who has his own interests and ambitions." His laugh turned to a sigh. "Ginsburg has always been my friend," he said, somewhat sadly. "But people change."

Lady Laura smiled—the seed had been sown.

Shortly afterward, Moses took his leave, feeling a little less lonely than he had earlier—talking things over with a friend did him some good, he thought, although he was still in an uncertain, anxious state.

13 August 1883

Three days later, without Moses's knowledge or permission, two of the leather strips were put on display in the great hall of the British Museum known as the King's Library, with the announcement in all the papers that the "general public are invited to see for themselves" this wonder of the ancient world. Moses took this as a sign that Ginsburg was on his side.

Lady Laura saw this as the moment to strike.

THIRTY-FIVE

London — Sunday, 16 March 1884

I HAPPENED TO BE STANDING AT the drawing room window, looking out at the wet streets and pavements, as Lord Parke's carriage rolled up in front of the Robinson's house. I immediately turned back into the room to inform Mary of the honor she was about to receive.

"My dear," I said, "now you shall at long last meet the mysterious and excellent Lord James Parke," I said. We were still luxuriating in the absence of her parents (at least, I certainly was), and it being Sunday, Mabel was attending a local church, where she was active in the choir. The Robinsons were not, on the whole, at all religious—my friend Mary being in fact actively opposed to such organized institutions—but they were nonetheless dutiful in the forms of polite society, and Mabel loved to sing. Just the two of us, therefore, were on hand to entertain Lord Parke.

Taking one more little peek out the window from behind the drapery, as I didn't want to appear over-eager, I was taken aback to see Lord Parke attending a beautiful young lady, with dark hair and a charming figure, from the carriage and up the walk to the front door. Not only *he* had come, but his affianced as well! It could scarcely be anyone other than the lady he had mentioned to me and John a few days ago. Well, well, this would be interesting too—I was, I admit, a bit anxious as to the kind of woman I felt he deserved versus the kind of woman he might be inclined (or required, per our brief exchange on this issue) to marry, given his position in society.

There was no time to further inform Mary of the additional visitor, so I arranged myself to awaiting their arrival in seeming insouciance, seating myself on a sofa and taking up a nearby journal, which just happened to be the latest edition of the *Palestinian Exploration Fund Report*, which Mary had managed to obtain the day before at my urgent request.

The butler duly announced the visitors—*Lord James Parke and Lady Emily Allerton*—and Mary and I rose to receive them. Lady Allerton was young and remarkably attractive, with dark hair and brown eyes that showed her to be both intelligent and possessing a sense of humor. She wore pale blue and white, as her youth and the season demanded, but it had the effect of freshness and health rather than the often insipid, studied appearance of purity and innocence that I had noticed before in young English ladies. There seemed from the first an affectionate and friendly sort of communication and relation between her and Lord Parke, which gave me no small amount of comfort.

Introductions were made with all due propriety, and after offering tea and pouring out cups and passing out plates, and settling the state of the weather, we turned to more important topics.

"I have informed Lady Emily," Lord Parke said, smiling at her, "of an overview of our adventures last week, in Paris and Rotterdam, and I assume you have brought your friend up to date as well, Miss Paget?"

"Yes, indeed," Mary answered with enthusiasm before I could speak. And I just must say, she was every bit as pretty as Lady Emily, although with a more captivating softness, perhaps, and naturally, a much more well-informed mind, in my humble opinion. I returned from my complaisant musings to hear Mary continuing.

"To think that in the space of a week, so many strange and untoward events could occur, and for you and Violet and John to go travelling about in order to investigate in person Mr. Shapira's sad demise," she said. "It is quite remarkable, and in such a cause, to face danger and distress."

"And there is more to come," Lord Parke said, nodding to me. "Miss Paget and I will be visiting Dr. Ginsburg at the British Museum tomorrow."

"We're hardly likely to encounter anything dangerous there, I imagine." I said, smiling wryly. But I was pleased at his alacrity. "You have secured an interview, then, so quickly!"

Lord Parke tilted his head in mock modesty. "I am a member of the Board, after all," he said. "He could hardly say no."

"And the interesting events keep occurring in another area of our investigation," I said after a moment, glancing at Mary, who encouraged me with a look to make the announcement.

"We think we have discovered the identity of the infamous 'Lady in Blue,' also known as the midnight prowler dressed in black," I said. "That lithe and resourceful woman who has dogged poor John's steps all this time."

Lord Parke looked astonished, and leaned forward eagerly. "Good Lord, Lady Emily and I also have an idea about who this woman might be! But, please, you go first!" He looked delighted at the coincidence of our investigations.

I nodded to Mary. "You tell them, my dear, as she is your acquaintance."

Mary colored prettily, and said, "We believe, from the description Violet has given me, that your Lady in Blue quite possibly could be a former schoolmate of mine, who lives here in London—Lady Laura Simmons-Hartley."

Lady Emily started and dropped her teacup back into its saucer, although thankfully it was nearly empty, and it didn't break. But our surprise at her shock was increased by Lord Parke exclaiming, "But that's exactly who we think it is, too." He turned to Lady Emily. "Emily, now, don't you think it is possible? Could Laura be involved somehow in all this?"

"What!" I cried. "Is she known to you both?" I looked at Mary, then back at Lord Parke. "Not that it should be such a surprise, that people in your circle should know each other, but...." For once, I was almost at a loss for words.

Mary, more attentive as a hostess than I, saw that Lady Emily was in some distress, and had leaped up to ensure that her fallen teacup had not splashed any liquid onto her dress. She poured another cup of tea, added sugar, and handed it to the lady, who drank it gratefully. We allowed her a few moments to regain her composure.

"I do hope you will forgive my bad behavior," she said, "but I had been trying very hard not to believe what Lord Parke and I came to imagine, after he had told me all that occurred. I have an engagement to see Laura—Lady Simmons-Hartley—later this week, and of course, I had no idea...how dreadful this all is!" She looked at Lord Parke in dismay, and he placed his hand over hers in comfort.

"We must remember," I interjected, "this is only speculation on our side, based on what little evidence we have, but perhaps you, Lady Emily, can tell us in more detail about the kind of person Lady Simmons-Hartley is, and whether this conjecture is likely to have any truth to it."

A somewhat awkward silence ensued, and as I glanced at Lord Parke and then Lady Emily, I could see that the young woman was struggling with the nature of my request—how could she possibly allow herself to share intimate details of her friend's life with complete strangers—especially if it might implicate her in criminal behavior? It was quite the dilemma.

"Emily," Lord Parke spoke in a low voice. "Perhaps if Miss Paget posed a few questions, you might find it possible to answer some of them within the bounds of propriety—but you can refrain from answering if you feel you cannot, in all good conscience, comment without exposing your friend?"

I was pleased at this evidence of Lord Parke's good sense as well as consideration for his fiancée's feelings and conscience, and hoped the lady might be persuaded to be a little forthcoming. I hastily started to formulate questions in my mind.

Lady Emily smiled, looking lovely again after the shock had turned her rather pale, and nodded her head. She looked at me with directness and honesty. "I will answer your questions, Miss Paget, insofar as I am able, and following the dictates of my sense of ethics."

I was especially pleased to hear her use the word "ethics" instead of "faith" perhaps, or "religion", although it suddenly occurred to me that she was, undoubtedly, a Roman Catholic like Lord Parke—presumably he could not marry outside of his faith, regardless whether that faith was adhered to in all its dictates. I thanked her and began my questions.

"Does your friend have an interest in biblical archaeology?" I thought I would start slowly, with issues that were not necessarily private and untouchable.

"Yes," Lady Emily said. "She has long had such an interest; in fact, I remember, some ten years ago, when she was nineteen, she travelled with a group of people from some bible society or other, to Jerusalem, and she came back raving about the antiquities she had seen there, and how she longed to go on a desert expedition herself."

"Did that ever happen?" I asked out of pure curiosity.

She shook her head. "I don't think so," she said. "At least, I never heard she had, although I know she went to France and Italy a number of times, looking at the ruins of ancient Roman forts and such."

Next step. "When she was in Jerusalem, had she ever mentioned to you meeting Mr. Shapira there?"

Lady Emily looked wary, but answered. "When Lord Parke told me the tale of what you all had experienced last week, and poor Mr. Shapira's death, I knew the name was familiar, and of course then recalled the scandal from last summer, but I—I," she paused for a moment, then continued, "I had completely forgotten all about it, but I recall actually having met Mr. Shapira, one time, while visiting Lady Laura at her home. I was there with her cousin, young James

Simpson—you have met him, Lord Parke—and Laura had invited Mr. Shapira to visit. I believe we talked a great deal about the scrolls and the biblical texts."

I pressed on. "Had you talked with her much about her trip to Jerusalem? Maybe she mentioned having gone to a souvenir shop, or bought some antiquities there?"

Her brow wrinkled; I saw that Mary and Lord Parke were leaning forward, listening intently.

A light seemed to break in Lady Emily's eyes. "I remember that she gave me a book of psalms, hand-printed quite beautifully, and with some pressed flowers for a frontispiece, and an olive-wood case to keep it in, that she said had come from the preeminent antiquarian dealer's shop in Jerusalem—and something about Bathsheba's Pool and King David—I don't recall it all."

I changed course abruptly. "Is Lady Simmons-Hartley an athletic sort of person?" I said.

Lady Emily wasn't a fool. "Do you mean to ask, could she slink around at night and climb through windows or down alleyways and run swiftly?" Her mouth tightened, but she decided to answer. "My friend has always been an able horsewoman and an indefatigable dancer; she has, the last five years or so," and here she hesitated a moment, but went on, "she has taken up fencing and certain Oriental exercises, I believe they call them *martial arts*, which she has told me, provides an excellent defense for a single woman who often travels without a male companion."

I could see that Lady Emily's own defenses were rising, and with a glance at Lord Parke, I decided to wind up the interrogation.

I smiled my most conciliating smile (I thought). "Your answers are clearly not any more than what anyone acquainted with Lady Simmons-Hartley, or the pages of the *Pall Mall Gazette*, would know about her. But I have one more question for you." I waited a moment. "Do you have any knowledge of her whereabouts over the last week?"

This question definitely gave Lady Emily pause, but at length she answered. "I am telling you no more than what her servants, or other friends, would tell you—she has been gone from London for about two weeks, maybe three—I do not see her as regularly as I once did, otherwise I would know for sure. But I do not know where she went when she left here."

Her answer struck a note that I had to follow up.

"And is there some particular reason why you and she do not see each other as regularly as you used to do?" I tried to make it sound like an innocent question, but I imagine that I failed entirely.

Lady Emily colored slightly, and answered coolly. "I'm sure I cannot say, other than that life often brings changes with it that affect one's relationships, however close they may have been at one time."

I could see I wouldn't get any further, and would have to perhaps trust to Lord Parke's ingenuity to tease a few more facts from his lady-love than I would be able to do.

Nonetheless, we parted soon after on friendly terms, Lady Emily having recovered herself well enough to invite both me and Mary to visit her at home, and Lord Parke pressing my hand with great fervor, and a promise to collect me promptly at eleven o'clock the next morning for our meeting with Dr. Ginsburg.

* * *

When our visitors had left, Mary and I looked at each other in amazement.

"Although I am not surprised that Lady Emily knows Laura," Mary said, using the name for her schoolmate that she was used to, "I actually wonder a bit at their having been friends, Laura being, well, Laura."

"Tell me more," I said, settling back comfortably on the sofa, and patting the cushion next to me to invite her to sit down. But she remained standing, and walked about the room, thinking and talking aloud.

"She said that they did not see each other as regularly as before," she mused. "And the very interesting knowledge of taking that instruction in, what did she say it was?"

"Martial arts," I prompted. I myself had dabbled a bit in some Oriental exercises, sitting cross-legged on a rug and emptying my mind—only I found it far too difficult, as I could not help myself thinking!

"As a woman who travels on her own," I added, "I can see the attraction to that—maybe I should look into it?" Mary glanced sharply at me, but ignored my attempt to get her goat, as the saying goes.

"I've been wracking my brain to find the incident that, I have to say," Mary confessed, "showed me that Laura had gone a little beyond 'eccentric' and was defying propriety in more serious ways. I think I put it out of my mind—but now I have recalled it."

"And what was that, dear heart?" I said, looking at her sympathetically.

"One day, about four years ago, something she said clearly indicated that she had become someone's mistress—or perhaps, just lover, as I don't think she was in any need of being 'kept', you know what I mean—" I did, but could hardly conceal my surprise that Mary knew about all those things—and she went on. "I received the distinct impression he was a Frenchman, was from Paris, and that he was also very involved in archaeology—but I couldn't bring myself to ask her any questions, although it was clear she was dying to talk about it."

"Perhaps," I said thoughtfully, "she couldn't resist telling Lady Emily about it, and that was what caused their cooling off?" I shook my head, thinking. "That brings back into the picture the Frenchman—who I am convinced is certainly Charles Clermont-Ganneau—who was with the blonde young lady at the Hotel Willemsbrug, and asked to see Mr. Shapira—her lover, no doubt, and therefore, also implicated in Mr. Shapira's death. We must find out if Lady Laura is acquainted with our monsieur Clermont-Ganneau—he seems inextricably mixed in with this whole case."

I sighed, and looked up at my friend to hear her response, but Mary had looked at her watch and now exclaimed, "We shall be late for our visit to the Grosvenor Gallery!" she said. "We must get there before it closes, this is the last day of the exhibit."

We hurried up to our rooms to change and ready ourselves for an excursion out into the town. Luckily, it appeared that the rain had stopped; the sun was shining weakly on the wet streets.

Well, I thought, as I hastily pulled on stouter shoes and a warmer shawl, no doubt Dr. Ginsburg can throw some light on this Clermont-Ganneau, and maybe we can come to the end of this maze of intrigue.

Frankly, I couldn't have imagined the half of what was still to come.

THIRTY-SIX

London — 13 August 1883

"MR. PRIME MINISTER, I AM DELIGHTED to meet you," said Moses, bowing to the grey-haired gentleman before him. Gladstone's face had a weariness that was etched into the granite-like structure of his whole head—massive, solid, and serious.

But his eyes lighted up when Moses escorted him to the vitrine in the King's Library that held the two leather strips of his Deuteronomy for display. Thankfully it was a sunny day, and the otherwise dimly-lighted library room, long and narrow with high walls filled with books, was illuminated well enough to appreciate the manuscript fragments in all their ancient glory.

"Ah, yes, I see, yes, yes, exceptionally interesting," Gladstone murmured as he bent over the glass, peering intently at the leather strips. Ginsburg had chosen two of the more legible strips for display, so that a number of characters could be seen.

"These characters are indeed very like the ones on the Mesha Stele, I can see that," Gladstone said.

"Yes, sir, the similarness is quite striking," Moses said, looking at him with admiration. "You haff acquaintance with the Moabite Stone then, sir?"

Gladstone nodded. "I have a photograph of it in my office," he said. "Such artifacts are an inspiration to us all, are they not, that there are always two sides to a story?"

Moses chuckled. "King Mesha would not haff imagined, I think, that his story of the great war with the Israelites would lie in wait for three thousand years before it could be told!"

Gladstone laughed along with him, and put a friendly hand on his shoulder. "I must say, Mr. Shapira, that your finding these remarkable remnants, and even more so, the amazing translation of the proto-Deuteronomy, are such boons to archaeology and theology that it beggars the imagination to think of what else might lie hidden in the deserts!"

Moses fervently nodded in agreement. He felt completely at ease with the great Prime Minister, and noticed with no little pride how the official bodyguards kept all the rest of the public far away from where they stood before the display. What an honor!

The Prime Minister spoke again. "I am particularly intrigued by the apparent presence of an extra commandment in your miracle of a text—how is it put again?"

"Yes, the eleventh commandment, we call it," said Moses; he recited, "*You shall not hate your brother in your heart,*" then added. "It can also be translated, *You shall not slay the soul of your brother.*"

Gladstone looked grave, and merely nodded his head. Then, looking around him, he said, "And where is Dr. Ginsburg? I had hoped to see him here this morning."

Ginsburg had declined to accompany him to the display, which Moses thought a little odd—but maybe seeing the Prime Minister did not rank highly in his old friend's mind; perhaps this was a sign that he wanted Moses to be the center of attention today.

Moses was ready with an answer. "He has been most hard working in his examining the manuscript, sir, so much I understand his family sends a messenger here from time to time, to make sure he is still alive! So you see, there is almost nothing that will tear him away from his work at this moment."

Gladstone smiled. "I am happy to hear it," he said, and turned his attention back to the display. He had a few more questions and comments for Moses, and the two discussed Deuteronomy and other biblical matters for several minutes, until the Prime Minister's secretary appeared at his side, murmuring something about his next meeting that day.

"Well, well, then, we shall take our leave, Mr. Shapira," Gladstone said heartily, shaking his hand. "Well done, very well done, sir."

Moses bowed and smiled, and walked with the great man to the door of the library, where throngs of people were impatiently waiting to be let into the room and see the display for themselves.

He felt as if he could go no higher on the ladder of his dreams.

15 August 1883

All the newspapers reported that the Prime Minister had viewed the Shapira Scrolls on display at the British Museum, and had talked with Mr. Shapira about them and other matters of biblical and archaeological interest.

But that was not all that appeared in the papers. Ginsburg's teasingly ambiguous comments and startling translations of the text were creating a firestorm of controversy among biblical savants across the Western world. Traditionalists decried the notion that "their" Deuteronomy was not as authentic as this supposedly earlier version. Skeptics of all stripes laughed at the idea that inked characters on sheepskin could survive in a damp and moldy cave for nearly three thousand years.

And many commenters, in letters and articles, were eager to remind the ignorant public that these so-called antiquities had been brought forth by none other than the infamous Moses Shapira, who had tried on previous occasions to foist fraudulent artifacts on credulous scholars—the Moabite Idols continued to wreak their curse on Moses's reputation.

The continuous rain of commentary and contradiction began to prey on Moses's equanimity. He finally demanded a meeting with Ginsburg—he wanted him to make a final decision, and soon.

They met two days after the Prime Minister's visit, in Ginsburg's office in the British Museum. This was not where the manuscript was kept, it was much too public a space—when Ginsburg was not actively examining them, they were carefully placed in cedar boxes and locked away in a vault, although on this day, there happened to be two of the strips laid out on the desk before them.

"My old friend," Moses began, "it seems to me that all this delay stirs up much talk and arguing not needful. My friends in Germany did not take so many days to see what they needed to see!"

Ginsburg leaned back in his desk chair, his chin resting on his hands, posed as if in prayer. He shook his head. "I must take the time I must take, Shapira," he said. "I daresay it won't be long now." He gestured to the two leather strips on his desk. "I have a question or two to ask you about something I saw on one of these strips, by the way."

Moses drew up his courage. "I am happy to discuss them, but first, I want to ask you if it should be a good idea to have a second scholar take a look at the manuscripts in addition to you?" At the startled look on Ginsburg's face, he hastened to add. "So that the whole burden does not fall on you—and does it not seem, perhaps, somewhat prideful, for the judgement of one man only, to determine such an important thing?" He held his breath then.

Ginsburg barked out a short laugh. "And who would you have as a second to me?" His voice reflected a mild contempt. "That scurrilous *dragoman* Clermont-Ganneau? Yes, he would do you a fine turn, you see, and me as well—taking all the credit as he always has done, regardless whether he would say *yea* or *nay*, with none of the work!"

Moses was amazed. "Why do you even mention his name? Do you think I want him to be near my scripts?"

Ginsburg picked up a letter that was lying on his desk, and tossed it over to Moses. "He has applied to me, in the name of the French government, to be allowed to see the manuscripts for himself, to help determine their authenticity." He snorted with greater contempt now. "He clearly assumes that a 'great scholar' such as himself can just ask and have—that we couldn't possibly deny him."

Moses quickly read over the letter; it was as Ginsburg had said. It was dated three days earlier, and mentioned today's date as the day Ganneau intended to visit Ginsburg at the museum.

No sooner had he finished the letter than there was a knock on the door, and Ginsburg's secretary announced a visitor: Charles Clermont-Ganneau. Within moments, their despised rival and nemesis stood before them, looking debonair and smug.

Moses was stricken into silence, and looked to Ginsburg to manage the situation. The museum official slowly rose from his chair; he did not invite Ganneau to be seated. It was exceedingly awkward, but Ganneau seemed to be determined to carry on as if they were all friends and colleagues and on the best of terms.

"How delightful that I find the two of you together," he said, giving the slightest nod of his head to Moses. "I trust that you received my letter, Dr. Ginsburg? And that I will be honored with the opportunity to view these fragments of leather, on behalf of the French government who, as you know, has an interest in such things, as do all civilized nations."

It was clear that he assumed they could not refuse him. But Ginsburg stood firm.

"Mr. Clermont-Ganneau," he said. "As I have not allowed any other scholars to work with me as I pursue my investigation of these manuscripts, I don't believe it will be possible for me, in all equity, to afford this opportunity to you."

Ganneau was silent, his eye fixed on Ginsburg. Then he looked down at the desk and saw the two leather strips.

"There," he said, pointing to them. "If I might just have a glance or two at those strips, it could be very quickly done." His eyes greedily took in every inch of the manuscripts.

Moses restrained the impulse to snatch them up, out of his rival's sight.

Ginsburg casually took a piece of paper from another part of his desk and laid it gently across the two leather strips. Moses bit his lip so as not to laugh.

"I would be concerned," Ginsburg said, "that such a cursory glance would result in a very odd translation of the little text that can be seen on these two artifacts," he said coolly. "It would not do to have competing translations at this point."

"Oh, as to that," Ganneau said, waving a hand, "I have no intention of any translation, my friend—I leave that all to you, as you have so far published in the papers! If there be differences to be determined, well, we shall leave that for a later time." He paused, again glanced at the desk, and resumed. "I am merely interested in the actual, physical, material state of these fragments, as a measure of their age and authenticity," he said, "which I believe I can, with my experience, determine after a short examination."

Moses looked at Ginsburg in dismay, and catching his glance, shook his head minutely. Ginsburg took the hint.

"I fear that the decision is not mine alone to make," he said, "and certainly not at a moment's notice. I must at the least consult with my superior, Dr. Edward Bond. I beg you to give me a day or two to consider whether your examination of the documents is advisable." He paused briefly, and smiled politely. "May I send you word sometime tomorrow? You are staying at the Savoy as usual, I presume?"

Ganneau drew himself up to his considerable height, and narrowed his eyes at the two older men. But he had a great deal of self-control, and was determined that he would ultimately win this battle, so he could afford to be gracious.

"Very well," he said, nodding his head, still without looking at Moses after that first glance. "I shall await your word, and depend on your adherence to scholarly principles to make the best decision."

He bowed abruptly and left the room.

* * *

A short note was delivered to the Savoy Hotel at seven o'clock in the evening of the next day, Thursday, 16 August. It read:

To M. Clermont-Ganneau

The British Museum regrets that it is impossible to grant your request to examine the Shapira manuscripts, at the express refusal of consent by Mr. Shapira as owner of the artifacts.

Edward Augustus Bond
Principal Librarian
(copy to C. D. Ginsburg)

Crumpling the note in his fist, Ganneau threw it across the room, cursing in gutter French. He immediately sat down at the desk in his hotel room and composed a letter to the *Times* of London to express his outrage. He described the Museum's refusal in stark terms, and added:

There was nothing to be said against this; the owner was free to act as he pleased. It was his strict right, but it is also my right to record publicly this refusal, quite personal to me; and this to some extent is the cause of this communication. I leave to public opinion the business of explaining the refusal. I will confine myself to recalling one fact, with comment. It was Mr. Shapira who sold the spurious Moabite potteries to Germany; and it was M. Clermont-Ganneau who, ten years ago, discovered and established the apocryphal nature of them.

He signed the letter with a flourish, and marched to the front desk to arrange for a messenger to take it post-haste to the Editor of the *Times*. Then he made his way to the Savoy's excellent restaurant, where he had no doubt Lady Laura Simmons-Hartley was already waiting for him.

THIRTY-SEVEN

London — Monday, 17 March 1884
At the British Museum

LORD PARKE'S CARRIAGE DREW UP before the Robinson's house quite promptly, and I hurried down the path to join him, my heart beating with excitement about our coming meeting with the famous Dr. Ginsburg.

"Good morning, my lord," I said as his footman opened the door and assisted me inside.

"It is a good morning, my dear Miss Paget," he said in return, beaming at me. The door closed on us and the coachman urged the team forward.

"Oh?" I said. He seemed to have something particular in mind. "And what makes it such a good morning?"

Lord Parke laughed, and replied with great gallantry, "Oh, of course, the opportunity to be with you on another adventure, you see," he said, grinning.

I looked at him narrowly. "But there is another reason...?"

He had the grace to blush slightly. "Lady Emily has been good enough to agree to set a date for our wedding, and the announcement will be in the papers shortly," he said.

"I congratulate you with all my heart, James," I said, seeing as we were alone—and this might be the last time I could address him so familiarly. "Lady Emily seems a splendid, intelligent and *simpatico* creature for you to align yourself with...and I can tell she is very fond of you."

"Fond! Yes, indeed, and I of her," he said, looking quite pleased. "I expect we shall rub along quite well." He then looked at me keenly. "She did say that she thought you were an unusually sharp mind, and although she found you a trifle terrifying, expressed the desire to know you better."

"Terrifying? Poor little me?" I laughed, actually rather gratified by the epithet. "Well, you may tell her the feeling is mutual—she is *formidable*, not only in French but in English as well."

We sat for a few moments in silent contemplation of their happy future. "But, James," I then said, "I have been thinking most intently about our meeting this morning."

"As have I," he said. "What do you think we should do about the disposition of the leather strips in our possession?" At that, he tapped a small case he had deposited on the floor, signifying that it held the manuscripts within.

I smiled. "As always, we are thinking of the same thing," I said, then grew more serious. "I have so many questions to ask of Dr. Ginsburg," I said. "And somehow I have the intuition that our possessing these manuscripts is a kind of leverage—do you not think so as well?—and that, as we are not *obliged* to give them up, at least not yet, because they are in fact, property belonging to John, we ought to retain them for a while—as a kind of assurance of future bargaining."

Lord Parke looked at me, I must say, with unmitigated admiration. "My dear Violet," he said, "Emily couldn't have been more precise when she called you 'terrifying'! I bow before such a formidable mind as yours, and agree entirely that that is how we ought to proceed."

I smiled, more gratified by his praise than I could almost admit, even to myself.

We talked over strategy and tactics the rest of the way to the Museum, and alighted before the steps of that temple of history and knowledge, fully armed for battle.

As we passed through the hallowed portals into the main hall, we chanced upon one of two persons in that institution with whom I was well acquainted—Edward Bond, the principal librarian. He started upon seeing me and Lord Parke as we walked through the foyer.

"Miss Lee! I swear, never so delighted to see you again—it's been too long a time!" He bowed, smiling, then directed his salutations to my companion. "And Lord Parke! I had thought of you as happily enjoying the delights of Paris, but here you are!"

We acknowledged his greeting, and I spoke first.

"We have an appointment with Dr. Christian Ginsburg this morning," I informed him, "about the recent, sad demise of Mr. Moses Shapira."

Mr. Bond's face fell immediately into a proper look of sorrow and concern. "Yes, yes, of course, I had heard, so very terrible, such a sad ending for an estimable man." Then he seemed to consider the import of my words.

"May I ask," he said, hesitating only a little, "Do you know Dr. Ginsburg? I mean, what possible connection do you have with Mr. Shapira, that you want to talk to Dr. Ginsburg about him?" But he hastened to retract his impolite query. "I apologize, it is not...I have no right to ask! But may I escort you, at least, to Dr. Ginsburg's office?" He smiled in relief when I nodded and accepted his offer, mentioning that I was as yet unacquainted with Dr. Ginsburg.

He led us to a plain wooden door on one side of the great hall, near the back, and unlocking it with a key he had on a ring in his pocket, he ushered us into the offices and archives of the great museum. A maze of hallways confused me utterly as we veered left and right, finally arriving at an office that had windows facing an inner courtyard—a brass nameplate announced it to be the domain of C. D. Ginsburg. The man himself sat at his desk; his door was open.

Edward Bond tapped lightly on the door frame, and as his colleague looked up, he stepped forward into the room.

"Dr. Ginsburg, here are your two visitors—you know Lord Parke, of course, and I am pleased to introduce to you Miss Vernon Lee, the noted author, and a frequent visitor to our library and research archives."

Christian Ginsburg stood and came around to the front of his desk—it was a small office, and the four of us made a sort of crowd in the space. He was a rather stout man, of middle height, and he had the scholar's gentle gaze, as if his mind was distracted with the perusal of ancient texts and hidden meanings. I would guess his age to have been in his mid-fifties—roughly the same as Mr. Shapira.

"Thank you, Mr. Bond, for escorting my guests here," Ginsburg said, nodding to his superior. Bond nodded amiably, and murmuring to me that he would be delighted to see me anytime, departed.

Lord Parke and I were invited to be seated in two chairs that faced Ginsburg's desk, and I took the opportunity to look around his office. In general, it was neat and tidy, although stacks of books and papers stood like pillars in the corners of the room, and some on the broad windowsill. His desk held the usual blotting pad with leather corners, a brass pen and ink stand, two receptacles for mail and papers, and three small figurines or statues that looked quite ancient, made of clay, perhaps, or carved from stone.

I could see that our host looked somewhat uneasy, and attributed it to Lord Parke's having relayed to him, when asking for the meeting, the general nature of our inquiries.

But unlike my approach to Lady Emily, I decided to be more direct—taking, perhaps, Inspector Cramer of Rotterdam as a model! "Dr. Ginsburg," I said, "I understand you have long been acquainted with Mr. Moses Shapira?"

He eyed me steadily. "Yes, Miss Lee," he said. "I first met Moses Shapira in Jerusalem, in 1872, when he welcomed me to that ancient city and showed me the places and things that general tourists never get to see." There was a note of sorrow in his voice, which prompted me to sympathy.

"I am very sorry, sir, about his unfortunate death—all his friends must feel the pain of his absence."

"He was an unusual man—brilliant, adventurous, restless, ambitious, but full of good humour and family feeling," Ginsburg said. "I counted him as a friend—as a brother."

I was finding it difficult to maintain a stern approach in the face of the man's evident fellow-feeling for Mr. Shapira—but nonetheless, there were things that required explanation. I felt Lord Parke's gaze upon me, and as I glanced at him, he spoke, proceeding as we had discussed.

"Perhaps we ought to lay before you a little of what our concern with Mr. Shapira consists," he said. "I had not indicated this in my telegram to you, or my note of two days ago, but we have in our possession what we believe are some of the leather strips that Mr. Shapira originally had brought to the Museum for possible purchase."

Ginsburg started at this, and stared in disbelief at Lord Parke. "May I, may I see them?" He fairly stuttered the words. "How did you come to possess them?"

"Certainly," Lord Parke said, and leaned down to pick up the case which held the leather strips. He extracted them carefully and folding back the heavy paper they were wrapped in, placed them on the desk before Ginsburg, who looked at them much, I imagine, as a father gazes upon his newborn son. Lord Parke very briefly related that they had been sent through the mail to a friend of ours who had met with and befriended Mr. Shapira about two months ago.

"But these are not all of the leather strips that Mr. Shapira originally showed to you, are they, Dr. Ginsburg?" I asked, leaning forward slightly.

"No, no, that is true, Miss Lee," he murmured, gently touching one of the scrolls before him. "This is but half of the fifteen scrolls we originally examined."

"And where are the others then?" I asked.

He looked up at me. "Why, they are here, in the vault of the Museum."

"And how did they come to be separated?" I said. "Why did you keep half of them here, when Mr. Shapira was clearly entitled to his property when he asked for it, especially as you had declared them forgeries?" I saw him wince at my directness, and thought it an interesting response—he looked, to my eye, ashamed, even guilty. "Why would the museum—why would *you*—want to hold on to them?"

"These are home questions," he said after he had collected himself for a few moments. He rubbed a hand across his forehead. "I'm not sure I am able to give you much of an answer."

"You sent half of the scrolls to Mr. Shapira when he asked for them earlier this year, in January," I said, my tone cool but not severe.

He looked surprised, then wary. "How on earth could you know that?" he asked. He looked at Lord Parke, then again at me. "What are you two playing at here?" He seemed suddenly angry. "Why should any of this matter to you? The poor man is dead, by his own hand—why cannot we leave him to rest in peace?" Then, in a sudden change, he was as quickly deflated as he had been roused. "I find it so hard to believe he would do such a terrible thing, and yet, perhaps he had given up hope." He looked sincerely distressed.

But I pressed my advantage. "And you went to see him, in Rotterdam, a few days before his death."

Ginsburg didn't seem to be surprised this time, and he nodded his head. "Yes, we met in the lobby of his hotel, and then went to lunch. It was, I believe, the Wednesday of the first week of this month." He fumbled in a drawer for his diary and, consulting it, confirmed the date. "Yes, the fifth of March."

"And what was the reason for this visit?" I asked.

Ginsburg looked uneasy once again. "I had something in particular to discuss with him." He looked as if wild horses couldn't drag another word out of him on that subject, so I tried another tack.

"Did you at any time go into his room at the Hotel Willemsbrug?" I asked, watching him closely. I hadn't been able to free my mind from thinking about Mr. Shapira's colorful carpet bag filled with documents, and how it had disappeared from his room.

He shook his head emphatically. "No, I was obliged to return to London that very evening, and I left the restaurant with him only to go straight to the train station; I presume he returned to his hotel." Again, there was a wary look in his eye. "Why do you ask so many questions about all this?"

Lord Parke spoke up at this point. "Dr. Ginsburg, we have been to Rotterdam, and we have spoken to the police there, and the hotel management, and we think—" He broke off momentarily, looking at me for support. I could see no reason not to present our conjectures to Dr. Ginsburg, although I hadn't quite yet excluded him from my private list of suspects. I nodded.

"We think," Lord Parke continued, "that Mr. Shapira may not have taken his own life—that he quite possibly met his death at someone else's hand." Ginsburg's eyes opened wide, and he stared in disbelief.

"And we think this," I added quickly, "not only from evidence we found at the site, but also because there have been two attempts to steal the scrolls from my friend's possession—once in his own home in Paris and once in Rotterdam—we can only conclude that someone wants them very badly and, perhaps, was willing to kill for them."

After a moment of stunned silence, a dark look passed over the scholar's face, and he slammed a hand on the table. "Clermont-Ganneau!" he cried. "That evil *dragoman* surely has had a hand in this!"

I was startled by his vehemence, but took notice of the word he used. "What exactly is a *dragoman*, sir?" I asked. "And why is it a name applied to Clermont-Ganneau?"

"It is a kind of semi-official go-between," he replied. "It is a term much in use a few decades ago, especially in the

East—it describes a man who knows several languages, is adept at negotiation and liaison—and deceit and betrayal," he added, his anger rising again. "Clermont-Ganneau, before he became the French Consul in Jerusalem, was such a one."

I took the risk of asking another, rather bold question.

"And are you at all acquainted with monsieur Clermont-Ganneau's companion, a young and beautiful blonde aristocrat of the London *ton*, who has an abiding interest in biblical archaeology?"

It was his turn to start again, and I felt the sudden stillness beside me, as Lord Parke held his breath.

Ginsburg looked from me to Lord Parke and back again. "Lady Laura Simmons-Hartley," he said, a trifle grimly. He put his head in his hands and groaned.

"What?" I said. "What is it, Dr. Ginsburg?"

His face showed the terrible thoughts coursing through his brain. "She came to me, here, sometime in February, talking about Shapira and how she was concerned for his health—she wanted to contact him, help him, but she didn't know where he was. And I happened, that very day, to have a letter from him announcing he was going to be in Rotterdam, at the Hotel Willemsbrug, for some weeks, but was currently visiting in Haarlem for a week or so—so I told her where he was, and that he seemed to be in good health, so she shouldn't worry about him."

I remembered what John had said about the stranger who had accosted Mr. Shapira at their dinner table, in Haarlem—it was doubtless Ganneau himself. What a close conspiracy these two lovers had! I mused about this information for a few moments, then I said, "But surely, she was not aware that any of the manuscript strips were in Mr. Shapira's possession? Didn't she think they were all here, with you?"

He shook his head, disconsolate. "When Clermont-Ganneau came here, late in January, he asked to see them, and he was shown the whole collection, the fifteen strips—but I—in my indignation and mistrust—let him know that Shapira had requested them to be returned. And I confirmed to the lady that I had indeed sent them to Shapira."

He lifted a hand and let in fall. "I had thought, previously," he said, "that there was some connection between them—between the lady and Clermont-Ganneau, but I dismissed it as unworthy of consideration." He shook his head. "They are in league together—they must be—to take the scrolls."

"But why?" I cried. "You have all judged these scrolls to be fraudulent, inauthentic! Why would Clermont-Ganneau, or anyone, want them so badly?" I looked at him severely. "And why did you then keep half of them when Mr. Shapira asked for them all?"

Ginsburg looked at us with sad eyes. "I am ashamed to say it, madam, but I believe that my judgement may have been—hasty. I have come to think that the scrolls may indeed be what Shapira said they were—an early, three-thousand-year-old version of Deuteronomy. I feel very strongly that I must examine them *all* again. I sent the ones in better condition to Shapira—those especially I must see again."

He paused, and sighed.

"And I think Clermont-Ganneau also believes the same," he said, and put his head in his hands once more.

THIRTY-EIGHT

London — Friday, 17 August 1883

THE EVER-CURIOUS LONDON PUBLIC, despite a mizzling rain and lowering clouds, still lined the sidewalk in front of the British Museum, keen to see the miraculous "ancient Bible" on display. The Prime Minister's visit had lent increased cachet to the honor of viewing the artifacts, regardless whether any viewer actually had the slightest notion of what they were looking at.

Charles Clermont-Ganneau had sent a private note to a more friendly colleague inside the walls of the great institution—Dr. Samuel Birch, an expert in Egyptology—and had thereby been escorted through a side door and thence to the King's Library, where he was able to more quickly approach the vitrine that held the Shapira Scrolls. He knew he might probably encounter Shapira himself, who was said to be present near the display nearly all day long, but as one of the general public, Ganneau certainly had as much right to be there and look at the leather strips as anyone else.

He was alone; Lady Laura had declined to attend with him, having viewed the scrolls earlier in the week, but that suited him well—he felt nervous and on edge, which always induced an irascible, unsociable mood in him that generally drove company away. Besides, they were still being discreet about being seen together in public.

The light in the great room was, unfortunately, quite dim, given the pervasive rain and clouds outside; the few hanging lamps, suspended from the extraordinarily high ceiling, did little to dispel the gloom. He drew near the vitrine, feeling nothing but contempt and disgust for the populace surging around him—ignorant sheep eager to be part of the latest 'thing'!

"Why, they are so small and dark!" exclaimed a young woman in front of him.

"Don't see nothing special about 'em," said her companion, with a sneer of assumed superiority. "Don't look like any Bible I ever seen."

Ganneau closed his eyes, blocking out the sight of other people, and edged closer to the display. He felt sure that an acute examination of the strips, however brief a time he had, would enable him to make a judgement as to their authenticity.

At last he gained the vitrine, and he planted himself firmly in the middle, so that people would have to step around him to see in. He maintained a fixed gaze on the two leather strips under the glass, not hearing the murmurs and words of indignation as people made their way past him.

After a few moments, he began to see what he had hoped for—evidence of exactly how these forgeries had been created! He had always, from the first, assumed they were fakes—they came via Shapira, did they not? That was enough for him to be suspicious on the instant.

The light was so dim that it was almost impossible to discern any writing on the leather strips, but he didn't care about the writing—if he could prove that the manuscripts— so-called—themselves were fakes, the writing and its

content wouldn't matter. He continued his examination—
the tops of the strips were straight and mostly even, as if they
had been cut from a larger piece of skin, while the bottom
edges were ragged and tattered. Other details began to surface under his avid scrutiny, and he wrote several notes in a
little notebook he had brought for the purpose.

After a time, he was alerted to rather more of a fuss
around him than previously, and tore his gaze away from the
scrolls to be confronted with a burly guard at his side, looking not at all apologetic, but frowning mightily at him.

"Move along now, sir, as you're disrupting the public as
wants to see these artifacks themselves, all right then? You
can go to the back of the line and start over if you want to
be seeing more."

Ganneau held his temper in check—he needed a little
more time—but he knew he could prevail upon Dr. Birch to
allow him entry again the next day. At least he had not en-
countered either Shapira or Ginsburg during his visit—considering what he thought he had found, he imagined he
would have a hard time of it to keep from gloating before
them and making a scene.

So he nodded briefly to the guard and walked quietly
away, although inside he was exulting. He was certain now
that he knew how Shapira had done it, and he was not inclined to go easy on the shopkeeper from Jerusalem, not this
time. He would expose the blackguard for the fraud he was,
and all the world would know that Clermont-Ganneau had
once more proven he was the elite expert in detecting archaeological fraud.

* * *

"But from so cursory an examination, Charles!" Lady Laura exclaimed. "Can you be sure that you are right?" She was standing before the fireplace in her drawing room, while Ganneau lounged on a settee near the window. It was late in the evening of the day he had gone to the British museum; they had dined at a mutual friend's home, where their liaison was understood and accepted without judgement or comment (Lady Laura having a reputation, of sorts, to maintain). Afterwards, they had come back to her Mayfair mansion to be alone to talk, and were now enjoying a cooled French white wine Ganneau had brought to her.

Ganneau frowned. "You do not think that I have the expertise to determine such a fraud?" But he wasn't really angry—he hadn't told her the whole of his discoveries.

She approached him quietly and sat down next to him, laying a hand on his arm soothingly.

"Tell me," she almost whispered. "Tell me what you found." Her alluring looks held the promise of a tempestuous night, and Ganneau took up her hand and kissed it.

"To be brief," he said, still holding her hand, a look of triumph in his eyes, "I believe that he took some very old pieces of leather used in synagogues—which he has collected for years, some of them three or more centuries old—and cut away those narrow strips at the bottom of a scroll, which explains why the top edges of Shapira's fragments are relatively smooth, as if cut off with a knife, while the bottom edges are ragged, as the bottoms of synagogue scrolls are."

Lady Laura sat, open-mouthed, hearing this explanation. She had seen many synagogue scrolls herself, and she had viewed Shapira's; they were as Ganneau described.

"There are other signs as well," Ganneau continued. "The sewing of the pieces together—if only I could examine the thread more minutely!—I believe they are of modern construction. There are faintly inscribed guidelines between the columns of writing, just as the synagogue rolls always have! And the letters themselves, the ink that is used—so very black and fresh-looking at some points, almost obscured in others—very clumsy, if you ask me, in the attempt to make the whole look old." He sniffed in contempt, and sipped at the remains of his wine. "Buried in sand, treated with spirits, stained and scorched and hidden away—pah! Amateurish stuff!" Then he laughed, harshly and gleefully. "What a letter I shall compose for the *Times*, revealing all!"

He gripped her hand so hard she almost cried out. "I will crush him!" he said, and drawing her close to him, he kissed her passionately, pulling at the neckline of her dress. They fell back on the settee in a fierce embrace.

Tuesday, 21 August 1883

From The *Times* of London

"On the 3d of the present month we gave an account of a remarkable manuscript brought to this country by MR. SHAPIRA, of Jerusalem, and written in a character which, supposing the manuscript to be genuine, would fix its date somewhere about the ninth century B.C. Since then we have published the translation of portions of it, and also MR. SHAPIRA'S account of the way in which it came into his possession. In first calling attention to the subject we pointed out the strong antecedent presumption against the genuineness of the fragments, a presumption resting upon the extreme improbability that leather should be found in excellent preservation after the lapse of twenty-seven centuries when skins known to date from the seventh century of our æra are falling to pieces, upon the dexterity with which ancient relics are forged, and upon the magnitude of the gains they may reasonably hope to secure in case of success. On those grounds we ventured to predict that MR. SHAPIRA'S treasure would undergo a particularly searching examination and would give rise to some rather keen controversy. Our anticipations have been fully verified by numerous communications which we have received, as well as by the interest excited in literary and critical circles. The manuscript has received that minute and respectful attention which is due to its alleged antiquity. An eminent Semitic scholar has been charged by the authorities of the British Museum with the task of deciphering it, transliterating it into Hebrew characters, translating it into English, and, finally, reporting upon its value. The work is one demanding immense patience, ability, and scholarship. While engaged in it DR. GINSBURG is obviously precluded from giving any opinion upon the questions which naturally present themselves to critics, and for the conclusive answer to which he is providing the material. Others, however, less bound to judicial reserve, have not hesitated to denounce the manuscript as a forgery; and M. CLERMONT-GANNEAU, whose letter we publish to-day, refuses even to admit that it is a clever forgery. He is prepared to show us exactly how the thing has been done, and even offers to provide us with a whole Pentateuch of equal antiquity if we will only find him enough synagogue rolls two or three centuries old to produce the requisite quantity of blank leather. He resembles the beneficent persons who come forward nowadays to show us by what simple means conjurors and spiritualists have hitherto imposed upon the credulous. Not content with assuring us of what we may, indeed, shrewdly surmise upon our own account, he insists upon robbing us of the harmless mystery that seems to attach to these ancient sheepskins even when we most stoutly refuse to assign them to the ninth century B.C. He is determined that we shall not only know the manuscript to be forged, but shall also track the forger through all his wiles and be compelled to admit that there is nothing wonderful or romantic about him."

Moses was beside himself with fury, but it was no less than what he would have expected from his arch-rival Ganneau. But he was further shocked and dismayed to see another letter, printed the same day, by his friend Captain Conder, who also wrote to the papers with his own estimation of the scrolls, after he had been allowed to examine them closely. His final sentence was damning: *"I had no hesitation in concluding that the supposed fragments of Deuteronomy were deliberate forgeries."*

This was a blow indeed, as Conder had previously been supportive of the scrolls' authenticity.

Ginsburg dutifully published his second installment of translation of the text, also in the same issue as the damning letters, but there was no indication from him at all as to the authenticity of the fragments.

The world of biblical archaeology was in turmoil, and scholars across Europe could not now refrain from publishing their opinions, many of them from savants who had not even had a glimpse of the fragments, or knew anything about Shapira other than the Moabite Idols scandal of ten years before. Some argued in favor of the ancient documents, but more were opposed.

Everything now depended upon Ginsburg.

THIRTY-NINE

London — Late Monday, 17 March 1884

Kensington, at the Robinson's Home

THE FIRST THING THAT MET MY EYES upon returning to Mary's house after the meeting with Dr. Ginsburg was a telegram addressed to me, waiting in the glass dish on the front hall table. I snatched it up, opened it and read it swiftly.

```
LONDON 17 MARCH 1884  12:05 PM

VP AM NOW IN TITE ST STOP COME FOR
TEA STOP MARY TOO STOP EAGER TO
KNOW LATEST STOP CHEERS JSS END
```

Grinning, I hastened to the drawing room to find Mary—and came smack up against George Robinson, her father, just exiting that room.

"Why, Miss Paget!" he said, attempting to smile and failing utterly.

"Mr. Robinson, how delightful to see you," I said. "Your wife's sister is better, I hope, so that you are come home again?"

A voice from inside the drawing room told me that Mrs. Robinson was within. "George, to whom are you speaking?"

I could just distinguish the low tones of Mary's lovely voice, telling her mama that it was probably I. Nodding my head in salutation to George, I swept past him and into the room, and heard the door close softly behind me. "Yes, indeed, it is I," I said, "and it is very good to see you in your home again, Mrs. Robinson. I trust your sister is better?"

"Thank you, Miss Paget," she said, smiling much more successfully at me than her husband had managed. I then turned to Mary, and handed her the telegram. She took it up eagerly, read it, and exclaimed, "Oh my, but yes, it's nearly tea time now, we should get ready to leave, Violet, quite soon." She handed back the telegram, and spoke to her mother.

"John Sargent has asked me and Violet especially to tea this afternoon, mama," she said. "On most important business, what I hinted at to you earlier."

"Oh! Well, if Mr. Sargent requests your presence, who am I to say him nay?" Mrs. Robinson said, with a good show of nonchalance. She looked at her daughter critically. "Wear your peach gown, dear, it always lends a glow to your complexion."

Mary rolled her eyes at this, although as her face was turned away from her mother and towards me, only I saw her amused irritation. As if John were a prospective suitor!

The two of us hastened upstairs to refresh ourselves and change into appropriate attire. As I stopped at my door, a few rooms down from Mary's, she spoke before continuing on. "I'm dying to hear everything from your appointment with Dr. Ginsburg!" she said.

I kissed her on the cheek. "And I am dying to tell you all!"

* * *

As it turned out, I thought better of telling the "all" of what I learned from Dr. Ginsburg, as Mary and I rode in the Robinson's carriage over to Tite Street; John was staying in a rented house there, with an art studio on the upper floor, in company with a fellow artist.

"I don't want to tell the story twice over," I protested. "Can you wait until we're with John, and then I can tell you both at once?" Of course she acquiesced—Mary has the most giving temperament of any person I've ever known.

As we drove to Tite Street, Mary produced a clipping from a newspaper she had been reading that morning, which she proceeded to show to me. It was dated the day before, Sunday 16 March, in *Reynolds's Weekly*. I read it through quickly.

"DEATH OF AN IMPOSTER. – A telegram from the Hague describes the sudden and melancholy end of Mr. Shapira, whose reported discovery of the oldest manuscript in the world excited the learned and startled the public some eight months ago. Deuteronomy on leather slips three thousand years of age did not long survive the scrutiny to which it was subjected at the British Museum. It was pronounced to be a forgery, and a very late forgery, too. The process by which the pieces of sheepskin on which the characters were inscribed had been made to assume the appearance of hoary antiquity was clearly explained, and Mr. Shapira ceased to attract the interest of mankind. He sank out of notice as completely as the Arab who, having brought him these alleged relics of the past, was seen no more alive. Now Mr. Shapira has shot himself in an hotel at Rotterdam. A card was found upon him describing him as an "agent of the British Museum residing at Jerusalem." His fate throws a new light upon the transactions which have made his name notorious."

I handed back the clipping to Mary, shaking my head. "Is this the first notice of his death to be published here?" I asked. She shook her head, and replied, "There were two very, very brief notices last Wednesday, the twelfth, mere sentences really, rather buried in the back pages. Mama brought them to my attention this morning—she always reads obituary notices." She gave a slight shudder. We were silent for the remaining few blocks of our journey.

* * *

John ran down the stairs and opened the door to us himself, there being no servants present, and we rejoiced to see each other, though only after a few days. His spirits were high— he had delivered "Madame X" to the Salon the day before, along with another fine painting, of the four daughters of a mutual friend, Edward Darley Boit, and he expected great fame and fortune to ensue upon the Salon's opening in April; I was 'wound up' as the saying goes, from the morning's visit; and Mary was so excited to be part of such an extraordinary event that she gave John a brief hug and a kiss on the cheek!! The look of admiration he gave her made me, for a fleeting instant, wonder if Mrs. Frances Robinson was more astute and canny that I had imagined. I put the thought aside immediately as unworthy of both parties.

When we arrived upstairs at the studio, we found that Lord Parke and Lady Emily had also been invited to join the tea party, and we met as old friends. I looked a question to Lord Parke and he, understanding my look, shook his head, and said in a low voice to me, "I have not spoken one word about this morning, Miss Paget—not even to Lady Emily—knowing we were all to be together this afternoon."

I smiled at him, highly gratified at his discretion. When we were all seated, Lord Parke and I took turns relating a good deal of what we had talked over with Dr. Ginsburg—and then it was time for questions.

"But you didn't say—why did Dr. Ginsburg go to Rotterdam to see Mr. Shapira early in March? And only for one day?" John asked. "Seems very strange to me."

"We thought so too," said Lord Parke. "And Dr. Ginsburg wasn't very forthcoming, although he did seem to indicate that he had wanted to consult with Mr. Shapira about something particular—ultimately, he did not choose to tell us."

"But you say that he has perhaps changed his mind about the Shapira Scrolls?" asked Lady Emily. "How extraordinary! Do you suppose he went to Rotterdam to tell Mr. Shapira of his new evaluation?"

"Yes, Lady Emily, quite extraordinary," I replied. "Lord Parke and I thought the same, but although Dr. Ginsburg would not say, it seems to be the most likely explanation for his visit."

"But wouldn't it rather give the lie to the idea of suicide," she persisted, "if Dr. Ginsburg told Mr. Shapira he now thought the scrolls were authentic—thus raising his hopes anew, both for his reputation as well as remuneration?"

(I had already approved of Lady Emily as Lord Parke's future wife, and her intelligent questions only ratified my decision.)

We all looked at one another, thinking about this. Mary spoke first. "Query whether Dr. Ginsburg may have been trying to persuade Mr. Shapira to give him back the scrolls in his possession—the half of them he had—to take back to London, *without* saying anything about having changed his mind about their authenticity—but Mr. Shapira refused?"

"After which," John chimed in, "could Dr. Ginsburg have decided to take the scrolls by force, and perhaps—one hopes—*accidentally* shot Mr. Shapira while doing so?"

I shook my head. "No, John, that won't do. We have proof that Dr. Ginsburg was back in London late that same night, and that he did not leave the metropolis again, so he couldn't have been present at Mr. Shapira's death. And besides, Mr. Shapira was seen and talked to by the hotel staff the next day."

"I must say that I don't believe Ginsburg had anything to do with Shapira's death," Lord Parke said with some vehemence. "And this is all so much speculation about what he did or did not say to Shapira when he visited him on the fifth of March—it isn't getting us anywhere."

He rose and went to the sideboard in search of something more to eat or drink. John rose also and joined him and, after a few whispered exchanges, John went to another cupboard and took out a bottle of whisky, at which both gentleman looked very pleased. They poured themselves glasses and returned to where we were all sitting.

"I say, John, don't you think some of us ladies would like a sip of something stronger than tea?" I smiled to alleviate what could sound like rudeness. "All this round and round is giving me a headache!"

Sherry was produced and glasses poured and served to all three ladies—Mary and Lady Emily thanking me particularly for being so attentive. We all laughed a bit and that eased the buildup of tension.

"It is my opinion," I said at last, gathering everyone's attention, "that we need to bring the principal parties in this situation face to face, with some kind of element of surprise or interest, and force their hand."

"And the principal parties being—?" Mary said.

"Dr. Ginsburg, of course, but also, most importantly, Charles Clermont-Ganneau and Lady Laura Simmons-Hartley." I sipped my sherry, feeling my headache ease.

Lord Parke looked thoughtful. "Ginsburg and Lady Laura, I expect, can be readily engaged." He looked at Lady Emily questioningly. "Didn't you say that you had an appointment with her this week? So we know that she is, at the least, in town?"

Lady Emily nodded. "I meet with her on Wednesday."

"But Clermont-Ganneau?" he then said, looking back to me. "He lives in Paris—how do you expect to get him to come to London, at short notice—and by what means of enticement?"

"Oh, there is no need for that!" I said airily, and looked at Mary. "My dear Miss Robinson has managed to gain information of his whereabouts in a most startling and underhanded manner! He is here in London."

Everyone was surprised, and looked over at Mary, who admonished my humour with a teasing glance.

"Oh, yes," she acknowledged, "very underhanded indeed! I read it in the newspaper this morning—he is here to address a meeting of the Palestinian Exploration Fund tomorrow evening, and is staying at the Savoy Hotel, where I'm sure we can send a message to him."

Lord Parke laughed and addressed me. "And just what are you planning, Miss Paget? I know you, you have probably every last detail written down already! Come, tell us what is to transpire, and what we all are going to do?"

I couldn't help smiling back, and then especially at John. "You, my dear John," I said, "are going to give a party, here in your studio, and along with Mary, invite all sorts of literary and artistic people, and Lord Parke will invite Ginsburg and Clermont-Ganneau and some other archaeological types, and…"

Lady Emily interrupted, but she was not smiling. "And I am to invite Lady Laura Simmons-Hartley."

That stopped me short, but only for a moment. "My dear Lady Emily—if you find you cannot invite her yourself, my friend Miss Robinson here is an old schoolmate of Lady Simmons-Hartley, and she can do the inviting." Mary nodded encouragingly.

Lady Emily thought this over, then smiled a little. "You are very good, Miss Paget, and I appreciate your consideration, but I would like to do my part in so serious a matter. I will personally invite her and beg her to attend."

"But what is to be the occasion for this party?" John asked. "What—beyond a mere social gathering—would induce all these people, particularly the *principal parties*, as you term them—to come?"

"Ah," I said, smiling again. "Nothing less than a private showing of the infamous Shapira Scrolls, which—especially in light of the poor man's recent demise—we will have it announced that they are to receive a second, even more thorough examination by worthy scholars and savants."

Everyone exclaimed over this idea as quite the thing to draw our suspects to the party, although I couldn't help admit to myself some trepidation as to the safety of the scrolls—or even one or more of us. After all, if one of the persons we suspected had indeed shot Mr. Shapira in a bungled attempt to secure the scrolls, what was to keep him—or her—from killing again?

FORTY

Jerusalem — Late August 1883

ROSETTE THREW DOWN THE COPY OF THE *TIMES* that the pastor, Mr. Green, had brought over for her to read. "This is atrocious!" she cried. "Infamous! It's simply the outcome of wicked jealousy!"

More than curious, Myriam picked up the paper and read through the article quickly, gasping as she read the sentence that portended their fate:

> "Others, however, less bound to judicial reserve, have not hesitated to denounce the manuscript as a forgery; and M. CLERMONT-GANNEAU, whose letter we publish to-day, refuses even to admit that it is a clever forgery."

She could not refrain from saying their hated enemy's name aloud, which elicited a terrible groan from her mother as she sat weeping in her chair.

"We are ruined, ruined!" she said, covering her face with her handkerchief and giving way to another burst of tears.

Myriam was so shocked she could hardly move, but hope, especially in the young, has a strong hold and soon she began to think that her father, surely, would be able to overcome his enemy, as he had done before. She attempted to soothe her mother.

"Dear mama," she said, rubbing her shoulders softly, "do not despair. Remember how Father has come out successful in the past—he was not held to blame for the idols, you remember—but I swear, these manuscripts of his, they are authentic! I was with him, day after day, as he worked to decipher them and make the letters become visible—he did not *make* them in his workshop!"

The more she thought about this, the more was she convinced that her father was correct about the age of these scrolls—he certainly did not create them himself! But, a moment's doubt entered in, perhaps that devil Selim had tricked him again, as he had with the Moabite idols and figurines! Could her father's reputation survive another incident of him being fooled like this?

It made her head hurt to think of all the variations of distress that were visiting upon them. She patted her mother's shoulder absently, but tried to reassure her, despite her own doubts.

"You'll see, mama, we will have a letter or telegram from papa any day now, telling us that the British Museum believes him, and has given him a cheque for a million pounds!"

But this only made Rosette shake her head, and cry all the harder. It had been several days since they had heard any news directly from Moses, and the newspaper article that their pastor, Mr. Green, had brought to the house to show them, was the first intimation that all was not going so smoothly in London.

"Let us go to the telegraph office ourselves, mama," Myriam said, thinking that perhaps taking some action might help them both. "We will send a telegram to papa, and beg him to write and tell us what is going on—surely one article by that horrid, horrid man cannot have so much influence as to ruin all our prospects!"

At length her mother was persuaded to calm herself, and they set off for the telegraph office. This was always an ordeal, as it was run by the Turkish government, and the clerks were at best indifferent, at worst, sneering and unhelpful. They were all ill-educated and officious, and Myriam was required to spell out every word and explain to them what each word meant—and, as her knowledge of Turkish was rather limited, this took a great deal of time and patience. In the end, what was sent to Moses in London was the following:

```
WE HAVE SEEN C-G'S ARTICLE IN PA-
PERS STOP PLS WRITE TO SAY ALL IS
WELL STOP LOVE AND BLESSINGS STOP
ROSETTE END
```

There was no reply that day, or the next, or the next. But in the next post there came a desperate letter from Augusta in Berlin, complaining bitterly about her father's long silence toward *her*. The school she attended told her the previous term's fees had not yet been paid, and they did not think they could accept her for the Fall term if the money did not arrive soon. Her bankers told her that nothing had been sent to them for some time.

"Oh! My poor Augusta!" Rosette cried. "The good God has indeed forsaken us!"

But there was more in the letter—Augusta said that the Schroeders, who had been so welcoming and friendly to her, were beginning to treat her coldly and without affection—

and even their son, her fiancé, was distinctly cool to her when they met, and talked of "changing circumstances" that might prevent their marriage!

This was a blow indeed, and Rosette and Myriam felt bereft of all comfort in their big, lonely house—people who had been honored to visit them now stayed away, and creditors instead camped on the doorstep with demands of payment.

They learned from subsequent articles in both the London and the Berlin papers, and from Augusta's letters, that there were still advocates in favor of Moses, although the preponderance of opinion seemed to be against him. In Germany the scholars who had examined the scrolls were especially furious, and hastened to publish that they had "never believed" in the first place that the manuscripts were authentic. Professor Schroeder was, perhaps, the loudest voice, protesting and claiming that he had actually warned Moses that the world would see through such an obvious piece of fakery!

The final blow came in a letter from the professor to Rosette, which urged her to enjoin her husband to stand up for himself, otherwise, he said, *"You will understand that if he cannot disprove all the accusations brought against him, we cannot possibly receive Elizabeth into our family, with its irreproachable record."*

* * *

Excerpts from the *London Daily News*, 22 August 1883, an article by an "unnamed expert":

MR. SHAPIRA'S DEUTERONOMY

"The interest both of scholars and the general public appears to be increasing with regard to the important questions raised by this manuscript, and as might have been expected, very diverse opinions are expressed with regard to its genuineness and value. Whatever may be the verdict eventually found, there can be no doubt that the arrival of the manuscript in this country will be long memorable in the history of literature. Dr. Ginsburg's work of examination and decipherment is not likely to be completed for two or three weeks; and meanwhile it may be well to hesitate before expressing an unqualified judgment....

...The portions of Mr. Shapira's manuscript exhibited last Friday and Saturday have been this week withdrawn from view. M. Clermont-Ganneau, whose name is well known in connection with the Moabite Stone, has published a letter, in which he claims to have proved that the manuscript is a forgery, and that it was written on slips cut from the margin of a comparatively modern synagogue-roll. He asserts that he has detected on one of the fragments the ending of the line which had served to guide the scribe who wrote the Hebrew roll, and which had extended on to the margin. This assertion will no doubt be fully inquired into. But the portion of the Deuteronomy manuscript examined by the present writer was written on leather of a thicker character, differing very considerably from that usually employed in synagogue-rolls.

Moreover, it is questionable whether on a purely speculative business it would have been worth while to mutilate and spoil a valuable roll. M. Clermont-Ganneau's evidence is also vitiated by the strong prejudice which he confesses he had previously entertained.

* * *

Excerpt from *The Standard* of the same day:

"The solemn farce of the 'Shapira Manuscripts' seems rapidly drawing to a close.... Indeed, our only wonder has always been how a fraud so transparent could for a single hour have imposed on the credulity of the experts who for the last three weeks have been wasting their learned leisure in discussing the authenticity of these scraps of dingy leather."

* * *

Myriam kept watch from an upper window for the mail cart coming down the Jaffa road—it was often two or three days late, what with rough seas and bad roads. It would take all the post to the post office, and then, as usual in the East, everyone would crowd around the door, calling out their names so the postman could look to see if there were letters for them.

She went there by herself, every few days, and braved the crowds of beggars and cripples along the road—she had no means to play Lady Bountiful these days, and felt ashamed and angry. Time and again she was handed a few envelopes, raising her hopes, only to have them dashed by reading someone else's name written there, and having to return them to the postman and wait some more.

No letter or telegram came from Moses Shapira; nothing came from him for them ever again.

FORTY-ONE

London — Tuesday, 18 March 1884

13 Tite Street – The Artists' Studios

WE DESCENDED UPON JOHN FAIRLY EARLY on Tuesday morning, before noon, although Mary had the foresight to send a note announcing our arrival, so we would not catch him in his dressing gown over breakfast. He welcomed us to the second floor, where he had his studio, and introduced us, on the way, to his fellow artist and American, Edwin Austin Abbey, an amiable, courteous young man who excelled in illustrating poetry and novels, and had lately been elected to the Royal Institute of Painters in Watercolors. He and John got on very well, and were very jolly in each other's company.

"You will forgive us, of course, John, for this intrusion," I said, as we settled ourselves on the chairs and sofa in the studio, "but there was scarcely any getting away by ourselves at Mary's house—as we didn't want anyone to know what we were planning—so we thought, why not come to the scene of the event? And here we are."

Mary drew out some sheets of paper from her large reticule, and a pencil, and was poised to take down names of guests. "We must do this quickly," she admonished. "If

Thursday is to be the evening, then we have no time to lose getting the invitations to our guests."

John nodded. "I assume you chose Thursday because Clermont-Ganneau will be engaged tomorrow night, and Friday evening is, no doubt, already in everyone's diaries booked for a play, or the opera, or some other such thing."

I smiled in agreement. "You show a commendable awareness of Society's schedules, John. That is indeed the case," I said. "Now, do you have any caveats or comments about guests? Mary and I have made our lists, and we think they are already quite complete." I handed him my list.

John thought a moment as he perused it. "I only bar married couples," he said, and grimaced. "And I imagine you can guess why." He handed the list back to me.

Mary looked nonplussed, but I guessed his meaning quickly. "So as to avoid the Caldecotts being here at the same time as Mrs. Callendar? That would be awkward, I admit. Very well, then." I turned to Mary. "There is a something or a nothing, as people say, between Mr. Caldecott and Mrs. Callendar," I explained. "Although I am inclined very strongly to vote on the side of 'something'."

Mary edited a final list for a few minutes, then read it aloud. "Mr. Henry James, Mrs. Stillman, Mr. Clifford"—

"Who is Mr. Clifford?" interrupted John.

"Oh, he's a portrait painter, like you John, only not anywhere near as good," she answered. "And he is the head of the Church Army operations in the slums—therefore, interested in biblical things, you know." John shrugged and Mary continued reading from the list.

"Mr. Theo Walter, Miss Charlene McCarthy, Mrs. Barstow, Mrs. Callander, Mrs. Mcloh and Mr. Walter Pater," she finished up.

"Don't forget Mr. Pater's sisters," I said. "He always goes about *cum ambolus sororibus.*"

John looked to be doing sums in his head. "That's twelve people right there—and with the three of us"—

"And Mabel," Mary said.

"And Mabel," John repeated, "and Lord Parke, Lady Emily, Dr. Ginsburg, Clermont-Ganneau and Lady Simmons-Hartley, that's twenty-one!" He looked around the room in dismay. "We can't fit twenty-one people in here, with food and drink and servers too."

Just then there came a light tap at the door, which was open, and Mr. Abbey begged entrance.

"I just want to offer my bit of space below, John," he said, "as you had mentioned you might be throwing a party, so I thought maybe you could use the room?"

"Excellent fellow!" John cried. "And in the nick of time! Yes, indeed, that would be capital, and of course, you are to be one of the party as well!"

I beamed at them both. "With the weather warming up as it is, it will be lovely to have access to the back garden through your studio, Mr. Abbey! How delightful!"

He bowed and smiled charmingly. "I shall be more than happy to attend the festivities myself, and only ask that I be allowed to invite two guests, in payment for the use of my studio—the two Misses Arnold, nieces of Mr. Matthew Arnold—will that be all right?"

"Absolutely unobjectionable," I said, and was joined by Mary and John in agreement.

"Now," I said, "before we can get this printed up—Mary knows a little printer who can do it quickly—we must determine how to word the special enticement that is to get our principal guests to this party." After a good deal of thought, writing down and crossing out and starting over, we came up with the final invitation:

Mr. John Singer Sargent
requests the honor of your presence
at his studio, 13 Tite Street, Chelsea,
at six o'clock in the evening
Thursday, 20th March
for a celebration and
special announcement regarding the
ancient biblical scrolls belonging to
the late lamented Mr. Moses Shapira.

The eminent scholar
Dr. Christian David Ginsburg
will be present
to make the announcement.

R.S.V.P.

"Quite satisfactory," John said, and all agreed.

Mary undertook to take the text to her printer and have cards made up, complete with envelopes, after which we would have a busy time addressing them and getting them in the late afternoon post. Every minute counted, especially with regard to our chief suspects, Lady Simmons-Hartley and M. Clermont-Ganneau. We trusted that Lord Parke was even now meeting with Dr. Ginsburg to persuade him to take part in this charade, and that he would be successful.

"Mary," I said, "I think it's entirely possible that Dr. Ginsburg and Lord Parke may have other scholars they think should attend, so please be sure to have extra invitations printed." Mary nodded and took her leave, promising to meet me at her parents' home as soon as humanly possible, where she and I and Mabel would address and post the invitations.

I looked around the room, and felt a little daunted by the idea of putting together a party with food and drink in less than three days—but once again Mr. Abbey came to the rescue.

"Dear Miss Paget," he said, with half a wink, "which I hope I may be privileged to call the august author Vernon Lee? I beg you will accept my assistance in planning the victuals and drinks part of this gathering?" His American accent, which in others I have found particularly nasal and grating, was melodic and cultured, and he was easy to listen to. "I have a most excellent cook at my house who is wasting away for want of anything to do other than serve up beans and toast for me of a morning—may I enlist her in planning for you and John?"

"Oh, my dear Abbey," John said before I could answer. "You are a savior!" He turned to me. "I have eaten some dinners at Abbey's and his cook is formidable. We shall have no worries about what we'll be serving."

We settled other details as the morning went on. At about noon, Lord Parke and Lady Emily turned up; they were introduced to Mr. Abbey, and Lord Parke reported on his successful talk with Dr. Ginsburg—the great scholar was at first reluctant to participate in our little scheme, but he soon saw the importance and seriousness of it, and was persuaded to take part from a deep sense of justice due to Mr. Shapira.

Lady Emily mentioned she would be visiting Lady Simmons-Hartley the next day, in mid-afternoon.

"Ah," I said, "then she is very likely to have received the invitation by then, but if not, you will be able to convey the request to her?"

Lady Emily nodded, looking rather serious, but determined to do her part.

Luckily, I was ready to depart at the same time as Lord Parke, and he graciously drove me to Kensington where I was just in time for a bit of luncheon with Mabel and Mrs. Robinson. Mary arrived a short time later with the printed invitations and envelopes, and we all sat down to accomplish our task with the satisfying result of posting the invitations by three o'clock.

Now, the waiting began, and I felt the tension grow hour by hour—the big question was, would Clermont-Ganneau accept the invitation, along with Lady Simmons-Hartley? And ultimately, a thought which none of us seemed to have asked aloud, what exactly did we expect would happen, and what would we do if "something" did happen?

FORTY-TWO

London — Wednesday, 22 August 1883

EDWARD BOND, THE CHIEF LIBRARIAN at the British Museum, was pacing furiously back and forth in Christian Ginsburg's office. He was holding a newspaper in his hands and pointing to it with an angry hand from time to time.

"My dear Ginsburg, you must now declare your opinion of these scrolls! We are in turmoil! An absolute storm of contention and baseless accusations—against us, here, in the Museum!—has been let loose in our world." He stopped his pacing and looked at his subordinate, who sat glumly at his desk. "I beg you, cease your examination and write a report, today."

Ginsburg slowly raised his eyes to look at Bond; he was weary to the bone, and the frustration and conflict he felt in his own mind about the scrolls—and his relationship to Shapira—showed in the tired planes of his face. He nodded his head. "You shall have it by the end of the day."

Bond looked relieved, then wary. "And you agree that it should be published in the papers as soon as possible?"

Ginsburg gave him a sharp, pained look. "Yes, of course, but under one condition—that I be allowed to give a copy of my report to Shapira before it becomes available to the papers."

The chief librarian looked as if he would object, but then nodded agreement. "It's only just," he said. He glanced around the room—the heat of August, although shielded by the trees in the inner courtyard, make the room fairly shimmer with warmth. "Well, then," he said gruffly, "I'll leave you to it."

Thursday, 23 August 1883

A large envelope was delivered to Moses Shapira at the Cannon Street Hotel the next day at noon. He was returning to the hotel after a melancholy late breakfast at a nearby café, where the constant flow of visitors to and from the great capital city ensured that no one was likely to recognize him as he sat over his eggs and toast and coffee. He was losing weight, and although he kept up his appearance with his beard regularly trimmed, his hair clean and combed, and well-made clothes on his back, his whole figure announced him as a disconsolate man.

As he passed through the lobby, he was reminded of how, just two weeks earlier, reporters and ardent biblical scholarly *amateurs* would surround him, asking questions and desiring his signature on the front leaf of their bibles. His attention was caught when he heard his name pronounced—looking up, he saw that the clerk at the front desk was beckoning him, holding out an envelope.

"This just came for you, sir," said the man, looking at him—so Moses thought—with a pitying eye. How would he be able to stand up under yet another scandal, in the eyes and minds of thousands, when this one man's condescension made him wish for instant annihilation!

He murmured his thanks, took the envelope, which he saw was from Dr. Ginsburg at the British Museum, and asked for his key. He trudged upstairs to his room. As he unlocked the door and stood looking at the well-furnished suite of rooms, another thought made him blanch, then turn red. He was almost out of money—and his banker in London had treated his last request for funds with a cool stare and a reluctant acquiescence. The hotel clerk's pitying look would soon turn to contempt, and he would be asked to leave—or possibly worse.

He sat at a table near the window and looked out at the summer day—a relentless sun, not a cloud in the sky, people scurrying by below, trying to stay in the shade of buildings and the few trees that grew near the railroad yards. London was hot and dusty, and it smelled of sweat and dirt and garbage. He closed his eyes and transported himself in memory back to the desert outside of Jerusalem, where he would ride his white horse, little Myriam settled in front of him, secure in his arms—the clear desert air rushing past, the scents of herbs and desert plants keen in his nose—how he longed to be home, right now, in his house, his shop, with his wife and children!

Moses looked at the envelope in his hands—it held whatever Fate was left for him in this world—he sighed deeply, and opened it. The first sentence almost killed him.

The manuscript of Deuteronomy which Mr. Shapira submitted to us for examination is a forgery.

This was followed by several pages delineating the evidence which proved the forgery to Dr. Ginsburg, both in the physical elements of the manuscripts and in the various mistakes and confusions of the actual text itself. Moses's astonishment grew as he read over the "proofs," and Ginsburg's conclusion that *"there were no less than four or five different persons engaged in the production of the forgery, and that the compiler of the Hebrew text was a Polish, Russian, or German Jew, or one who had learned Hebrew in the North of Europe."* He could not have pointed the finger more clearly to Moses than if he had named him outright.

Stunned, Moses sat still in his chair for nearly an hour—he could hardly think—he wanted to stop breathing. At length he took up a small piece of writing paper, a note, that had been included with Ginsburg's report—it was from Ginsburg himself.

My dear Shapira, I apologize most profoundly for the pain this will cause you. This report will be given to the newspapers for publication on Monday, 27 August. Sincerely, C. D. Ginsburg

Indignation and wrath rose in Moses's chest to counteract his misery—and he snatched up a pen and a slip of the hotel stationery. Surely his old friend—his former friend—must have known much earlier than today what he thought of the manuscripts—surely he could have warned Moses much earlier? And avoided all this publicity, which just served to feed the public controversy and lead to scandal? He had to respond to Ginsburg somehow, and he wrote blindly, just as the thoughts came to him.

Dear Dr. Ginsburg! You have made a fool of me by publishing and exhibiting things that you believe them to be false. I do not think I shall be able to survive this shame, although I am yet not convince that the MS is a forgery unless M. Ganneau did it. I will leave London in a day or two for Berlin. Yours truly, M. W. Shapira."

He sealed the letter and immediately rose and took it down to the front desk to be posted. He caught a glimpse of himself as he passed through the lobby with its huge mirrors in golden frames—he looked like a wild man, his hair sticking out where he had pulled at it, his clothes disheveled, his eyes bloodshot and staring. He hurried back to his room as quickly as he could, and started making plans to leave for Berlin at the first opportunity.

What he would do when he arrived there was anyone's guess. He just needed to be out of London before the newspapers were available on Monday. Despite every setback, he still believed that the manuscripts were genuine—and he felt a determination growing in him to show these prejudiced savants they were wrong.

* * *

Moses had left the city long before the first edition of the Monday *Times* was available, and it was a blessing he was not there to read it. The Editors wrote:

> "We publish this morning Dr. Ginsburg's report on the Shapira Manuscript. It is to the effect we anticipated from the first. The manuscript is pronounced to be beyond all question a forgery."

But the worst indignity of all—and how it happened is open to speculation—the newspaper published the note that

Moses had written to Ginsburg, and added the Editor's condescending comment:

> "He is so disappointed with the results of his bargain that he threatens to commit suicide. This, we venture to think, he will not do. He has survived the Moabite pottery fraud, and he will probably survive this new one. His wise course will be to return to Jerusalem, to follow up the fraud, and so endeavor to trace it to its origin. The story in its entirety will be so strange that it will be received with a welcome which will go far to make up to him for his present disappointment. If he has no story to tell, we can only profess ourselves sorry for him; consolation we have none to offer."

It was unlikely—and therefore another blessing—that Moses ever saw the horrid cartoon in *Punch* a week or so later, that played upon all the worst prejudices held by Britons and Europeans, of the deceptive, cunning Jew interested only in making money, and the enlightened Englishman exposing his fraud to the public.

PUNCH'S FANCY PORTRAITS.—No. 152.

MR. SHARP-EYE-RA.

SHOWING, IN VERY FANCIFUL PORTRAITURE, HOW DETECTIVE GINSBURG
ACTUALLY DID MR. SHARP-EYE-RA OUT OF HIS SKIN.

FORTY-THREE

London — Wednesday Late Evening, 19 March 1884

Lady Laura's Drawing Room

THE DRAWING ROOM FIRE HAD BURNED LOW by the time Clermont-Ganneau was expected at Lady Laura's Mayfair mansion; she had sent the servants—all but her butler—to their beds and awaited her lover in quiet, if cooling, solitude. She had not seen him since they parted in Rotterdam, and she was nervous about meeting him tonight—she held some secrets quite closely, and she suspected the same of him. Their partnership was breaking up, in more ways than one. She was going to have to be exceedingly careful with her canny, ruthless lover.

Her meeting earlier in the day with her friend, Lady Emily Allerton, had been a severe test of her nerves, and she feared she had not acquitted herself well. It had been some time since they had met, and the first few moments were awkward. But Lady Emily, ever perfect in politeness, smoothly began talking of familiar people and events, but then, when she noticed the invitation to the evening party being given by John Singer Sargent, open on the sofa where she sat, she had exclaimed that she was going to be there, too. Her fiancé, Lord James Parke, was on the Board of the British Museum, and was keen to attend.

They then spoke very briefly of the tragedy surrounding Mr. Shapira and his fraudulent scrolls, and speculated only a little about what the announcement might be that Dr. Ginsburg was going to make.

Lady Laura had feared that her manners were not equal to quell the agitation she felt upon discussing these things—she had not known that her friend was engaged—and to Lord Parke! And that they were both friends of that painter, Sargent—and he still had the scrolls in his possession! Her mind was in a turmoil, and she tried to appear nonchalant about her pursuit of biblical archaeology, which Lady Emily asked her about, indicating that she had lately not been very much interested in such things. Lady Emily did not mention anything about having met Shapira the summer before, in Lady Laura's drawing room; perhaps she didn't remember? And Lady Laura didn't bring it up.

Fortunately, two other ladies were then announced, and the general diffusion of topics and the serving of tea and cakes allowed her sufficient cover to regain her equanimity. Lady Emily had pressed her hand in a most friendly way when she left, and had murmured that she looked forward to seeing her at Sargent's studio the next evening.

Lady Laura was roused from her reflections by the butler opening the drawing room door and announcing her visitor. She steeled herself to act, as she always had with him, the part of the dependent lover.

"Charles!" she cried out when she saw him. The butler had already discreetly withdrawn. She threw herself into his arms and he patted her back lightly, speaking in low tones in French to *calm herself, all would be well.*

"Might I have some of that Scottish whisky you keep?" he at length requested, gently extracting himself from her grip. He looked into her tearful eyes, shaking his head slightly. "You look as if you could use some yourself, *ma cherie.*"

She nodded and allowed him to retrieve the decanter and pour out two glasses for them. After handing her a glass, and drinking half of his own, he shivered slightly and glanced at the fireplace.

"Oh, my dear!" he admonished, and adeptly built up the fire again so the room began to warm. He then sat next to Lady Laura on the sofa and pulled up a woolen blanket, lying half on the floor, and draped it around her shoulders, then began to chafe her cold hands. She began to revive after a few minutes.

"Ah, there are those English roses in your cheeks," he said, then sat back, took up the remainder of his whisky and, downing it quickly, poured another dram for himself.

"Tell me what is upsetting you so much, *cher Laure,*" he said.

She stared at him, blinking in the dim firelight. She called up all her acting abilities. "Have you not seen the newspapers? Do you not know?" Looking at him intently, she said, "I see that you do—you *do know* that Shapira is dead, yes? And by his own hand? And yet," she continued, with a hint of contempt in her voice, "You do not care one whit, do you?"

"We were always at odds, he and I," Ganneau said, twisting his glass in the firelight, sending sparks of light through the amber liquid. "His methods were beneath contempt—amateurish and deceptive, and I expect his past sins were lying very heavily upon his head. I am sorry for him that he should have decided to end it this way—very sorry for his family, I swear—but I cannot say that I was surprised to hear it."

"But he was in good health, when I saw him in Rotterdam!" Lady Laura blurted out. "Although not cheerful, he did not seem to me so desperate as to take his own life!"

Ganneau met this outburst with a deadly silence. "You—*saw*—him?" He said it slowly, still turning the glass in his hand, and fixing his gaze on her face, now pale with uncertainty. "This you did not tell me."

"I—that is—you remember, after he refused to see us at the hotel, that I said perhaps I should try to see him myself." Lady Laura fed the spark of anger that Ganneau's indifference to their colleague's death—and he was, after all, their colleague—had lighted in her. She pulled back from him on the sofa and sat up straighter, arranging her dress around her like a shield.

"Yes, I remember that," the Frenchman said, continuing to keep his gaze on her, "but you did not tell me that you had accomplished it."

With a swift motion as she threw aside the wool blanket, Lady Laura rose and walked to the fireplace. "There wasn't time—you were leaving that afternoon, by a different train, to return to Paris quickly." She turned to look at him from the greater distance, calmer and collected now. "And besides, nothing came of it."

"What had you hoped would have come from meeting with him, Laure?" It was said smoothly, but she could see she was going to have to be very careful—Ganneau was canny, with an almost sixth sense alert for undertones and nuances—for lies. For the first time in their relationship, she felt a *frisson* of fear. He was a dangerous man, and she was playing a dangerous game.

"Why, as we discussed, persuading him to sell the leather strips—as curiosities, as souvenirs, if you like—as a way of helping him recoup his losses," she recited this explanation as if she were quoting her lover from an earlier conversation. "Surely you recall that was how we talked about approaching him?"

Ganneau seemed to relax a trifle, and sipped at his whisky. Lady Laura, gaining confidence, moved closer to pick up the decanter and refill his glass, but as she reached for it, he suddenly grasped her wrist in a strong grip.

"What happened between you when you met him? Did you go to his room?" He softly growled the words, and gave a quick turn to her wrist, but she stifled a pained cry.

"Charles," she said, sternly and with great dignity, "let go of my arm, please." After a moment, he opened his hand and she took a step back.

"If you must know," she said, slowly walking around the room, "I did go to his room." She gave a low laugh. "Those foolish clerks at the desk, they had no idea that I was even there!" She glanced at Ganneau. "You know how invisibly I can get about, don't you? Well, it worked a treat at the Hotel Willemsbrug."

Ganneau abruptly seemed to lose interest. "And so you didn't get anything from him? Too bad, all that talented skulking about for nothing."

She gazed steadily at him, then shrugged. "He didn't have the manuscripts—he had sent them away to someone."

He then rose from the sofa and walked over to stand before her. He raised his hand to her face—she managed not to flinch—but he merely stroked her cheek with one finger. "Too bad for him," he said. "And for us." He paused and asked, mildly, "Do you have any notion who might have the manuscripts now?"

Lady Laura kept her gaze steady. "He would not say, and I do not know who has them now." Too late, she realized by the flare in his eyes that he knew she was lying. She had never told him about her attempts to take the scrolls from Sargent in Paris, and again in Rotterdam.

"Oh?" he said, sounding careless. He stepped back and retrieved a note from a pocket of his coat. "Then you didn't receive an invitation to this odd little *soirée* that Singer Sargent, the painter, is holding at his studio tomorrow evening?"

He waved the card at her and waited.

Defeated, Lady Laura dropped into the nearest chair. "Yes," she said wearily. "I received an invitation as well—and"—she broke off. She didn't want to bring up Lady Emily's visit to her this afternoon—she didn't want Ganneau to know about that connection.

"And what?" Ganneau said sharply.

"Nothing," she said, then, "are you going to attend?"

Ganneau seemed to be thinking it over. "Yes," he said decisively. "And so are you, my dear," he said. When she didn't protest, he continued, walking back over to her and, taking her by the hand, brought her to her feet. "We may very well have need of your *invisibility* again in this matter." Kissing the back of her hand, he let it drop, and just stood for a moment, as if deciding something.

"I must say, dear one," he said in a soft drawl, watching her closely, "when *I* saw him that night, he was in a terrible state."

She visibly started at the import of his words.

"You? *You*—saw—Shapira?" She reached to grasp his meaning. "After I was there? You stayed in Rotterdam? But how? Why?"

Ganneau smiled. "How indeed? Why indeed?" he echoed. "You are not the only one who can slink about as if invisible." He turned serious quickly. "There were some—documents—he had with him that I needed to see, and other issues between us that required some, shall we say, negotiation." He paused, then smiled again, faintly. "Colleague to colleague, you understand."

Lady Laura gazed at him in growing horror. "Charles! What are you saying? Charles, did you—did you murder Mr. Shapira?"

His brows shot up in pleased surprise. "I'm highly gratified that you think I am capable of such a thing, my dear!" he said, making a mock bow to her. "It seems my reputation as an adventurer has sunk into you quite deeply."

He moved toward her, leaning in, and kissed her cheek. His lips were cold. He whispered to her, "I know what he said to you—he said it to me as well." He paused. "When he saw you for what you are, that day in Rotterdam, did *you* drive him to his death, my dear?"

She gasped, and pulling back, she raised a hand to slap him, but he caught her wrist again, and laughed. "You may have cause to feel differently," he said, "but my conscience does not reproach me for anything." Then he bowed properly, and let himself out of the room.

Lady Laura's first thought was that his final statement was not inconsistent with the possibility he had actually killed Shapira.

FORTY-FOUR

Rotterdam — Wednesday, 5 March 1884

Last Days at the Hotel Willemsbrug

MOSES SHAPIRA WATCHED FROM HIS HOTEL ROOM window as Christian Ginsburg walked up the street toward the hotel. He had known the man for more than a decade; had shared important discoveries with him; had spent long hours discussing ancient Hebrew texts and marvelling at the artistic and intellectual abilities of long-dead scribes and rabbis. They were both born Jews—they had both converted to Christianity—a tie that, however unspoken, bound them together in deep ways. They had both, in their own paths, been successful—until the scandal of the scrolls had broken the arc of Moses's rise, and catapulted Ginsburg into celebrity status, for whatever that meant in the rarified air of biblical scholarship.

It seemed that discovering frauds, Moses considered, was a more certain way of gaining a reputation for cleverness and acuity than grinding away at translations of obscure texts, as Ginsburg had previously done. That same path had certainly served Clermont-Ganneau well, at Moses's considerable expense.

Moses turned away from the window and prepared to go down the stairs and meet his visitor in the lobby. He glanced around his room—his carpet bag gaped open on a chair, stuffed with documents, letters, and maps of various cities he had visited in recent months: London, Berlin, Amsterdam. He bent down to close the carpet bag, and his eye caught the glimmer of his good luck talisman that he kept in a little pocket inside the bag: the Star of David shekel embedded in cedarwood; he had cut it away from the goatskin headband after his last expedition, to take it with him on this journey with the scrolls. He drew it out and held it in the palm of one hand, while touching it lightly with his fingers. He felt his distance from Jerusalem as a constant ache in his heart; he had begun to doubt, at times, if he would see the beloved city again. He placed the coin back in its little pouch and wondered, sadly, if it would bring him good luck now, when he needed it so desperately.

On his desk were the seven leather strips of his original set of fifteen of the Deuteronomy; Ginsburg had sent them to him in January. He had asked for all of them, but Ginsburg had begged him to leave half the strips at the British Museum, as he had some thoughts of re-examining them, and promised to return them to Moses in good time. Moses did not press him, at the time, about what he meant by that. He thought with some gratitude that Ginsburg had sent him the strips that were in the best condition, the most readable. He covered the leather strips with their heavy cloth wrappings, so they would not be so exposed, and left the room.

* * *

The two men sat over the remains of a late lunch at a restaurant that was nearer the railway station than the hotel, as

Ginsburg was scheduled to return to London that evening. The scholar took out his pocket watch and consulted it; he had a little time left.

Moses watched him with a careful eye; their long discussion had both eased their mutual awkwardness and inflamed their mutual wariness of each other—a wariness that did not amount to actual distrust, and certainly not even dislike—their friendship was of too long a standing for that.

"My friend," Moses said at last, after long minutes of silence while they sipped at their final coffees, "your sudden arrival, and you leaving so soon, seems to me strange and not like you, and yet here we sit, all this time, and you have not come to what it is you are wanting to tell me, no?"

Ginsburg set his cup down carefully, his pale, whiskerless face growing rather pink.

"I'm not sure how to say this," he began slowly, "but I fear that others—one other in particular, I need not say his name to you—may attempt to get hold of the scrolls for himself. He came to the Museum in January and insisted on seeing them, to make another examination, you see."

Moses nodded. "I was asked then, by letter, to allow Ganneau to examine the strips that were there." He shrugged. "I saw no reason to keep him away, I even thought perhaps he was going to change his mind." He laughed, soundlessly and without mirth.

Ginsburg nodded. "He had applied to Dr. Rieu for the permission—I was not informed ahead of time—but when I heard that he was on the premises, examining the strips!" He shook his head in dismay. "I impulsively rushed in and tried to stop the proceeding, but only succeeded in making myself look foolish, like an old dotard anxious to protect his darlings."

"Do you know what he thought of what he saw?" Moses was curious, and suspicious.

Ginsburg shook his head. "I didn't want to ask him." He shrugged. "I told him that you had asked for the manuscripts to be sent to you, and that this would be his last chance to see them. I had no contact with him after that."

Moses was silent, wondering what he should say. Ganneau *had* approached him already once, that night in Haarlem, some weeks ago now—the night he made the acquaintance of that generous, friendly artist, Singer Sargent. It warmed his heart to think of the artist, the talk they had together, the wonderful dinner. But Ganneau—Moses had refused to listen to anything he had to say, and told him to be on his way, he wanted nothing to do with him—and the hateful man left with a sneering *au revoir.* He had wondered then how the Frenchman had known where he was to be found; now he presumed that somehow the man's connections in London had revealed where Shapira was—perhaps Rieu, who was friendlier to Ganneau than the others.

Ginsburg was watching him, and then leaned forward suddenly. "I just say this to keep you on your guard—if he were to approach you—you must keep the manuscripts safe, and if it cannot be done here, send them away to someone who can guard them."

Moses was puzzled by his tone and his warnings. "Why does anyone want my scrolls?" he said. "When you—and Ganneau—and all the world is set on saying they are frauds, and me as well?"

Ginsburg looked down into the dregs of coffee in his cup, and cleared his throat. "I have sometimes wondered, these past several months," Ginsburg said, talking slowly and with hesitation, "whether I—if it were possible that I—was too hasty"—he broke off, shook his head. "No, it was not haste that compelled my hand to write what I did—not haste, but ambition." He could not, apparently, bring himself to look up into his colleague's eyes.

Moses felt a tiny flicker of hope, then fear mixed with it, as he considered what Ginsburg was trying to say. He waited, nearly holding his breath, not moving.

After a moment, Ginsburg said in a low voice, "It has occurred to me, as I look over all the statements scholars have made—and only the ones who actually saw the scrolls, themselves, and worked on possible translations, of some or all of the characters—as I read those statements, it seems to me that so much of it is steeped in fear, the fear of change, the fear that what is known is wrong, and that one must give up a cherished notion for something new, something perhaps less comfortable." He shook his head, in anger at himself. "I followed like a craven recruit when I should have led the charge like a captain."

Moses had strained to hear every word, weighing his friend's tones of regret and sorrow with the scarcely believable meaning of his speech. He could bear it no longer.

"What is it you are saying, my friend?" he asked.

Ginsburg finally looked up, apologetic and shamed. "I have come to believe that I may have wronged you, my friend Shapira, and that those scrolls of yours may very well be the valuable ancient scripts you have always said they were—a proto-Deuteronomy that, if true, would have a tremendous impact on the world of biblical scholarship."

Moses was stunned, and did not try to hide his feelings from the scholar who sat with him. He put a hand to his forehead and closed his eyes. Tears leaked out slowly from under his eyelids, and he didn't even try to wipe them away. He was so very tired; it had been so very long since he had heard words of encouragement or friendship. After all these months of wandering, like his ancient ancestors in the desert lands—was God going to allow him to enter his own Canaan, unlike the original Moses, who had died in view of the Promised Land and was buried in an unmarked grave?

When he opened his eyes, he found Ginsburg looking at him anxiously, and he pulled himself together to speak.

"I thank you for your truth now, Ginsburg my friend," he said. "It warms my heart."

Ginsburg relaxed slightly, but then looked at his watch again.

"I must go meet the train," he said. But he still sat there, and spoke again. "And, soon, I hope you can return to London, with the rest of the scrolls, and maybe together we can work on them again—and that will help us see what should be done next."

Moses could only smile and nod his head; he felt incapable of speaking aloud. They both rose from the table and clasped hands, then embraced as brothers. Ginsburg gathered his things and set off for the railroad station, after paying the bill for their lunch. His parting words held a stronger warning. "I have reason to believe that your enemy is on the lookout for you—be safe, and keep the scrolls safe."

Moses made his way back to the Hotel Willemsbrug, his mind and heart at the same time lighter and yet, also heavier with an unknown dread—the fear, perhaps, of expectation and hope that might too soon be again betrayed and snatched away from him. He hurried his steps as he realized he had left the Deuteronomy fragments unguarded in his room—he would have to think quickly about how to keep them secure. He believed that Ginsburg's warning about their common enemy was valid; Ganneau's thwarted attempt to speak with him in Haarlem might drive him to more extreme methods.

He considered the possibility that he could just pack up and leave Rotterdam, head for Berlin, or perhaps even go home, to Jerusalem. But he had very little money, not enough even for a third-class ticket to Berlin—and he doubted whether there would be anyone in that city to welcome him. He winced as he thought of his poor daughter Augusta, bearing his shameful neglect of her school fees, and the likely disdain of Schroeder and his family—he hadn't given much thought to that before. Ginsburg had told him money would be forthcoming from some purchases that the British Museum had approved, so he would be obliged to wait here, in Rotterdam, until the funds were available at the bank. He was paid up at the Willemsbrug through Monday, so it was at least a place to stay until he could determine what and where his next move would be.

Moses decided that he must get the scrolls to a place of safety, and soon, and he nearly ran the rest of the way to his hotel. He was so anxious to get to his room that he did not even greet the desk clerk, as he usually did upon returning to the hotel, but only asked for his key and hurried up the stairs.

FORTY-FIVE

London — Thursday, 20 March 1884

The Party at the Studio

THE CROWD HAD SWELLED TO SOME THIRTY PEOPLE or more by the time our party was in full swing. I'm not sure how that happened, but then, one person decided to bring along a sister or brother, and another person (actually, John did this) found that Oscar Wilde and his fiancée Constance Lloyd happened to be taking a look at a house Wilde had just bought, two doors down, and he persuaded them to join us. Mr. Abbey was imposed upon for another couple of daughters of aged literary lights, and so there you are, full house.

But with no less than five official hosts and hostesses— myself, Mary, John, Lord Parke and Mr. Abbey—there were no gaps in welcoming guests and showing them about— some to the back garden, champagne coupes or glasses of ginger beer in hand, others to the upstairs studio, to gaze upon John's unfinished portrait of Lady Playfair, still others admiring Mr. Abbey's watercolors and illustrations, on display in his studio.

We were quite a lively group—and I felt it all over in my nerves and especially my stomach. How was it all going to end? The principal guests had not yet arrived—Ginsburg, Clermont-Ganneau and Lady Laura Simmons-Hartley—and my attention was continually diverted from various conversations as I kept my eye on the door, anxious for their arrival.

The Shapira Scrolls—the ones that had been sent to John—were encased in a locked vitrine in the principal room on the ground floor, behind a heavy velvet curtain. We five had planned beforehand that one of us was to stand near the curtain at all times; it was currently my post, and as it gave a clear view of the front door, I was able to maintain guard and keep watch for our important guests.

Lord Parke happened to be on hand just at the moment that Dr. Ginsburg arrived at the door, so he was able to usher him in, get him a glass of something good and a plate of food, and lead him out to the garden. Mary came up to me from time to time.

"Isn't there something I can get you, Violet?" she asked, as always thinking of others. She glanced at her watch. "It's almost seven, then I can relieve you and you can walk about and get some fresh air."

I was about to thank her for her kindness when a little stir at the door caught my eye, then riveted my attention: a most extraordinary couple had just entered—larger than life, I would have to say—a tall, very handsome and very arrogant gentleman dressed to the height of French fashions for men, and at his side a vision of blonde loveliness in a shimmering, peacock blue gown and cape—they could be none other than Ganneau and his paramour, Lady Laura.

Where was Lord Parke? Or Lady Emily? Surely they should be the ones to greet these guests? But I had momentarily forgotten that Mary and Lady Laura had been schoolmates, so as I turned to her she was already moving forward to greet her friend. I watched avidly as she approached the couple in the doorway, who were divesting themselves of their outerwear to one of the trim, adorable little models John had hired for the occasion.

"Lady Laura, you are most welcome," Mary said in an admirably friendly voice. "I had assured Mr. Sargent that you would be interested in this event, and I am so glad to see that I was correct. It has been too long since we have met." And the two ladies cordially pressed kisses on each other's cheeks, while (I noticed) Clermont-Ganneau quietly took in Mary's radiant beauty.

"Mary, it has indeed been too long," Lady Simmons-Hartley said; then turning to her companion, "May I introduce you to monsieur Charles Clermont-Ganneau? Miss Mary Robinson, the acclaimed poet and author of a splendid biography of Emily Brontë."

"Absolutely delighted!" cried Mary as she held out her hand. She continued in French (her French is excellent, much better than mine, which is, I admit, more than good), and the three of them slowly moved into the room, speaking rapidly and laughing at some witticism of Ganneau's. Mary had been instructed to find a way to nonchalantly inform them that the scrolls were to continue at the studio for the next day or two, as John considered himself as their guardian, if temporarily.

I saw her help provide them with drinks and move toward the garden, where I could see, through the studio windows, that Lord Parke and Lady Emily were chatting gaily with a small circle of friends. I couldn't determine where Dr. Ginsburg had got to. After a little while, Mary once more appeared at my side, ready to take my place on guard before the velvet curtain, and greeting new guests, although by my private count, I believe that nearly everyone we had invited had arrived.

"I think we are free to allow any stragglers to let themselves in," I said. "After all, we are in the heart of Bohemia, are we not? Where all forms and regulations of polite society are set at naught?"

"I don't think even you believe that, Violet," Mary said, "despite what you are busy writing in *Miss Brown*." But a kind smile took any possible sting from the hint.

"Well, especially now that all our most prominent— guests, I should say, although I almost said suspects!—have shown themselves, we shall be able to get on with the chief event of the evening." I looked around again. "I wonder where Dr. Ginsburg is?"

I was prevented from looking for him as Mr. Henry James caught my attention—he was gingerly descending the stairs from John's studio, his brow wrinkled as he winced from his typically too-tight shoes—and I hurried over to meet him.

"Dear Mr. James," I cried, and he looked up only when he had gained the solid floor, and fixed his mild grey eyes upon me.

"Dear Miss Lee," he said, nodding politely. "What an entertaining society you all have gathered here this evening." A gleam in his eye told me he was, as usual, taking in every detail the guests had to offer—clothes, faces, conversation, reactions and silences, pairings and flirtations. I briefly wondered what he thought of the contrast between me in my high-collared, black brocade and the two Robinson sisters, fairy-like and charming in their lovely white frocks. What would he make of a friendship with such contrasts?

We stood for a moment together, looking at the crowd. "I hope you will forgive the impertinence," I said to him in a low voice, deciding to seize the opportunity, "but I beg to be allowed to dedicate my first novel to you, Mr. James, as a great inspiration to writers of fiction." I looked at him hopefully, although I certainly didn't expect he would decline the request. "I am titling it *Miss Brown*."

"I am deeply honored," he said, and bowed to me. "It is a good title."

John came bounding down the stairs just then, and caught us up in his enthusiasm. "Shall we start the main event, then?" he said. But then he was diverted by seeing Oscar Wilde and Constance coming towards us, and held out a hand to them.

I had met Wilde before, but not his fiancée, and while introductions were exchanging, I noticed that after a brief nod, Henry James managed to slip quite away from the Irish Presence. I rather liked Wilde; he so slyly mocks everything, especially when he seems to be praising it.

The ebb and flow of guests soon parted us, and John and I sought out Lord Parke and Dr. Ginsburg, to finally get to the point of this soirée. I admit to feeling both impatient and in dread of the event, but high-ho, as the English say, the hunt was on and we could but ride to flush out the fox.

We engaged Mabel to run upstairs and let everyone who was in John's studio know that Dr. Ginsburg was going to be making his announcement shortly. Mary did the same for people out in the garden, and finally, John, his voice carrying through the noise of conversation and laughing, called the company to order.

The downstairs space was just about large enough to hold everyone, with some people lounging on the stairs and looking over the banisters. We had shepherded Dr. Ginsburg to a place in front of the velvet curtain; I was stationed to one side, prepared to pull the curtain open at the appropriate moment, and Lord Parke was standing next to Dr. Ginsburg, in order to introduce him. He caught my eye and winked discreetly.

I couldn't help but see that the Frenchman Ganneau and Lady Simmons-Hartley had stationed themselves very near the front of the crowd, though off to the side a bit, so as to command a full view of the proceedings. That his very presence served to intimidate Dr. Ginsburg was not apparent, but I noticed that the English scholar paled slightly when he caught sight of his detested colleague.

Lady Emily caught up a fork and tapped it lightly on her champagne glass, bringing about a respectful silence. Lord Parke smiled his thanks to her, and began to speak.

"Ladies and gentlemen, you are all most welcome to this special evening of Art and Science—our hosts, Mr. John Singer Sargent and Mr. Edwin Austin Abbey, have delighted our eyes with a display of their fine paintings and sketches, and now we come to the 'science' part." He paused for effect, and became more sober.

"No one who was here in London last August will have forgotten the intense, public discussions over what was to become the scandal of the Shapira Scrolls—manuscripts said by their owner, Moses Shapira, to be the earliest known writing of the book of Deuteronomy, some three thousand years old." He paused again, seeing many heads nodding in agreement. "You can also not have missed the most recent news of the sad death of Mr. Shapira, in Rotterdam, about ten days ago, and I know I speak for many of us when I express our sorrow that a once-prominent person, who discovered many ancient scrolls and statues of real value to scholarship, should have met his end so tragically."

There were a few murmurs and whispers at this, and I couldn't help but look at Ganneau and his lady—his face held an undisguised smirk of satisfied contempt, while hers looked shaded and a bit sad.

Lord Parke continued. "We have here tonight a portion of those scrolls, which you will all be able to see in a few moments, and about which we will hear a statement from Dr. Christian David Ginsburg, scholar and Semitic expert at the British Museum. I give you Dr. Ginsburg."

The guests politely applauded, and looked expectantly at Ginsburg as he took the center stage.

"I am here tonight, ladies and gentlemen," he said, his voice firm, "to announce that a new examination of the Shapira Scrolls will be undertaken by me, and other scholars, in light of some new evidence and ideas that have prompted us to take a second look."

Some people looked surprised and interested; others looked as if they wondered why they should care. Ganneau's brows lowered and a red flush began to creep up his neck.

"I say this with the full disclosure that I am by no means declaring that the scrolls are, after all, authentic, and as ancient as Mr. Shapira claimed they were—but I *am* saying that they deserve another examination, and it is very possible that the conclusion to be reached may be very different from the one that was announced by so many, including myself, last August."

He nodded to Lord Parke that he was finished, and that the curtain could be drawn aside. But before I could start, a cultured voice rang out over the room.

"I must insist on speaking!" Of course it was Ganneau. All eyes turned to him. "This is a travesty, and an insult, and nothing but a publicity stunt to further the base ambitions of a second-rate scholar! The poor man is barely cold in his grave and you bring him forward for mockery even after his death! Shame on you, sir, shame!"

Ganneau smiled in smug triumph as the other guests gasped and began to murmur. I whispered to John, who stood near me, "The Germans have a word for a man such as he—*backpfeifengesicht*—a face badly in need of a slap." John suppressed an appreciative grin.

Apparently Ganneau had said his piece, but as he took Lady Simmons-Hartley by the arm to lead her out the door, I thought I saw her stiffen, as if to reject his grasp; but not being the kind of person to make a scene (I conjectured), she allowed herself to be escorted through the crowd and away.

I pulled aside the curtain, and the room exploded with noise and exclamations and calls for more champagne as people surged forward to look at the scrolls.

But the trap was set, and now the real waiting would begin.

FORTY-SIX

Rotterdam — Thursday Morning, 6 March 1884

Last Days at the Hotel Willemsbrug

THE LEATHER STRIPS HAD BEEN UNDISTURBED, when Moses had returned from his lunch with Dr. Ginsburg, and now, the next morning, they lay in their cloth wrappings on the desk in his hotel room. He contemplated them with mixed feelings of sorrow and concern. He was determined to take seriously Dr. Ginsburg's warnings of the day before, but he was puzzled about what to do. He wandered once more to the window, and was standing there when he heard a gentle tap on his door.

"Yes?" he called out, suddenly apprehensive.

"It's Angela," said a young woman's voice, and he relaxed. The maid, come to tidy up. He strode to the door and let her in, smiling as he did so. She was a cheerful, pretty, hard-working girl, and she was very pleasant to him.

"Good morning, my dear," he said, showing her in and closing the door. "I am afraid I will be in your way some today, as I am not going out so soon."

"That is no problem, sir," she answered, smiling back at him. "You're easy to get around, and there's not that much to do." She proceeded to make her rounds of dusting and sweeping, remaking the bed and straightening up, exchanging towels and soap.

Moses had returned to gazing out the window, almost forgetting the maid who moved quietly around the room. He started with a low cry, however, a moment later, as he watched two people approach the hotel from across the street. The man happened to look up, his eyes searching the front of the hotel, and Moses was not quick enough to step back from the window—he saw, and was seen by, Charles Clermont-Ganneau, his nemesis. The woman with him was none other than Lady Laura Simmons-Hartley—a discovery which sent a piercing pain through his whole being. Her glorious blonde hair floated free under a small blue hat, and the electric blue of her gown and cloak seemed to reflect all the feeble sunshine that the grey sky had to offer.

"What's wrong, sir?" he heard Angela saying. She may have said it twice before she gained his attention.

"What's that? Oh, nothing, child, nothing," he said, quite distracted. Would they dare to just come to his room? Would they not have to apply to the front desk, and send up a message?

Not five minutes later there was a discreet knock on his door, and he heard the youthful voice of the bellboy. "Message for you, Mr. Shapira, from the front desk."

Puffing out a breath of relief, he opened the door, told the boy to wait, and read over the message—a Mr. Eglantine, indeed! He almost laughed. He shoved the note in his pocket and said to the bellboy, "Tell Josef that I am not at home to this gentleman, not now, not ever." He gave the boy a penny and watched him scamper back down the hall.

More discreetly now, he watched from behind the curtain to the street below. Soon he saw the two visitors leave the hotel—and indeed, Ganneau's eyes once more scanned the windows, searching for a sign of his quarry, but eventually gave up and walked away, Lady Laura beside him.

Moses went again to his desk, and gathering up the scrolls, wrapped them carefully in their cloths, and placed them inside another bag made of cloth.

Angela was still in the room, making up the bed.

"My dear," he said. "Do you know if nearby is some shop to buy paper to wrap a package? And some string? Something I have to send by post." His English always came out worse when he was distressed.

The maid thought a moment, then nodded. "There is a little stationer's shop on the street behind the hotel— Schmidt's, I think it is, sir—he would have what you need."

Thanking her, he threw on his overcoat, took up the bag of scrolls and opened the door. He would take the back stairs, through the door right next to his room, and leave the hotel secretly—he feared his enemy might be watching the front.

"Angela, my dear girl," he said, looking at her with affection—he had told her before that she reminded him of his dear Myriam, they were about the same age—"could you please do me the favor to not come tomorrow? I must be alone and quiet a few days."

"Of course, sir," she said, nodding. "I understand. I will lock your door when I am through. And as I won't be in on Saturday or Sunday, why then, I'll see you bright and early Monday morning, won't I, sir?"

"Yes, yes, of course you will," Moses said, looking at her intently. "I wish for you all good things, my dear, and that you will always be happy and good." He patted his pocket to make sure he had his key, and then he left the room.

* * *

His errand accomplished, Moses turned with a heavy heart to walk back from the post office to the Hotel Willemsbrug. He wasn't sure why he had followed the intuition he'd felt about sending the scrolls away—and to Paris, to a person not well known to him—but he felt satisfied it was the right thing. Regardless, it was done, and there was no going back now.

He found he had little appetite, but he stopped on the way back at a little café he'd been to several times since moving into the hotel, and ordered coffee and a sandwich. It was long past noon, and the day was growing dark. He should go back and get started again on the most recent sets of manuscripts he was transcribing—a Torah from a Russian synagogue, very old, some six centuries, and difficult to read.

He decided it was safe to arrive through the front door, and, nodding to the young man there—not Josef, someone taking his place for the evening perhaps—he trudged up the stairs. He didn't think he'd come down for dinner tonight; his stomach was nervous and upset.

As he was turning the key in the lock, a small shadow stepped out from the recessed doorway to the back staircase. It was Lady Laura Simmons-Hartley, her electric blue garments changed for a slim-lined dress and cloak of black, and a hood gathered over her sunny golden hair.

"Shapira," she whispered, and put a hand out to touch his arm, but withdrew it when he flinched.

He looked quickly up and down the hall—there was no one in sight; in fact, he didn't think there were any other guests on this floor, as he'd never heard or seen anyone. Clearly, she had seen him leave from the rear of the hotel, and used the stairs herself to come up to this floor.

"Come inside, quick," he whispered, and opening the door, motioned to her to go before him. Once inside, he locked the door and put the key on the desk, while Lady Laura threw the hood back from her head, letting her blonde curls fall across her shoulders. She was looking intently around the room, as if searching for something in particular.

"What are you here for?" Moses asked, standing quite still in the center of the room, not even taking off his overcoat. When she didn't answer, he scoffed at her. "Did your paramour Ganneau send you to make love to me? And take my documents?"

"I am no thief!" she said with some asperity. "Do you think I would take something from you, who have been my friend and colleague? And why do you mention Clermont-Ganneau?"

And more than that, Moses thought, and wondered that she did not say *that* aloud. No matter—everything was changed now. He held his temper—and his sorrow—in check.

"I saw you with him, with mine enemy," he said. "You thought to come up here, but why? To make me feel worse is not possible."

Lady Laura gazed at him with sad sympathy. "Oh, my dear Shapira, you have been so unjustly treated, you must know that is what I think."

He regarded her with suspicion. "What you think and what you do are different things," he said slowly. He thought of Ginsburg's warnings, and his suggestion that even Ganneau may have changed his mind about the authenticity of the scrolls. He watched her narrowly, and wondered at her coolness when she took a small bottle of Toquay wine from her reticule and proceeded to open it at the washstand.

"I think this calls for a bracing cordial," she said. There were two small glasses face-down on paper doilies on the washstand; turning them over, she poured some of the golden liquid into each one. With one in her hand, she walked away and looked at Moses with a smile meant to be encouraging. Her face was pale, but two flushed spots appeared high on her cheeks, and her lips looked unnaturally rosy, as if she had put rouge on them.

"What are you here for?" he said again. He felt the weight of his overcoat heavy on his shoulders, and unbuttoned it, shrugging it off and draping it over the back of the desk chair. Lady Laura stood nearer the window but, he noticed, not so near that she would be seen by someone looking up from the street below. His mind worked quickly.

"He doesn't know you have come here, yes?" he said. She glanced at him, and moved further back from the window.

"That is the case," she admitted. "He has gone back to Paris. I am to go back to London tomorrow."

"How can I trust what you say?" Moses said, a note of sorrow creeping in. "You are partner with him, the man who ruins me, over and again, a man who sneers, his lip curled, as is said in the Psalm."

She turned her face away, but spoke in a low voice. "Won't you have a drink with me, Shapira? Please?"

Moses felt a moment's pity, his heart relenting to hear the suffering in her voice. He walked the few steps to the washstand and took up the glass. For a moment, it crossed his mind that it was poison he was about to drink. He felt his heart break, and quaffed it down in one gulp.

She smiled then, and raised her glass. "To the best days gone by," she said. He nodded, and put his glass down on the washstand again, but Lady Laura held on to hers, sipping at it slowly

"How can you be with such a one?" Moses said in reproach, his anger mixing with his sorrow. "You, so curious and interested—what devil's trick does he play you? To make you love him?" He shook his head, keeping the tears at bay. "You haff broke mine *herz*, to see you with him."

She looked up sharply at that, then shook her head. "It is a kind of love, a painful and aching love, but so be it, it binds me to him, and I cannot help myself." She stood still and silent, a look on her face as if she were amazed at the words she had spoken aloud, as if she had never thought or said them before—and now stood face to face with them. She downed the remainder of the liqueur in her glass.

Moses felt the darkness of her captivity wave over him, and shook himself to withstand it. *Remember Ginsburg's warnings*, he told himself.

"Does he want my poor scrolls?" Moses asked her directly, watching carefully.

After a moment, she nodded. "Yes, he wants them," she said. She looked at Moses with a wan smile. "Will you give them to me—never mind him!—will you do this for me?"

Moses was struck by her sweetness and her woundedness; that man held her so tightly in his grip she couldn't even breathe, much less think for herself. It steeled his resolve, however, to thwart his enemy, even though it might further injure her—but it also might set her free.

He shook his head. "I send them away," he said. "I send them to—to a friend."

She stared at him, unbelieving. "You gave them to someone else? Who? That dotard Ginsburg?" Her voice rose in sudden fury. "Who else deserves them more than I, and Ganneau? He at least knows what they are worth!" She froze suddenly, as if she'd said too much, but she pressed on. "You are ruined, you can never regain your reputation now—why don't you just accept that and let someone else take their chance?"

Moses watched her curiously, through a mix of grief and pain at her condemnation, but he felt no need to defend himself. "How did you even know I am here?" he said, his suspicions returning in force.

A knock on the door halted their conversation, and putting a finger to his lips, Moses stepped to the door and opened it part way. It was the bellboy, with the late afternoon post. Moses stepped outside the door, almost closing it, and accepted the small pile of mail. But then he spoke to him. "Son, please tell Josef to hold any more mail or packages for me for the next few days, I do not wish to be disturbed again—I have told Angela not to come in to tidy up tomorrow—just have him keep my post at the desk, I will come down for it eventually."

When Lady Laura saw that Moses had stepped into the hall, she quickly moved over to where his coat hung from the back of the chair, and began looking through his coat pockets—clearly he had just come back from an errand; and after having parted from Clermont-Ganneau in the street, she had doubled back, gone to the rear of the hotel, and watched Moses leaving with a small package. He must have gone to post the scrolls to his friend!

Her fingers touched a piece of paper in an inner pocket of his coat, and she drew it out—it was a post office receipt for a package mailed to Paris—no street address, just a badly spelled destination: *The famous portret painter, John Sarjeant, Paris, France.* She folded it quickly and put it in her pocket.

The door opened slightly as Moses was finishing up his conversation with the messenger, and Lady Laura stepped over to the washstand as Moses began to re-enter the room. She knew who Sargent was; she even knew some of his friends. He wouldn't be hard to find. She would make for Paris directly—and she wouldn't tell Ganneau she was there—it would be a surprise for him—how he would laugh! All this went through her mind swiftly as she re-capped the liqueur bottle and put it back into her reticule. Taking hold of a little hand-towel on the washstand, she wiped her glass and replaced it, top down, on its little paper doily.

Moses had come back into the room and was looking at her keenly, with half a glance at the open carpet-bag on his desk, but he seemed satisfied that nothing had been disturbed.

Lady Laura lifted her chin, self-consciously assertive. "I think we have nothing further to say to one another," she said, and made as if to move toward the door, but Moses stepped in front of her.

"I could wish that we would part a different way," he said haltingly; he couldn't help the tears that moistened his eyes.

That she was affected, he could readily see. But that she would not give in, would not change her feelings, was also clear.

"I could wish that, too," she said softly, surprising him. "But I fear this will be our last meeting, ever, Shapira," she said, his name on her lips sounding like a sweet caress.

He stepped out of her way, and bowed his head so he wouldn't see her walk out the door.

FORTY-SEVEN

London — Thursday Late at Night, 20-21 March 1884

At the Studio

WE HAD GONE OVER OUR PLANS until we were thoroughly tired of thinking, but it was necessary to be prepared for anything that might happen. I insisted that Mary and Mabel return to their parents' home—I would never forgive myself if by placing them in danger they would suffer some injury, and naturally, even if that didn't occur, their parents would dislike me even more. So John and Lord Parke and I—and Mr. Abbey, whom we couldn't exclude because it was his property as well as John's, but who was a stalwart American and a good man in a pinch, as we would find out—so, the four of us stationed ourselves in hidden places around the ground floor, in sight of or close enough to the scrolls in the vitrine to interrupt any attempt to take them.

We'd had quite a debate about whether to close the velvet curtains or leave them open. I argued to keep them closed—why make it easy for a potential thief? And wouldn't they expect we would conceal them?—but John thought that they might obscure our own view of anything going on, and said we should draw them back. In the end, my views won out, and the heavy curtains were closed.

I should have kept my mouth shut.

Lord Parke and I pretended to leave after the party was over, sometime around ten o'clock (Lady Emily had departed much earlier) but we shortly circled around and entered through the back of the house, with John waiting at the garden gate that opened to the mews. Lord Parke and I stayed out of range of the windows, and we kept conversation to a minimum. John and Mr. Abbey—I might as well call him Edwin, as we all became fast friends after that night—made a show of standing at the front door, smoking and talking and having a last drink, then tamping the fire, turning out lights, and each one going off to bed. Shortly before midnight, the house was completely dark and quiet. This being Chelsea, however, the noises from the streets continued for another hour or so, carriages with singing revelers, quick steps on the pavements, a drunken passenger hallooing up to the driver as they passed.

Then all was completely quiet.

Although I sat comfortably enough on a straight-backed chair, hidden in a recess of the staircase on the ground floor, I felt every itch and constraint multiply and grow in severity as I endeavoured to keep still. My eyes had grown quite accustomed to the dark, although the rooms were particularly black and full of shadows, as the gas lamps on the street were too far away to help lighten up the interior of the house. It was so quiet I could hear the tick of the dying coals in the fireplace.

Edwin was stationed in his studio, directly across from the scrolls in the vitrine; John was near the door to the garden—there were only two doors, that one and the front door, so we assumed the thief, whoever he or she was going to be, would come through one or the other; and Lord Parke stood guard at the front door, standing against the wall so that if the door opened, he would be concealed behind it, as well as behind a large-leafed plant, which helped to hide him further.

We had agreed to allow any intruder to enter the house unmolested, as we wanted to catch him (or her) in the act, so to speak, so we would be certain it was the scrolls they were after.

I had nearly pitched forward on my hard chair, my eyes closing in sleep, when I heard the sound of the garden door opening. We had decided not to lock that door—but someone coming in that way would have to get through the gate with its sturdy lock, or leap over the high garden walls—obstacles enough, we had thought.

Well, someone had done all that, and was now about to enter the house.

I could almost feel my colleagues all holding their breath as a small and dark shape slipped like a shadow into the room that opened to the garden. Surely it was the blonde—surely that was Lady Laura! The thief glided across the floor, making no sound, and the shadows hid her form exceedingly well—she passed by me as I sat shrinking into my own shadow of the staircase, not daring to breathe. She all but disappeared as she approached the velvet curtain— its soft darkness seemed to bar any light from coming near, and she melted into it as if she had literally passed through the barrier like smoke through an open window.

I could neither hear nor see anything. There was no movement, no sound, not even the scrape of a lockpick in the vitrine keyhole. Damn those curtains! Why had I persuaded everyone they should remain closed! I was desperate to move, to cry out, to do *something* to break the stillness. Was the thief going to get away in this almost liquid night air?

Suddenly, a shout—from John, still near the garden door.

"Hie there, you!" he cried, and as I rose from my chair, I saw him, his form large against the dim windows that faced the garden, leap at a small shadow that was making for the door. There was a crash and a grunt, a muffled cry.

Lord Parke dashed from behind the large plant, holding a lantern which he quickly and efficiently lighted, while still making for the garden room.

The flare of gaslight was in a very real way not at all helpful, as it blinded us by focusing our eyes on its light and throwing everything else into shadow. I felt rather than saw the small form break away from John and dash toward the front door.

"Oh no, you don't!" I cried, and ran forward to intercept her. At that moment, Edwin stepped out of the doorway to his studio, looking much larger than he appeared in daylight, and caught the fleeing figure in his arms. She cried out, started kicking and beating at him. I grabbed a large coat from a hook near the staircase and ran to the struggling duo, holding the coat before me and ultimately throwing myself on the smaller form as she still struggled with Edwin. Finally, she was subdued, and Edwin and I held her down until she stopped moving about.

John and Lord Parke lighted several more lamps around the rooms, and we all came to stand before our quarry. John lifted the coat and there lay Lady Laura, her blonde hair escaped from her black navy man's tight cap, bleeding a little from a cut on her cheek, and looking altogether miserable and resigned to her fate. A small carpet bag lay beside her, open, and the leather strips were stuffed inside. She had almost—*almost*—gotten away with them.

* * *

Soon we were seated around a dining table in the garden room, lamps lighted, the fire going, and hot tea in our cups and biscuits on a large plate before us. No one had as yet said anything, especially Lady Laura, who had refused any food or drink and just sat sullenly, her eyes closed.

Lord Parke looked at me, one brow lifted in a question. I nodded—he should start, he was the one most acquainted with Lady Laura—they were the most like.

"Laura," he said slowly, and waited until she opened her eyes and looked at him. "I think an explanation would be most helpful."

She narrowed her eyes at him. "Are you going to call the police?" It was bravado, I could see; she was really frightened. I spoke up, softly.

"Do you think this is a matter for the police?" I said.

She looked at me, puzzled, then pulled at her lower lip with her teeth. She shook her head. "No."

"Then tell us what is going on," Lord Parke said. "This doesn't have to end badly for you."

I know he was trying to be encouraging, but I shook my head slightly at him. Lady Laura shrugged; she looked completely weary. "I don't even know where to start," she said.

"Then let us help you," John said suddenly. He leaned forward—he was sitting across the table from her. "Was it you who broke into my studio that night, looking for the scrolls?"

"Yes." She raised her head cautiously.

"How did you know that I had them?" he said.

"I saw your name on a receipt in Shapira's room," she said, and added, with the ghost of a smile, "despite his bad spelling, and it wasn't hard to find you in Paris."

"So you may have been the last person to see Mr. Shapira alive," I said. It sounded brutal, but I wanted to test her.

She looked troubled. "I—that is—I wasn't the last, no," she said. She closed her eyes tightly, then opened them again, seeming determined now. "I have no desire to protect him—Clermont-Ganneau told me he went to see Shapira in his hotel room," she said, defiantly. "Later in the evening of the same day I saw him, on the Thursday before his death."

"Did you know this at the time?" Lord Parke asked.

She shook her head vehemently. "I thought he'd already left to return to Paris—that is what he was supposed to do. I was to leave the next day."

I regarded her thoughtfully. "Did Ganneau know that *you* went to see Shapira?"

She answered with a quick negative. "I only told him that later, here in London—that's when he told me that he had seen Shapira too."

We were all silent a moment. There was the sound of truth in her voice, but I wasn't ready to absolve her yet.

"Do you think Ganneau could have killed Mr. Shapira?" I asked.

She looked puzzled. "*Could* have? Do you mean, is he capable of murder? Yes, I truly believe that—but, *did* he kill

Shapira?" She shook her head. "He said he did not—actually," she stopped to correct herself. "What he *said* was that his *conscience did not reproach him* for anything he had done—that was his answer when I asked him if he had killed Shapira." She looked at each one of us.

"That doesn't leave out the possibility that he *did* kill him," John said. We were all silent for a moment.

"I thought the police in Rotterdam determined that Shapira had killed himself, shot himself with his own gun," Lady Laura said, almost in a whisper.

Lord Parke answered. "Yes, that is their official position, and I don't believe they think they have any evidence to controvert it."

I was growing impatient to get to the heart of the matter. "Why did—why *does*—Ganneau want the scrolls? Did he send you here to take them? And were you going to deliver them to him tonight?"

Lady Laura looked at me appraisingly; she had regained some composure, especially, I think, because she felt more confident that we were not going to turn her over to the police. "You are a friend of Mary Robinson's," she said.

I acknowledged it with a quick nod of my head, but gave her a look that meant, *I'm still waiting for answers.*

"Charles thinks it's possible the scrolls may be authentic after all—he doesn't trust Ginsburg," she said, shrugging. "He just wants to see them again, to examine them undisturbed, and be able to come to his own conclusions. That's what he has told me."

This comported with what Dr. Ginsburg had intimated to us earlier in the week.

"And tonight?" I said sharply.

She was resigned. "Yes, I came here at his request," she half-smiled at the word. "His orders. And he is expecting me at the Savoy early this morning." She looked around the room dully. "I wonder what he'll do when I don't show up?"

I was thinking about something Lady Laura had said at first—that she had no desire to protect Ganneau. "Is he blackmailing you, Lady Simmons-Hartley?"

She started, and looked at me with quiet anger, then shrugged. "In a manner of speaking, yes. My reputation..." her voice trailed off.

A sudden but quiet knock on the front door startled us all; I nearly jumped out of my chair. Lord Parke rose and went to answer it—we could hear low voices talking back and forth, then finally Lord Parke's voice saying, "Good man, excellent work. Now go get some sleep if you can."

He came back into the room, a grim look on his face.

"Lady Simmons-Hartley," he said, properly addressing her this time, "I can inform you that your presence at the Savoy will not be required. Clermont-Ganneau has left the hotel and is half-way to Dover by now, enroute to Paris."

"How do you know this, James?" I cried, forgetting propriety in the shock of this news.

"I had my man watching the Savoy, and Clermont-Ganneau, this whole evening, and he witnessed him leaving the hotel with all his baggage, and heard the direction he gave the coachman."

I turned to the others in dismay, but particularly to Lady Laura. "Lady Simmons-Hartley, why do you think he would depart before knowing you had accomplished your mission, and the scrolls were safe in his hands?"

We all looked to her for an explanation. After a moment, she spoke. "I can only guess, knowing how Charles thinks, that he set someone to spy on me—and this house—someone who saw that I entered but did not come out—the lights all on, people shouting and talking. He could only come to one conclusion, that I had been caught in the act. That I had failed to complete my mission."

With this summary, she seemed to be struck with a sense of her situation, and started to weep, putting her hands to her face.

"What will become of me?" she cried. "I will die of disgrace!"

Lord Parke, John and I exchanged glances. Edwin had remained silent all this time, but surprising us all, he spoke in a gentle voice.

"My lady," he said. "We are not the police, and we do not have the power to arrest you," he said, glancing at first John, then me. I nodded encouragement. "You were prevented from taking anything from this house, and your actions, though wrong, have caused no harm. I do not believe that anyone in this company is inclined to take this matter to the authorities, or to allow it to be publicized."

She looked up then, scarcely daring to hope. Lord Parke took her hand. "It is true, Laura, you have my word on it."

"And mine," John said solemnly.

"And mine as well," I said. I caught up the bag in which Lady Laura had placed the scrolls, and handed it to Lord Parke. It was a plain cloth carpet bag—not, as I had so hoped, a colorful tapestry like the one the maid Angela described as belonging to Mr. Shapira. Indeed, that would have been entirely too tidy a resolution!

"Are we agreed?" I said, and everyone nodded. I turned to Lord Parke, and handed him the bag. "Please, my lord, tell Dr. Ginsburg we are grateful for his help, and we wish him well in his further examinations of the scrolls. May it bring about a vindication of Mr. Shapira, and restore his reputation to him, in all justice."

"Amen to that," said Lord Parke.

FORTY-EIGHT

From the 1919 Memoir of Myriam Shapira Harry

Jerusalem — 15 March 1884

WE HAD TO SELL ALL OUR HORSES, and dismiss all the servants except my dear Ouarda—no money had come from my father, or been put in the bank, for several months. We were three lonely women in a dismal house, slowly being emptied of all its furnishings. No one came to visit, and we even stopped going to church, it was too humiliating.

As to the shop, everything was in such disorder and so out of joint, that, although the great cases had arrived as usual, no one had dared to unpack them. The season had been an unusually good one, and although there had been crowds of pilgrims, no one felt any interest in pressing the sales, and all the employees had grown hopelessly slack.

There was no money to pay the rent and the overdue fees for Augusta's schooling. Dr. Schroeder had written that they were "obliged" to give up the association with our family, and the engagement with his son was broken off. Augusta went to live with a relative of my mother's, and her letters were bitter and angry—they made my mother cry for hours after she read them.

We managed somehow, with me working very hard to keep up the small sales of pilgrim's souvenirs at the shop, until one day, early in the Spring, in March, there was such glorious weather that I took a holiday from the shop, and allowed myself the treat of lounging about in the picturesque garden of our villa, as I had so often done in happier times. Although I was old enough to know better, I climbed the almond tree, listening to Ouarda softly singing a lullaby below me, as she sat at her sewing on the flagstones. I felt happier than I had in many a day, soothed by the springtime weather, and the birds singing in the trees.

All at once my joy faded—down below inside the house, I heard the heavy tread of several feet on the flagstones, and the sound of low, subdued voices. Climbing quickly down the tree, I brought myself on a level with the dining-room window and looked through it.

As usual, my mother was sitting in her armchair, working on some mending, but now I saw three men in black coats coming through the door with very solemn faces. The trio consisted of the British consul, the German banker, and our pastor Mr. Green.

I watched them, as each sat down on the edge of his chair, forming a half-circle round my mother. And I noted, too, how the garment she was mending slipped from between her hands and how her anxious eyes seemed glued on the somber faces surrounding her.

I could not hear a word of what they were saying, they spoke in such low, subdued voices, and Ouarda was singing now so loudly too.

My mother gave a piercing cry, and all the men closed around her. As I jumped from my tree, they noticed me through the window, and called to me, "Quick, quick! Bring some water and some vinegar too!"

I ran into the room with some water but my mother had recovered herself quickly, and though her lips quivered in her deathly white face, she managed to dismiss her visitors with quiet dignity.

"The Lord will strengthen me to bear this heavy blow," she said. "I thank you gentlemen for coming to see me."

And as the three men filed out of the room, my mother drew me towards her, and clasping me passionately in her arms, she sobbed out, "Your father is dead! Your father is dead!"

I wasn't to learn the worst of it all for several days, until the sad, sad truth became more widely known throughout the city. The local Jewish paper, which had always viewed my father with suspicion on account of his conversion to Christianity, was particularly harsh, and I learned later, had many of the actual facts wrong.

Jerusalem — 31 March 1884

Excerpt from the Havatzelet newspaper

"The apostate Shapira, a resident of our city and the proprietor of a book shop here, who is known infamously regarding the forgery of Moabite jars, has recently committed suicide during his stay in Rotterdam.... The police broke down the door and came into the room and found Shapira lying dead upon his bed surrounded by a stream of blood, for he had taken his own life and killed himself with the barrel of a rifle."

* * *

Rotterdam! What kind of a city is Rotterdam, to die in and to be buried in? I remember when my father and I used to ride out in the mornings near the Plain of the Philistines, and go past the Mussulman cemetery, and he always said, "It must be pleasant for the dead to be there in sunshine." So I looked up that city in my geography book and read, *"Rotterdam, a flourishing commercial centre intersected with innumerable canals."* A vision of a cemetery rose before my eyes, with all the graves soaked in water, and their headstones and crosses shaking unsteadily in the wet earth.

How tragic my father's fate had been! After having lived in Jerusalem and looked down on Bathsheba's Pool, after roaming through the deserts, to die at the other end of the world in the land of fogs and innumerable canals!

I opened my atlas, on which Europe showed as an extensive continent, brightly coloured, and dotted with the names of so many, many places; and then, far away, ever so far away from Europe, I found the pale, narrow strip, which represented my own country, squeezed in between Arabia and vast Africa, like a miserable outcast ashamed of its own existence.

And yet how cruel the people could be in that wonderful, all-powerful Europe. All the sorrow, all the treachery that has ever clouded my life has come from Europe. Holland with its Rotterdam, where my papa died; England with its London and the British Museum, where he was so falsely accused, after he had been so feted; then there's Berlin, with those hateful Schroeders who had thrown Augusta over; and Paris, where Clermont-Ganneau lived, the heartless villain who has ruined us all. I'm sure he had his part to play in my father's death.

And people say that Palestine is an uncivilised country, where every one dies of cholera and sunstroke, if they are not murdered! Papa was always running risks amongst the Bedouin, and was exposed to all sorts of infection, but nothing ever happened to him here. He met his death in Holland, in that Europe which considers herself so far advanced in all the branches of modern culture, and so civilized!

And he died there because the people were so wicked and so cruel that they broke his heart.

My mother said we had to move to Germany, to live with her relatives. I think she was happy to be moving 'home' as she said, and it was good to see Augusta again—they comforted each other. But it was never my home. I never found comfort there.

The bishop was kind enough to say prayers on our last Sunday in Jerusalem for the repose of my father's soul, seeing—as he explained—that Papa was presumed to have had a fit of temporary insanity, and therefore could not be held to have committed a mortal sin by killing himself. There was some small comfort in that.

My mother and I stood in front of our house, watching the poor remains of our belongings being carried out to the wagon that was taking us to the docks to board our ship for Trieste; from there, we took a train to Berlin. There had been just enough money left, after paying off all our creditors, for second-class tickets, and a little bit more to help us find rooms in Berlin when we arrived. We were wearing very shabby mourning clothes made by a poor but generous Armenian tailor. I had blackened a straw hat of mine, and dyed some daisies with ink—clutching a sheaf of palms, I felt like an angel of death.

My beloved Ouarda, her veil wrapped round her head, had already set out for her native village, after we parted with heart-breaking sobs on both sides. She tried to encourage me by saying I would get used to Berlin and Europe and forget this wretched country and never want to come back.

But as the driver cracked his whip, and the carriage began to move, I said aloud to my mother, as though taking a formal oath, "If I forget thee, O Jerusalem, let my right hand forget her cunning."

EPILOGUE

THE FRUSTRATION AND DOUBT SOWED by that perplexing and tragic case lingered with me for many days—and for John as well. He went back to Paris soon after the night we caught Lady Laura—I scarcely saw him while he was in London, as Mr. Henry James had taken hold of him and was parading him around to all the important (and wealthy) people who might commission a portrait. But the Salon was about to open and he had to be there for Varnishing Day. I won't go into detail here about the outrage and scandal that his *Madame X* created in those hallowed halls, and the gossip that filled the soirees and dinner parties of Paris for weeks on end—I'll save that for the next mystery, which I think I'll call *"Carnation, Lily, Lily, Rose"* because it's all about John's time at Broadway and the crazed, murderous things that happened there while he was painting that glorious image— and besides, everyone knows all about *Madame X*—and ultimately, it only boosted his reputation and made him even more in demand as a portrait painter—so much so that he at one point declared he'd "never do another mug!"

But there are a few straggling threads that I feel must be tidied up, about the whole Shapira case. One is that, for all that I ever heard, the Shapira Scrolls never saw the light of day again, certainly as far as the general public were concerned. Ginsburg at the British Museum had charge of them, but apparently he never made any further announcement about their authenticity, and other more interesting events occurred to take the notice of the general public away. I *did* hear from Lord Parke a few years later that they were being sold at auction, as an oddity and a curiosity, for about twenty pounds, and that was the end of that.

However, I was never quite satisfied as to the nature of Mr. Shapira's death, not at all content thinking it was suicide—or if it was, he was somehow pushed to it, out of spite or cruelty or even extortion! Lady Laura was no longer a suspect in my mind, nor of course Dr. Ginsburg, but that arrogant Clermont-Ganneau was right at the top of the list—still is, after all these years—and one thing in particular keeps me thinking that he had a definite hand in Shapira's demise. You can deduce what you like from this small clue.

About a week or ten days after the party at John and Edwin's studio, I received a little package and a letter—I was still staying at Mary's, although about to leave on an extended tour of the industrialized sections of northern England, with some female activist friends—as I say, I received these things and opened them quickly, my curiosity all aflame. The package held a small object—an old silver coin, with a Star of David on one side, embedded in a frame of some kind of fragrant wood. I turned eagerly to the letter— it was from Lady Laura Simmons-Hartley—which was brief and to the point.

Dear Miss Paget,

Two days ago I received this talisman by post from Paris, with no note, but I am sure it came from one whose name I would not gladly write nor speak. I recognized it immediately as a "good luck charm" that was the property of the late Mr. Shapira; I had seen him hold it and toss it about on numerous occasions.

I can only say, I do not believe he would have ever parted with this object willingly. I am sending it to you as someone who will understand its significance, and if one can do nothing, it is at least a reminder to you how diligently you and your friends tried to bring about justice for Mr. Shapira.

Sincerely,
Lady Laura Simmons-Hartley

I held the small object in the palm of my hand, and marvelled at the sight of it and all that it meant. But Lady Laura was right—this was not any kind of evidence that the authorities could bring to bear on a murderer—or perhaps, one who only stood looking down at a poor man whose life had fled, and afterwards, made off with an unsent letter and a colorful carpet bag of documents and curiosities such as this talisman, and then mistakenly slipped the room key in the wrong box. I placed the old coin in its wooden frame carefully on my desk, and leaned back to contemplate the tragic fate of Mr. Moses Shapira and his ancient scrolls.

May his memory be for a blessing.

Violet Paget
Il Palmerino
Fiesole, Italy – 1928

AUTHOR'S NOTE

The notorious scandals of the Shapira Scrolls and the Moabite Idols in the mid-to-late 19th century have haunted the reputation and legacy of Moses Wilhelm Shapira for 140 years, and the debate over the supposed forgeries continues to this day. Several books have been written, some very recently, that lay out the known facts and the speculations about Shapira and his treasures. Please consult the bibliography at the end for more. It is important to note that these events took place at a time when European domination of Middle Eastern countries resulted in the removal and possession of many cultural artifacts; some of these artifacts have been returned to their country of origin, while others remain in the acquiring countries' museums.

The Eleventh Commandment, however, is a work of fiction—an historical novel, and the fourth mystery in my series featuring John Singer Sargent and Violet Paget (aka Vernon Lee) as amateur sleuths. I have tried to write close to the facts of the Shapira case, but the involvement of John and Violet is a fantasy all my own. However, I have little doubt that they were aware of the scandal at the time. But I like to say, History tells the Facts, and Novels show the Truth. So, my apologies to scholars who will notice with raised eyebrows some deviations from absolute fact, but I hope that my own deep regard for finding the true humanity in every person's story will lend credibility to this mystery.

Mary F. Burns
San Francisco – 2022

REALITY AND FICTION

The people mentioned by name in all the sections about Moses Shapira are real, historical characters: his family, the academics and scholars, the Bedouin sheiks and Selim; the only exceptions are incidental characters such as maids, butlers, hotel clerks and the like. In the Sargent/Paget sections, those mentioned by name are also real, even Inspector Cramer, with the exception of Lady Emily, Lord Parke, and Lady Laura (but the "Lady in Blue" is real, as Myriam Shapira Harry describes in her memoir—I just gave her a name).

I have tried to stay true to the actual events and timing of Moses Shapira's life and discoveries—the summer and fall of 1883, in particular, accurately describe his journeys to Berlin and London, and the events that occurred there. The quoted sections from the newspapers are the real thing, as is the Punch cartoon. Although conversations are of necessity imagined and therefore fictional, there are numerous accounts (meeting minutes, newspaper articles) that report what was said at certain meeting and gatherings, which were very helpful to reconstructing actual conversations.

Where are the Shapira Scrolls now? Although Violet Paget could not, of course, know anything other than that the scrolls were sold at an auction, the search for the Shapira Scrolls continues to this day, and as you can see in the *Selected Bibliography* below, books and articles are still being published about where they might be now, and how to determine the authenticity of the leather strips, based on the evidence available from those extraordinary few weeks in Berlin and London.

Matthew Hamilton, an independent manuscript researcher in Sydney, Australia, to whom I owe a huge debt of gratitude for his time and information, generously provided this summary for me of the "sightings" of the manuscripts after 1884:

- Auction at Sotheby's was in 1885
- Exhibited at the Anglo-Jewish Exhibition in 1887
- Advertised by Quaritch (an auction house) in 1887
- Sold in 1889 to Philip Brookes Mason who also exhibited them in 1889.

Mason died in 1903 and the fate of the scrolls subsequent to then is still a mystery.

PICTURE GALLERY

Mr. Shapira, British Museum, 20. Aug. 1883.
Sketched in the British Museum. W. Simpson

Moses Wilhelm Shapira, c. 1883

Maria Rosette Shapira, c. 1904
nom de plume: Myriam Harry

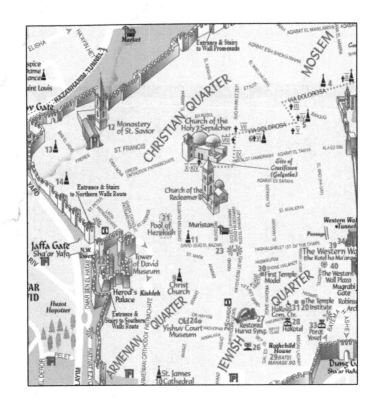

Map of Old City Jerusalem. #21 "Pool of Hezekiah" is the site of "Bathsheba's Pool", so-called in Moses Shapira's day; the back windows of his shop on the Street of the Christians looked out on this pool, an old reservoir. The Jaffa Gate is to the left and the Tower of David is just inside it; the Anglican (Jewish) Christ Church is to the right and slightly below the Tower.

The Mesha Stele, or "Moabite Stone"
discovered in Moab, 1865.

Items from the Shapira Moabite Collection

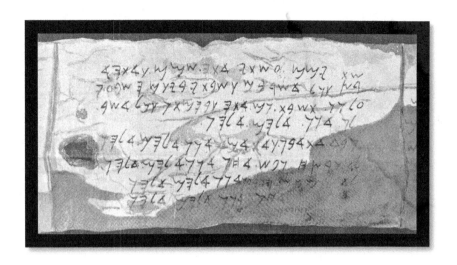

Artist's drawing of a fragment from the
Shapira Scrolls, c. 1883

Charles Clermont-Ganneau

Christian David Ginsburg

SELECTED BIBLIOGRAPHY

Colby, Vineta. *Vernon Lee: A Literary Biography*. (Charlottesville and London: University of Virginia Press, 2003).

Dershowitz, Idan. *The Valediction of Moses* (Mohr Sieback, 2021)

Harry, Myriam Shapira. *The Little Daughter of Jerusalem*. (New York: E. P. Dutton & Co., 1919). Translated from the French by Phoebe Allen.

Nichols, Ross K. *The Moses Scroll: Reopening the Most Controversial Case in the History of Biblical Scholarship*. (Saint Francisville, Louisiana: Horeb Press, 2021).

Reiner, Fred. "Tracking the Shapira Case: A Biblical Scandal Revisited" *Biblical Archaeology Review* 23:3, May/June 1997

Rigg, Patricia. *A. Mary F. Robinson: Victorian Poet & Modern Woman of Letters*. (Montreal & Kingston: McGill-Queen's University Press, 2021).

Sabo, Yoram. "Shapira & I" (Film, 2014). View at: https://vimeo.com/99821693

Schuessler, Jennifer. "A Fake? Or Biblical Gold?" (*New York Times*, March 28, 2021), Arts & Leisure Section/Culture, pp. 1, 8-9.

Tigay, Chanan. *The Lost Book of Moses: The Hunt for the World's Oldest Bible*. (New York: HarperCollins Publishers, 2016).

ACKNOWLEDGEMENTS

The idea for this novel was ignited by an article I read in the *New York Times*, March 28, 2021, titled "A Fake? Or Biblical Gold?" by Jennifer Schuessler, summarizing the story of the Shapira Scrolls, and discussing the most recent research about them by scholar **Idan Dershowitz**, School of Jewish Theology, University of Potsdam, Germany, who posits that they may have been authentic after all. Professor Dershowitz graciously published a detailed academic paper for free at academia.edu, titled "The Valediction of Moses: New Evidence on the Shapira Deuteronomy Fragments"; he also published a lengthier book on the subject.

I use the word "ignited" quite deliberately because I felt such a burst of energy and delight while reading this story, and almost immediately realized that I had the basis for my next Sargent/Paget mystery! After several months of research (still ongoing, in a way), I started writing in September 2021 and kept it up until the book was finished in January 2022. I can't even number the websites I looked up and the links I tracked down on the internet, but I owe an enormous debt of gratitude to four people in particular: first, **Matthew Hamilton,** an independent manuscript researcher in Sydney, Australia, who was an enormous help and support to me (and to the authors mentioned below, as a key contributor to their own researches) giving generously of his time and encyclopedic knowledge of the Shapira affair, which he has been studying and researching for two decades and more. I am also obliged to **Chanan Tigay**, for his *The Lost Book of Moses* (2016). Mr. Tigay is an award-winning journalist, former Investigative Reporting Fellow at the

University of California Berkeley, and now a professor of creative writing at San Francisco State University. His persistent, single-minded focus to track down the true story of the "leather strips" and their owner Moses Shapira produced an exciting book built on his amazing journey of nearly two years. Also, **Ross K. Nichols'** *The Moses Scroll* (2021) covers much of the same ground as Tigay, but with added facts and perspectives that, for me as a novelist, provided rich ground for my imagining who Moses Shapira was and what happened 140 years ago, much of which still remains a mystery. Finally, I am grateful to **Yoram Sabo**, a film producer and director in Israel, whose excellent film *"Shapira & I"* was the delightful and poignant fruit of his nearly thirty years' search for the Shapira Scrolls, and gave me a very visual and emotional sense of the places Moses Shapira visited right up to his tragic end.

I thank my faithful beta readers Jay Miller, Stephanie Cowell and Robert Densmore, who always provide insights and encouragement, and who love Sargent and Paget almost as much as I do. And I am grateful to my husband, who understands so well when I lock myself in my office and emerge after some hours each day while I'm writing, dazed and introspective and in need of a glass of wine.

OTHER BOOKS BY MARY F. BURNS

Portraits of an Artist:
A Novel about John Singer Sargent

The Sargent/Paget Mysteries

The Spoils of Avalon – Book One

The Love for Three Oranges – Book Two

The Unicorn in the Mirror – Book Three

Other Historical Fiction

Isaac and Ishmael: A Novel of Genesis

J-The Woman Who Wrote the Bible

Ember Days

Of Ripeness & The River

Short Fiction Series: A Classic & A Sequel

In the Cage by Henry James + *At Chalk Farm*
Crapy Cornelia by Henry James + *The Grace of Uncertainty*

Non-Fiction

Reading Mrs. Dalloway

To see book trailers, contact the author, and order these
books, please visit the author's website at
www.maryfburns.com

Made in the USA
Monee, IL
04 May 2022

95902317R00207